Knock Knock

Knock Knock

by

S. P. Miskowski

Omnium Gatherum
Los Angeles CA

Knock Knock
Copyright © 2011 S.P. Miskowski
Cover design and illustration © 2011 Russell Dickerson

ISBN-13:978-0615580708
ISBN-10:061558070X

omniumgatherumedia.com

1.2

First Edition

Praise for Knock Knock

"Along with Brendan Connell's *The Architect*, I rate *Delphine Dodd* as the best novella I read in 2012, and *Knock Knock* as the best book I read in any category." —Peter Tennant, *Black Static*

"Beautifully written and relentlessly suspenseful, it's a great book to curl up with on a cold winter's night. Just be sure to keep the doors locked and all the lights on!" —Lucy Taylor, *The Silence Between the Screams*

"...more than a great read; it is a fascinating meditation on the nature of horror. There are supernatural elements to the book, yes, but the setting (an impoverished, ruined logging town) and the main characters (three school girls with hopes and dreams made improbable if not impossible by their realities) are a beautifully rendered commentary on the cyclical nature of real-world human tragedy." —Molly Tanzer, *A Pretty Mouth*

"With her distinct voice, Miskowski takes you deep into the back woods of America, where shadows chase you and people do the unthinkable." —Angel Leigh McCoy, Wily Writers

"Eventually the story achieves a momentum all its own, rushing headlong to a shattering finale, and the prose, which Miskowski uses with such care and accuracy throughout, in the final pages attains a fever dream intensity, so that we can't trace any clear divide between reality and the skewed perspectives of the characters, the two blurring into each other, everything viewed through a blood red filter and in the light cast by flickering flames." – Peter Tennant, *Black Static*

For Rosalie and Karolee on the long winter nights.

"I shut my eyes and all the world drops dead; I lift my eyes and all is born again."

- Sylvia Plath

Part One

Part One

The Girls

At first the spell was nothing but a game designed by little girls. As far as they knew, it was only of interest to the three of them. They never imagined what they did that afternoon would matter to anyone else.

For most grownups in Skillute, Washington in the late 1960s few events rose in significance above the routine of work, Sunday worship, and the weekend six-pack. The prospect of someday joining this world of quietly unhappy adults made the three girls long for useless adventures.

They were awkward, slender, average height, age eleven to eleven and a half. They came up with the idea to swear an oath against having babies after another girl, whose mother was overdue with twins, whispered a few mortifying details of the pregnancy while they slouched in the darkened back row of their classroom during a hygiene film.

"For two whole weeks Mama hasn't moved off of the couch. Just sits there all day breathing."

The girl affected a ragged intake of breath.

"Grandma brings her ice chips soaked in Budweiser."

"Why?" Ethel asked.

The storyteller was poor, her green-plaid cotton dress threadbare at the collar and cuffs. After each question she grinned before doling out another bit of knowledge, savoring the discomfort of her audience.

"That's to stop the pain when Mama's gums bleed. They get so raw they break open and her mouth fills up with blood. Then she's got to spit into a cup."

"Sick," Beverly whispered.

"All she does is cry and tell Grandma these twin babies

are a curse, and if she could she would cut that man from Wenatchee."

The girl wrinkled her nose. She held her hands up in a loose circle around her neck.

"Mama's ankles are this big around. She can't sleep at night, and she can't wear shoes because her feet are all swollen up."

Mrs. Coffey shushed the class from her dim corner at the front of the room, near the chalkboard. A few silhouettes moved restlessly in the flickering light. The girls ducked lower in their seats.

"Her hair kept falling out of her head until she was bald except for one patch on the side."

"Did it grow back?" Beverly asked.

"Yeah," said the girl. "But now there's hair on her stomach, too, like the fur on a dog's belly."

"No!" Ethel said.

The girl nodded: It was true.

"Grandma shaves it off, but it grows back thicker every time."

"I've never heard of that," Beverly said.

"Doctor says it's pretty common," the girl informed them.

Now Ethel and Beverly turned to Marietta, whose aunt was a midwife and a fortune-teller. They waited while Marietta made up her mind to speak.

"Some pregnant women grow hair in places they didn't have it before," she said solemnly. "That's true."

A shiver ran through the group. All turned their attention to the film screen at the front of the room, where a young woman with pigtails was demonstrating the proper way for a lady to wash her hands in a public bathroom.

The conversation had its effect on all three girls. Later that day, during lunch break, Beverly announced:

"I'm not ever going to have fur on my stomach. That's not even human."

She sniffed disdainfully and picked at her bracelet,

turning over each miniature charm until all the painted shamrocks faced outward. The bracelet accentuated a single stroke of pink polish dabbed on each of her nails.

"We're doomed," said Ethel.

All three girls looked down at their untouched sandwiches on the cafeteria table: Egg salad, peanut butter with grape jelly, liverwurst. Knowing what they knew about the world and what it held in store for them had ruined their appetite. They could only sigh and stare at the food with jaded smiles. They were considering never eating again.

"I'm telling you both right now: I won't let my ankles get bigger around than my whole neck!" Beverly said. "That's never going to happen. Never."

Her determination inspired the others. They nodded and, just like that, it was decided.

"How can we make sure we won't have babies?" Ethel asked.

Both girls turned once more to Marietta. Her seriousness, her violet eyes and the lank, black hair framing her face gave her a dramatic air that would have prompted teasing if most of her classmates weren't afraid of her.

"We could have an accident," she said.

"What kind of accident?" Ethel asked.

"No," Beverly interrupted. "I'm not doing that. Come on, Marietta, doesn't your aunt know something we can take, or do? Something that doesn't hurt."

"Maybe there's a way," she said. "Sometimes women ask my aunt for a remedy. That's after the fact, though. This is different. I'll have to look it up in the spell book when she's out of the house."

The other two exchanged a sly look. Marietta went on:

"We can swear an oath. If we use the right spell, it might work."

"Might?" Beverly said.

"It's my aunt that's got the healing power."

"Well, that's no good," said Beverly. "She won't help us."

"If we all say the oath and if we use blood, it could work."

"Blood?"

"A spell is the most powerful when it uses the woman's blood," said Marietta.

"She means from your period," Beverly explained to Ethel.

"I know that," said Ethel. She paused and then admitted: "I don't have any."

"I don't either," said Beverly. "And Marietta?"

Marietta shook her head. No. Not yet.

"But that's the point," Beverly said. "We have to take the oath before this thing gets us."

"You're right," said Ethel. "Once we start to bleed, we can have a baby any time. Then we might as well be dead."

They were silent for a moment.

"What can we do?" Ethel asked again.

"Well," Beverly began. "What if we cut our fingers for blood, and say the oath somewhere that's got its own power, a secret place?"

"In the woods?"

"That's all I can think of," said Beverly.

Ethel looked away.

"Don't be a sissy," Beverly told her. "Miss Knocks is just a fairy tale. If the place has any power it's only because people believe it. You don't believe in a fairy tale, do you?"

"No."

"Then it can't hurt you. On the other hand, if you swear an oath and you believe it, maybe it comes true."

"You think so?" Ethel said.

"Why not?" Beverly said. "It's the power of positive thinking."

Marietta considered this and said: "I'll look up the spell as soon as I can."

The kids outside this tiny social circle considered Marietta strange, if not dangerous, and they kept their distance. Her mother was long gone. Nobody could say where. The girl never knew her. Her aunt was Delphine Dodd and they lived in a bungalow near the railroad tracks.

Delphine was old, thin as a spindle, with black eyes that sparkled like obsidian. Her house reeked of weeds and incense.

Local women paid Delphine for potions, herbal remedies, and spells. They also asked her to tell the future. Women found their way to Delphine if their family doctors were too expensive or too likely to say no to what they wanted.

Most of Delphine's remedies were cheap. Sometimes they were unnecessary. The ailments women brought to her door varied, but only a few of them were actually sick. Some of them felt they had married badly and they were too ashamed to go back to their families. Others worried that they were too old or ugly, and would never be loved by anyone. Some of the women married men who beat them or cheated on them. After having a sympathetic older woman dote on them for a few hours with hot tea and incantations and the fragrance of rose-scented candles, most of the heartsick women felt better. Naturally Delphine had a good number of regular clients.

The herbal recipes and charms came to Delphine through a long line of midwives. She had practiced these arts since she was a child, even younger than her niece. She could offer any one of hundreds of spells from longevity to fertility, spiritual cleansing, enhanced memory, and more restful sleep. Each spell was accompanied by an herbal formula.

Readings were a different matter. Delphine didn't charge people money to tell their fortune, she said, because that would be the wrong thing to do. Her clients gave her tokens of appreciation. Her predictions only came true about half the time, yet she had a reputation for being reliable. The women who consulted her tended to believe what came true and forget the rest.

Marietta inspired gossip at school with her stark appearance and because people wondered how much of her aunt's gift she inherited. It was rumored that Delphine used the girl as an assistant in even the most delicate procedures, but no one ever confirmed this by admitting they had consulted the midwife to end a pregnancy. Whether it was true or not, grownups regarded young Marietta with wariness and children were careful not to insult her to her face.

One story at school was that the weird girl with lavender eyes had made a grease fire break out at Jessup's Diner just by staring at the kitchen door. On another occasion she had blinked at a passing lumber truck and its load of maple logs had come tumbling down onto the road.

By fourth grade no one spoke to Marietta except Ethel and Beverly. Being friends with her was the most mysterious part of their lives, the only thrilling and spooky thing they knew aside from *Dark Shadows*. They swooned at the prospect of anything different, even frightening, if it seemed glamorous. They wanted to be part of something darkly romantic and beautiful. Barring that, something peculiar would do. Marietta and her strange pedigree would do.

Beverly was soft looking and perfectly groomed, but not truly pretty. Her nose was a bit too long and her lips were a bit too thin. She sensed that she would never be naturally feminine, and she was learning to be content with excellent posture and an enviable wardrobe. She spent a lot of time choosing and matching accessories. She coveted nice dresses and trinkets. She was becoming a snob about it. She would soon be mortified to discover that her mother was secretly stitching Casual Corner store labels into her blouses and dresses, each piece of clothing home-sewn according to a McCall's pattern.

Ethel's appearance was only mentioned when she was compared to her mother, and then people sighed and said it was a shame. Too bad, they said, she didn't have her mother's pale blue eyes or honey-colored hair. Too bad she didn't stand up straight. Too bad she dragged her feet when she walked. Too bad her fine-looking mama Shirley was mostly known for the men she drank with, loggers and timber buyers and passing salesmen. She wasn't picky about the men or the booze, and it was commonly assumed that her husband wasn't Ethel's real father.

The second bell rang. A few students loitered in the cafeteria. The girls scooped up their uneaten sandwiches and headed for the double doors. As each passed, she tossed the dreaded lunch into an aluminum trashcan and turned away with a mournful expression.

Marietta was as good as her word. By mid-week she had secured the information they needed.

That Friday after school they crossed the deserted kickball field in single file. They clambered up a wide incline clotted with ground ivy and then hurried on. They had to hike for a quarter of a mile, slightly more uphill and slow going across the darkening floor of the forest.

Finally they reached a stand of old growth where they could no longer see the outer edge of the woods. They couldn't hear the intermittent traffic that led north to the freeway. There wasn't even a thin break in the encircling Douglas fir and red cedar. The bracken was heavy here. They picked their way carefully through nettles and twigs to a small clearing and looked up at the motley ceiling.

All around lay a quiet part of the forest the girls had never seen before. They had only heard of it as the background to fairy tales about Miss Knocks. People said she walked here late at night. Miss Knocks with her long arms reaching up into the trees to pull children down to the ground. Miss Knocks chasing kids out of the woods, scooping them up in a pillowcase and hauling them away into the night. She was part of the folklore everyone in Skillute knew. Part myth, part fireside tale, Miss Knocks kept children wondering and watching shadows, at least until second or third grade.

The girls claimed they were too grownup for these tales. Yet they had chosen this location for its promise of dark magic and secrecy. Now in the shadows of the forest they suddenly felt the restless stirrings of fear. They were too stubborn to say so, but they were anxious to be finished and on their way home.

It was mid-October. The forest was several degrees cooler than the outer world. The girls began buttoning their bulky sweaters by the time they had settled on the exact spot.

"I'm cold," Beverly grumbled. "How long will this take?"

She pulled a white beret out of her sweater pocket, put it on her head and tweaked it to one side.

"Let's get started," Ethel said.

"Did everyone bring a piece of string?" Marietta asked.

They opened change purses and lunchboxes and scrambled in pockets. Finally each girl produced a string.

"Come on, let's say the oath," said Beverly.

"Does your string come from something that belongs to you and only to you?" Marietta asked them.

"Yes," said Ethel.

"It has to belong to you, for the spell to work," said Marietta.

"Of course it's mine," said Beverly. "It's a shoestring from my old sneakers. I don't wear them any more. Does that matter?"

"No," said Marietta. "It can be something old. But why is it so clean and white?"

"I washed it," Beverly said and made a "tsk" sound with her tongue.

"Why?" Ethel asked.

"I'm not taking an oath on a dirty old shoestring."

"What's yours?" Marietta asked Ethel.

"It's a strand of rickrack from one of my dresses. Doesn't fit any more, so I pulled this off the hem."

"Good," said Marietta. "That's good. My string is a silk ribbon."

She held up the black silk for them to see.

"That's pretty," said Beverly. "Are you sure you want to waste that?"

"If the spell works, it isn't wasted."

"Okay. Okay. Can we start? I'm freezing! Can't we hurry up?"

Beverly stamped her feet in place.

"You've got to do this right, or it won't work," Marietta reminded her.

"Probably won't work anyway," Beverly said. "If I have to stand out here in the woods for a while, we have to have a fire. It's too cold. My knees are bumping together!"

They agreed to light a small fire to get them through the ceremony. The sky had darkened steadily. Now it verged on a downpour. But in this patch of the woods the trees had been untouched for more than a century. They bowed in and laced overhead. There wasn't a sliver of pure sky between the branches undulating, entwined above.

Ethel crouched to clear a spot in the dirt. She pushed back fallen leaves, and made a face when she accidentally scooped up a banana slug. She scraped her hand clean on a moss-covered trunk then picked the stray dots of moss from her palm.

"Hurry up," said Beverly. "What should we set on fire?"

Ethel sighed and shook her head. Beverly always had the grand ideas. Then Ethel and Marietta had to figure out how to make them work.

"Well?" Beverly asked. She was wearing a layer of lipstick she had surreptitiously applied after school. That morning she had swiped the tube of Coral Pink from her mother's pocketbook.

"Okay," said Ethel. "Over there's a pile of wood chips."

Ethel had spied a fallen branch lying atop and partly concealing a nest of cedar shingles. She hopped over the broken logs and helped herself to three shingles that seemed intact. She had to shake off dirt and beetles. Then she slapped away a bit of moss stuck along the edge and placed the shingles in a rough triangle in the space she had cleared. She was about to start rubbing sticks together when Beverly reached into her pocketbook and produced a Zippo lighter.

"Where did you get that?" Ethel asked.

"None of your business," said Beverly.

The girls crouched, and Beverly popped the lid on the Zippo. She flicked the thumbwheel and held the flame against the corner of the cedar shingles. Once the flame took to the edges the girls leaned in and blew on the shingles to keep them going. At last the girls stood and gathered around the meager fire.

"Now what?" Beverly asked.

"Now take this pin," said Marietta.

She held a straight pin between two fingers, pinching it carefully to avoid being burned, and barely touched it to the fire. Then she stood and pricked her index finger with it.

Ethel and Beverly winced at the sight of red-black blood forming a liquid pearl on the tip of Marietta's finger. Before they could say anything she ran her finger along the black silk ribbon. After the ribbon absorbed the drop of blood she handed the pin to Beverly, who drew a sharp breath and pricked her own finger, then touched the shoestring with it. Ethel did the same with her piece of rickrack.

"Do as I do," said Marietta.

She took the black ribbon now and tied two knots in it. Then she crouched and dug a fistful of dirt from the ground, placed the ribbon in the hole she had made and covered it with the dirt. Beverly, who was still shivering from the cold, quickly tied a single knot and buried the shoestring.

"How many knots did you make?" Marietta asked her.

"What difference does it make? A knot is a knot, right?"

Ethel considered this. Then she tied four knots in the rickrack and buried it. When she finished the other two were staring at her.

"Might as well be safe," she said.

"Why?" Beverly said. "You think a squirrel might dig up your rickrack and untie it?"

"You shouldn't make fun of the spell," said Marietta.

"You should hurry up," said Beverly. "Say the oath and

let's get out of here."

In turn each repeated the oath they had spent most of the week writing:

"On my soul and by the name of Miss Knocks in the heart of these woods, I swear to never let another one such as myself issue forth from the sacred temple of my body."

Each girl, in turn, grinned at this bit. They were a little embarrassed by the word "body" in relation to themselves, but they were also proud of the time they'd spent writing the oath. They had stolen phrases from TV shows and from books at the school library, combining them into a speech that was impressively solemn when spoken on a cold afternoon in the gloomy woods.

"By all that is sacred to me, I will keep this vow until my whole life is over and done."

Ethel was the last of the three to repeat the vow. Despite the density of the canopy overhead one raindrop fell through, cold, plump, and glistening, onto her face as she began. It quivered there, broke, and ran down. She looked up with a grimace. The raindrop coursed the length of her neck and dribbled inside her cotton dress. High in the trees there was a pattering rain, but it would take time to soak through the canopy.

Marietta broke the circle, jumped and turned around. She looked over her shoulder and stared off into the shadows.

"What?" Beverly asked. "What happened?"

"Did you see it?"

"See what?"

The other two stared at Marietta. Beyond the dark layer of leaves, above the branches and debris swaying over them, the blackened clouds moved and thunder rolled in. The clouds seemed to jostle and murmur overhead. Beverly's voice broke through the rumbling sound:

"Fire!"

Several leaves had blown flat against the small arch of cedar shingles and stuck there. Catching the flame and then dislodging, the leaves tumbled across the forest floor, conjuring a thin corridor of smoke as they rolled. The girls stamped their feet at the leaves outside the circle, but it only stirred up more smoke.

"We can't put it out!" Ethel screamed.

A clap of thunder made all of them jump.

"The rain can put it out," Beverly said. "I don't care. Let's go!"

"Rain's not even touching the ground here," Marietta said.

Beverly wasn't listening. She turned away from the other two.

"I'm late for supper! Let's go!" She yelled.

She leapt free of the encircling smoke and darted off through the woods, back the way they had come. Ethel and Marietta went on stamping at the dirt and leaves, burying the shingles with a shallow pile of dirt. They kept scratching their ankles and calves on stray nettles as they worked. The smoke rolled up around them, making it hard to breathe.

Ethel peeled off her sweater and began swatting the ground with it. She took a step following the flames, and another step. Bundling her pitifully charred sweater, she pressed it against a clot of weeds at the base of a cedar and held it there while smoke rolled out underneath. When it seemed that the fire was extinguished she lifted the sweater. Something on the ground caught her attention, and she poked at it with a twig. Then she let out a cry.

Marietta crowded next to her and peered over her shoulder. Both girls gazed down at what was unmistakably a slender, blackened jawbone protruding from the earth in the spot where Ethel had chased the fire. Like tiny hematite chips several crooked, human teeth jutted from the bone. Neither Ethel nor Marietta moved.

Finally Ethel said:

"Who do you think it belonged to?"

Marietta shook her head.

"I don't know," she said. "Could be really old. Maybe there was a cemetery here, or a logging camp. Or it might be a Cowlitz relic."

"Should we take it?" Ethel asked.

Marietta shook her head. She pushed some leaves and dirt over the jawbone and patted them into place.

"No. Whatever was buried here ought to stay put," she said. "Leave it alone."

Ethel hesitated.

"It's a bad sign, Ethel. Leave it alone."

The smoke was rising once more and shifting in the air around them. Smoke shimmied out of the leaves under their feet. Everything seemed to be moving at once. Every scrap of the forest shuddered. More leaves were starting to smolder. A spark shot up from the cedar shingles and Ethel screamed:

"We have to go!"

They ran, with thin fingers of smoke winding upward in the woods behind them. They tore through ferns and shrubs that cut their legs. Back through the fir trees and undergrowth, across the leafy floor grasping at their ankles, down the ivy-covered incline. Marietta slipped and fell on her backside. Ethel scooped her up under both arms and pulled her the rest of the way. They hit the kickball field running.

"I have to go home! My aunt's going to be mad if she finds out!" Marietta shouted.

Then she took off and left Ethel standing on the muddy field. The sky split open, tearing like a sheet, letting the rain down. Ahead of Ethel, across the field, Marietta turned and called to her through the torrent. Ethel couldn't hear the words. She could only see Marietta's mouth gaping.

Ethel looked down at her mud-spattered dress and the charred sweater hanging, sodden and ruined, from her right hand. Marietta shouted again. This time her high, keening voice cut right across the field:

"Don't tell anyone!"

Marietta turned away and Ethel took off running. All the way home she practiced what she would say if her mother questioned her about a fire in the woods:

"Must have been lightning split a tree, but I wasn't there, so I don't know."

Marietta

To an unfamiliar eye the town of Skillute would have appeared dense with cedar, western hemlock and Douglas fir. The timber companies were still thriving. The lumber and aluminum firms were making money and hiring help almost every quarter. Their employees commuted from five counties for good jobs they considered themselves lucky to get.

To people that had lived in Skillute all of their lives, however, the gaps and scars on the land were visible. Some of the routes cut by three generations of timber companies had been abandoned. Others were never used, leaving wide gravel roads to narrow and dwindle away, leading nowhere. In a few spots these routes were marked by new growth, with alder springing up along forgotten paths.

Here and there the hills were split in half, leaving their interior exposed. The stratified walls ranged as high as twenty-five or thirty feet. From their dirt hundreds of tree roots emerged and dangled in the air.

Longtime residents of Skillute and nearby Kelso and Longview tended to be tight-lipped, hardworking descendants of loggers and farmers. They were self-sufficient and proud of it, and they kept to themselves as much as possible. They repeated time honored cautionary tales for the benefit of their kids, who didn't listen. Boredom made the children restless but their parents didn't worry overmuch. Experience would trim their wings.

Out of the five thousand or so residents only a handful of people knew how the legend of Miss Knocks began. One of these was Delphine Dodd, and what she knew she would eventually pass along to her niece as the girl grew up and was able to make sense of it. What Marietta knew from the start was that the last stand of old growth in Skillute, the place Miss Knocks was said to haunt by night, was strictly off limits.

"Did you bury it?" Delphine asked at least ten times.

"We buried it," Marietta answered every time.

Her hands trembled at the memory. She could still feel the smooth arc of the blackened jawbone against her fingertips. Despite herself she had yearned to keep it. She knew her aunt would have flown into a rage, although she wasn't sure why.

She didn't dare tell about the spell or the oath she had taken. Casting spells on her own was forbidden, too, and the excuse that she did it to please her friends was worse than no excuse. Delphine lectured Marietta constantly about not taking outsiders into her confidence, and the old woman considered anyone who didn't share their name and lineage to be an outsider.

Marietta never intended to tell her aunt where she had been that day. The old woman sensed it the second she looked at her face. She knew the girl had seen something, touched something. So Marietta decided on a partial truth. She told her aunt about the woods and what she had found, in the hope that Delphine might explain it to her.

"How deep did you say you buried it? Did you touch it?"

"Yes."

"You touched it with your bare hands?"

"I had to. Only to cover it with dirt."

"How deep did you bury it?"

"Deep enough."

"How would you know what's deep enough?"

"I put dirt over it. I buried it and I ran away."

"You never go there again. Do you understand?"

"Yes."

"Look at me and promise. I told you a hundred times, and you nodded: yes, yes. And then you didn't do what I said. How can I believe you?"

"We just wanted," Marietta began.

"Don't want. That's what brings women to misery. Hear me? Want nothing. Every woman who comes to me comes in despair over something caused by a man. I'm not telling you to hate men. Just keep your wits. Don't long for things you don't need. Why did you go into the woods?"

"We got lost. We were playing hide and seek, and we walked too far, is all."

"Why do you tell me lies? I'm your keeper, Marietta. The only person you can trust. What were you doing there?"

"Nothing. We got lost playing a game."

"You're too old to play games. What were you doing?"

"We got lost."

The old woman sighed. She looked the girl in the eye.

"There's wickedness, Marietta, dark as night. There are things that are wicked and if you touch them, they know you. They know where to find you now."

"I won't go there again," Marietta promised.

Delphine didn't answer. She burned the clothes Marietta wore that day, and cleansed the house with incantations and with burning chicory wood and sage.

Ethel

Ethel ran along the dirt path toward the trailer where her family had lived since her dad lost his job as a foreman at the paper mill. Drinking on the job, the boss said. Her dad said the boss was a liar, but the company let him go. A few months later the bank claimed their house. That was when the real trouble started.

Ethel didn't mind the trailer. Her mother Shirley said it was trashy. She said they were living like hicks. They couldn't even afford one of the mobile home parks over in Longview, and Shirley said that was as low as anybody ought to go. Instead they had to get by on a vacant lot owned by a relative. They were a charity case.

"Someday we're leaving this goddamn town," Shirley said every time she got drunk. "We'll pack one suitcase and clear right out!"

After several months the paper mill was busy enough to add a night shift. They re-hired Ethel's dad for the late shift, but only at half what he was making before. The boss warned him that one mistake would be his last.

"Mouse or man?" Shirley asked her husband at least once a week. "Are you a mouse or a man, Newie? What kind of man crawls back to people that treat him like dirt?"

Newell Burney held his tongue until he had a couple of shots of vodka. Then he reminded Shirley that he earned every penny they had, and she didn't lift a finger if she didn't feel like it. He told her to go ride some other jackass, if she could find one. Here he would smile in an ugly way, leering at his angry, young wife until Ethel had to look away from both of them.

The dirt path ran alongside the woods. The rain had let up for a moment, but the wind still whipped Ethel's brown hair across her face. Voices chirped from the darkened fir trees, the forest-muffled noise of frantic birds. She hated birds, especially owls.

Once, when she was seven, she had seen a screech owl swoop down in moonlight and disappear into the lower depth of a grassy trench. The owl emerged seconds later, with a shriek and a mighty flap of its wings. It held a field mouse clasped tight in its left claw, and as it climbed the air beside Ethel, preparing to take full flight, she saw in one blink the terror-struck eyes of the mouse caught in the owl's momentum, snatched clean out of its world.

She had stood there, in the middle of the road, breathing hard, with her ribs aching. She wanted to outrun the awful rush of wings, so she spun with her arms out, again and again, until she fell sideways and was sick in the grass. When the ground stopped spinning, she saw it again in her head: the mouse forced quiet in the owl's grip.

Against her will and despite a vain desire to be grown-up, Ethel scurried along, facing forward the way the little kids in school said you were supposed to:

"Keep your eyes to yourself. Be home before dark. Or Miss Knocks might find you and catch you in the woods with her long, long arms."

Ethel tried to think of other things while she hurried home, but her imagination kept circling back. She didn't like to admit she still felt afraid of Miss Knocks, afraid of the way Shirley lowered her voice when she told the stories. In Shirley's hands Miss Knocks became a hateful, hungry thing nesting in treetops. At night she was looking down, licking her lips and waiting for the chance to drag little girls like Ethel to her tree house, surrounded by the ink-black sky:

"Chh-shh! That's the sound of another child's skin catching fire! Chh-shh!"

Whenever Shirley made this sound the hairs on Ethel's

arms tingled. Shirley always looked away, licked her dry lips, and laughed.

Today every strand of Shirley's hair was sprayed stiffly into place. Her mascara was already starting to smear. A cigarette dangled from her lips, unlit.

"I told you: don't get stains on your school dresses or you can do your own damn wash!"

Shirley caught Ethel as she darted up from the path to the concrete back steps of the trailer. She swung a wooden spoon with one hand and clubbed Ethel on the back of her left thigh. A welt formed, the color of a new strawberry. She followed Ethel into the trailer, waving the spoon and shouting:

"I'm not bothering any more! Hear me? You get your clothes filthy playing kickball at that damn school, and see who does the laundry! Not me!"

The scent of drugstore cologne clung to the furniture. It was called Eau de something, and Shirley said it came from London, England, where people knew how to have a good time.

Shirley was dressed to go out: crisply ironed, pleated mini-skirt; a cotton blouse with shaggy ruffles; chunky go-go boots that zipped up the side; a shocking pink scarf tied over her spray-stiffened hair to keep the rain off. Nothing went together and most of it was out of style by a couple of years, but Ethel wasn't going to point this out. Every time she noticed a thing like that, Shirley went wild.

"You say you're better than me? Go on, then, little girl. You're so smart? I'll show you smart."

Ethel said nothing about her mother's outfit. She went to her room, peeled off her wet dress and changed into a hand-me-down pair of red corduroy slacks and a ratty t-shirt. Most of her home clothes were from the Salvation Army. Her school clothes came from Sears because Shirley wasn't about to let "those dumb hick kids" make fun of her daughter's appearance. That would mean Shirley didn't know how a girl ought to dress.

Ethel went to the kitchen, got a can of pineapple slices out of the fridge and peeled back the wax paper covering it. She slurped the leftover pineapple juice from the can. The heavy sweet syrup made her teeth hurt. She grimaced and took another swig.

Without saying goodbye Shirley put her lipstick and wallet into her good purse, left the trailer and slammed the front door. A few seconds later, Ethel heard the crunch of go-go boots on gravel as Shirley dashed through the rain to the car. Now it was coming down hard.

The gears began grinding away on the beat-up Impala in the yard. Her dad was forever fixing it up for her mother to drive another fifty miles until it broke down. Then Shirley would scream that he couldn't do anything a hundred percent, and he was old enough to be her grandpa. She said he was keeping the car the way it was on purpose, keeping her trapped here. Late at night she would stride off into the woods to smoke cigarettes until she was freezing and worn out. She'd come back with bloodshot eyes and Ethel could hear her crying, a sort of throaty whisper, late into the night.

This evening mud and wet gravel sprayed the outside wall, telling Ethel she wouldn't see her mother for a few hours. Her dad was working. She was free. She decided to eat grilled cheese sandwiches with Pepsi for supper. And she could watch cartoons on the portable TV if she reshaped the ball of foil attached to the antenna.

Tonight she was happy to be on her own. It was *Star Trek* night and she could stay up late. There was only the rain spattering the trailer outside, and Ethel lying on the couch in the blue glow of the little TV.

She lay on the couch after cartoons and the early news ended. Next came *High Chaparral*, then *The Name of the Game*, and then Ethel's favorite, *Star Trek*. After that was nothing but the news and weather.

Finally the buzz of the TV signal began to lull her into drowsiness. She tried to let go all the way and sleep but her brain kept buzzing. She watched the TV sideways with her head resting on a flat, velveteen cushion.

Shirley was probably at the nearest tavern with one of her boyfriends. Newell would sneak a couple of shots of vodka at work on his break. Ethel didn't want to know these things. She didn't want to be their daughter.

Some nights, half sleeping, dreaming of wings and black sky, Ethel pretended her parents didn't exist anymore. With their fights and name-calling and Shirley's habit of wandering off into the woods to sulk, they were like children. They threw the kind of tantrums Ethel wasn't allowed to throw. And when they made up, it was worse. They would lock themselves in the bedroom with the TV and a case of beer for hours at a time while Ethel played alone outside.

By now the fire in the forest might have gone out by itself. Maybe people would be talking about it down at the tavern, and Shirley would remember the stains on her dress and sweater, and figure out what Ethel had done.

No matter what happened, her story was ready: Miss Knocks set the fire. This was a perfect lie, because Shirley would have to admit that Miss Knocks was made-up, if she wanted to punish Ethel. It was the kind of plan Mr. Spock would like. Its logic would overload Shirley's mind, and smoke would pour from her ears, and she would no longer compute.

The TV buzz infected Ethel's dreams. She lay awake and asleep at the same time, no longer in the room but sensing the electric hum faintly beneath everything. Leaves swirled around the room and out the door. A cloud of smoke lifted its head snakelike and whispered in her ear:

"Sure as you're born."

Vaguely from beneath the TV hum another noise emerged, a scratching sound: distant, quietly insistent, and then distinct. It seemed to move slowly but evenly down the length of the trailer, from the bedrooms at the end, past the kitchen to the living room, to the couch. It stopped there and stayed. It was coming from directly beneath the couch.

Ethel opened her eyes and lay still, listening for a sound she hoped to identify as a branch blown free in the storm and stuck under the trailer. But now the scratching climbed deliberately and methodically up one wall, over the trailer roof, and down the other side, where it stopped.

"Squirrel," she whispered. "Raccoon."

Again the scratching unmistakably made its way across the trailer on the underside. Inching its way beneath the living room until it was, once more, directly under the couch where Ethel lay.

She turned to look out the living room window. Framed by the glass, a good seven feet off the ground outside, the top half of a face was pressed against the glass, eyes in shadow, nostrils expelling air in short bursts that fogged the glass and cleared, fogged the glass and cleared, in rhythm.

Ethel bolted upright, scattering cushions and upsetting the plastic dish on the table. She ran to the hall closet, yanked the door open, and shoved aside her father's fishing boots. She climbed inside and pulled the door shut behind her. In the close dark she could smell the rubber boots, the salty skin of an old raincoat, the musty scent of storage and un-swept corners full of dust, hair, mouse droppings, and dirt. Breathing hard, she sank down against the coats and boxes, but she held onto the doorknob, keeping it shut tight.

Nothing moved. Only rain spatters and the sigh of the wind came from outside the trailer.

She was still sitting in the closet, leaning back and holding the door shut, half-asleep, hands aching where they clenched the doorknob, when she heard the engine of her father's truck. Once she knew her father was home Ethel opened the door and ran out as fast as she could, all the way to her bed. She jumped in and started snoring. If she believed she had been sleeping and dreaming all along, it might be true. It would be true.

The front door squealed on rusty hinges. Her father's hacking cough followed, then the metallic snap of his cigarette lighter. Next the fridge door opened and closed. These were his usual sounds. He would drink a beer and wait for Shirley to come home.

Even the thought of the argument that would follow wasn't enough to keep Ethel's eyes open. She drifted down and in. She let herself tumble into deep sleep. Faintly, as the world slipped away, she caught the lingering scent of her father's cigarette in the next room. She dreamed of smoke trails, winding out the window and through the crackling woods.

"Breathe!"

Was it her father's voice?

"Breathe! Come on, honey! Take a big breath for me!"

Ethel inhaled. A sharp pain shot through her chest. She felt sick. She had to clench her jaw not to vomit. Pain came rolling up from her lungs and her stomach. She coughed hard, opened her eyes, and stared straight up at the morning sky. A dark-eyed junco went zigzagging across her view overhead.

"I think she's good," she heard someone say. "She's going to be okay."

She heard other voices and the crunch of gravel. She tried to turn her head. Her neck felt stiff and her head throbbed. She tried to sit up but a hand touched her shoulder and the voice said:

"Take it easy, now. You're all right. Take it easy."

The next thing she saw was light, not the light from the sky but a blue and red flicker. It bounced across the outside wall of the trailer, which was black and charred. Smoke was drifting from the door and the windows. She turned her head in the other direction and saw stretchers, two of them, covered with blankets, waiting to be loaded into an ambulance.

"Where's my dad?" Ethel tried to ask, and found that

her throat was raw, tasting of blood like the time when she had her tonsils out.

"Take it easy."

The man talking to Ethel wore a uniform. He tried to smile at her, but his eyes didn't smile. He looked down at her with what seemed like pity.

"You've just got smoke in your lungs, sweetheart. You'll be okay. Everything's going to be okay."

She looked again at the covered stretchers. Before she could form a real thought about what was lying beneath the blankets, the words came into her head:

"Over and done."

The Girls

"Gangly" was how Beverly Sherman's mother described Beverly and her friends at fourteen. The previous year she had called them "string beans" and before that they were "nothing but puppies." Just to be precise in her contempt, Beverly looked up "gangly" in a dictionary and reported to the other girls. As they suspected, the term was not flattering.

"Going on fifteen," each of the girls said, whenever people asked their age. "Almost fifteen. Pretty soon." Even though their birthdays were months away.

It was a humid, overcast Saturday morning in early summer. The forecast was good but also notoriously unreliable.

Mrs. Sherman had packed sandwiches for them. Now she stood next to the car saying goodbye.

"Look at you girls!" She shouted. "Gangly as all get-out!"

Beverly, Ethel, and Marietta stretched out their skinny legs in the back seat of the Bel Air. They wore cotton skirts and sleeveless blouses with sandals. Their swimsuits and shorts were packed in a canvas bag in the trunk.

In the front seat Ethel's Aunt Constance smiled indulgently at Mrs. Sherman and fanned herself with a road map. They were getting a late start. If the weather were good Long Beach would be crowded by the time they arrived.

"They're growing up so fast," Constance said.

Three sets of solemn eyes gazed at her, framed by the rearview mirror. None blinked.

"No," said Mrs. Sherman. "They're taller, but they're sure not growing up. At least mine isn't."

She handed Beverly a ten-dollar bill through the back seat window. Then she stood up straight and smiled her broad, pink smile.

"Look at you! Just a gaggle of gangly girls going up to the beach!"

Mrs. Sherman laughed. She stepped back from the car and waved goodbye. The girls turned and watched her grow small in the back window as the Bel Air picked up speed.

Constance always sat alone in the front seat on road trips. She hummed or sang along with the radio. The girls liked to chat and they didn't like to sing.

"Your mama thinks we look funny," Ethel said, once they were on the road.

"She thinks everybody looks funny," Beverly said. "She has nicknames for all of her friends, behind their back."

"Like what?" Ethel asked.

"Toad Neck," said Beverly. "That's for the cashier at Jessup's."

The other girls grinned. Beverly went on with the list of women her mother liked to mock.

"Half-Price, that's Carolyn Price, the Sunday school teacher, because she likes a bargain too much. Shiftless is my aunt Polly. I used to think it was because she doesn't wear a slip, but it's more than that. She stole my mother's boyfriend in high school. And your aunt has a nickname."

Beverly lowered her voice and the other girls leaned closer to hear. They tilted their heads just a bit and lowered their eyes.

"Mother calls her James."

Ethel and Marietta shared a blank expression. Then Ethel figured it out.

"Oh, like a chauffeur on TV! 'Home, James!'"

They all nodded. Constance was humming along to a Broadway show tune on the radio. She gave them a wink in the rearview mirror.

"Well that's a rude thing to say," said Ethel.

Her aunt was the only family she had left. Her father's middle-aged sister moved from Longview after the fire that killed Ethel's parents. Constance said it was easier for a grown woman to start over in a new town than to expect a girl Ethel's age to change schools and friends, after all she had been through. She sold her house in Longview and the lot she owned, the one the Burneys had been living on, and bought a decent little place in Skillute with a garage and a good-sized back yard. She ran a tailoring business from home.

"She only ever sees your aunt when she's behind the wheel, taking us to school or the beach or a movie."

"Connie drives us around to be nice," said Ethel. "Your mom's kind of mean."

"Cry me a river," said Beverly. "I have to live with her."

They passed through the stately old town of Astoria with the prim clapboard houses Beverly called "claptrap." A little over an hour later they stood in the back aisle of Marsh's Free Museum staring into the glass aquarium that housed the remains of Jake the Alligator Man.

This was always their first stop as soon as they reached the peninsula. The girls couldn't explain their fascination with Jake, whose shriveled and blackened body, human from head to waist and alligator from waist to tail tip, was the main attraction at the souvenir store. Their attitude was one of revulsion mixed with pity, and there was something more, an affection, as if the creature in the display tank were a cousin they had to greet on every trip despite his hideous deformity.

"He looks lonely," Ethel said.

"He doesn't look lonely. He looks dead. He's dead."

Beverly reminded Ethel of this obvious fact on every trip. It was another part of their ritual. Each time they went to the beach, they visited Jake. Ethel always noticed how forlorn the half-man, half-alligator seemed, and Beverly always said:

"He's dead."

This time she added:

"And he's lucky he doesn't have to look at all the out-of-towners. That woman at the checkout stand is wearing the ugliest muumuu I've ever seen. Oh boy. Her bald husband is taking a picture of us. Like we're part of the exhibit! Turn your back to him."

The sun they had hoped for never broke through that day. A storm was coming. Most of the tourists had snatched up their lawn chairs and towels and children, and fled indoors. Marsh's was nearly empty. The bald man crept closer to the girls, with his camera lens aimed at them.

"If you all look this way and smile, I can get a real good shot," he said. "Then I can mail the picture to y'all later."

Without turning around Beverly said to the man:

"Do you think we don't have any pictures of ourselves?"

She shook her head and gave a little snorting laugh.

"If you take that picture," she told him. "We're going to scream and tell the cops you asked us to take off our clothes."

The sound of shifting and groaning floorboards indicated that the man was hurrying back to safety. His wife was fishing for a wallet inside an enormous beach bag, to pay for a basket of seashells.

"These will be so pretty in the bathroom," she said merrily.

"Why do they buy those things?" Beverly asked.

"Mementos," said Ethel.

"So they can remember the day," Marietta added.

Beverly laughed.

"The day she wore an ugly dress and they hated each other and he tried to take pictures of three girls he'd never even met?"

They wandered outside and down the sidewalk. They bought root beer at the general store next to Marsh's, and decided to stroll along the boardwalk in the cool drizzle. They agreed it was just their luck to have rain at the beach on a day that was forecast as a beauty.

The air was heavy, damp, and pearl gray. It was hard to tell where the ocean ended and the sky started.

Aunt Constance would be waiting at the rented bungalow. By the time they returned she would have everything ready. A fire would be blazing in the cast iron stove and she would be knitting. The girls would roast hot dogs indoors. Then they would make s'mores and play canasta. Late at night they would listen to Constance tell spooky stories about lighthouse keepers and ghost pirates and women from the sea.

"Where do you think Jake really came from?" Ethel asked.

They passed a weathered fence. Then they began to cross at a diagonal the grass-speckled approach that led from the boardwalk past their bungalow and on to the sea.

"Maybe a circus," Marietta said.

"I don't know about that," said Beverly.

"Well, he must have been a freak," Ethel suggested. "So where else would he come from, if it wasn't the circus?"

Beverly considered this. The call of seagulls carried across the water.

"It's got to be one of two things," she said at last. "He was a boy his parents kept hidden all his life, maybe in a barn or a shed. When he died they couldn't bury him in a church graveyard like normal kids, so his parents wrapped him up and gave him to the museum."

"Why?" Ethel asked.

"As a warning to other people, everywhere."

"A warning against what?"

Beverly sighed. She held the root beer can to her lips and breathed against it, making a small arc of condensation. At last she said:

"Against whatever bad things his parents did. They must have done something that was - "

She searched for the word. The other girls waited.

"Taboo," she said.

"What's the other thing?" Ethel asked. "Where else

could he come from?"

"My aunt says he's a regular boy, sewn to an alligator's tail," said Marietta.

The other two looked at her. Marietta was becoming more taciturn these days. Yet every now and then she would burst out with a statement that seemed crazy enough to be true.

"In a way," said Ethel. "That's worse. It means that somebody cut him in half and threw away his legs, so they could turn him into a half-alligator."

All three stopped to consider the implications. They sipped their root beer and walked on.

"If that's what happened," said Beverly. "Do you think he was dead or alive when they sewed him together?"

"Dead," said Ethel. "I hope he was dead."

A cormorant waddled across the width of the sandy approach ahead of them. Its feathers were black as oil. It gave a grunting call and hopped a few steps toward the sea, away from the girls.

"But the alligator part is charred just like the boy part," said Beverly. "You think somebody went to the trouble to find a burnt tail, to match the burned-up face, or the other way around?"

Ethel was watching the bird on the beach. Suddenly Beverly flushed pink from ear to ear.

"Sorry, Ethel," she said.

"That's okay."

"I forgot."

"It's okay."

Sharp and fast, something flew through the air and struck the cormorant. It gave a loud cry and lifted its wings, but it was too late. A second rock whistled across the sand and hit the bird in the head. It fell hard against the sand and started shrieking, turning over and over but unable to stand or fly.

The girls watched a boy of nine or ten come from the left, whooping and laughing. He was closing in fast on the cormorant. The bird was coated in damp sand now and it slowed with each attempt to right itself, but its cries still pierced the air. The boy drew up next to it, lifted a stick of petrified wood and struck the bird with it. In its death throes the cormorant lay streaked with blood against the sand.

Ethel and Beverly stood frozen, too shocked to move. They stared at the boy, who only now seemed to notice the group watching him. He gave them a defiant smile, and lifted the stick once more. It was a pointless gesture because the bird was near death. Yet he raised his arm higher than before, showing off now that he knew he had an audience.

Marietta stepped ahead of Ethel and Beverly. She kept walking toward the boy until only about fifty feet remained between them. The beach and boardwalk were deserted but for the four of them. Marietta kept walking until she could see the boy's face clearly and he could see hers. He shook the stick overhead for emphasis and then brought it down one last time on the broken bird.

All three girls heard it distinctly. As though no other sound occupied the air, not the ocean waves, the breeze, the cars passing on the wet and glittering road behind them. The only sound they heard was the clean, hard snap of young bones breaking. This was followed at once by a scream so shrill that Beverly and Ethel had to drop their soda cans and cover their ears.

Only Marietta listened to the full-throated wailing of the boy, whose arm was fractured in three places. Only Marietta stood watching as he fell to the sand next to the dead cormorant, writhing and screaming for his mother who would soon hear him from their bungalow and come running to her boy in his agony. Only Marietta smiled.

Marietta

Blood flowing, warm crimson between her thighs. She felt it coming out of her in clots, then in streams. Heated by her body, it came thick, tinged with the scent of copper. Blood would run down her legs if she let it. If she stood still as an evergreen, feet stuck in the ground, shards of light cutting the shadows on all sides. She dreamed of standing so for days, weeks, or years in a darkened forest. Giving over, simultaneously, to the forces inside and out. It was her one soothing thought, the one that brought balance.

Blood broke the pain in her head and her back. First came the tension in her neck, then the pain like a sewing needle stuck through the back of her head, wriggling behind one of her eyes, trying to propel it from the socket. Then the cramps came, deep in her abdomen, a vise tightening all day until she couldn't stand up. She was blinded, doubled over, gripped by a force ancient and unyielding.

The curse. She had never known why the women who visited Aunt Delphine called it that, but now she knew. Time stopped and all objects froze while this torture worked its way through her.

Delphine brewed ginger tea, mixed in a good dose of brown sugar, and made her sip it while she lay in bed with a warm compress across her stomach. This was soothing to her, being cared for, but nothing took the pain away until her period broke with a final crescendo so excruciating that she thought surely she must die. Then with the flow of blood the vise loosened its grip and sharp pain gradually gave way to an ache. The ache brought dullness of mind, stupor, but that was better than what had gone before.

Now she could lie in Delphine's room among her candles and magic boxes and jars of herbs, propped up on silk pillows in the pale sunlight. She tried to skim books, to no avail, then magazines. She couldn't make sense of them. When she sat quietly her mind flooded with pictures.

At first she thought she was recalling images from the magazines, but she soon realized that the pictures inside her head were preventing her understanding anything placed in front of her. The scenes in her head were moving, crowding out what was before her eyes. So she gave in. She closed her eyes and sank into blackness, and the visions took hold of her. The pain in her head ceased, the blood swelled and coursed from her body, and she watched as terrible and splendid things occurred.

She thought she had no control over it. She tried many times, but she couldn't will herself to see what she wanted to see. Gradually she learned that everything she saw would happen soon. She had to wait for it. It was like watching the planchette glide across a Ouija board. She was connected to the movement, but she couldn't say how.

A week before one of their trips to the beach she had seen ebon wings bloodied in sand, blackened driftwood etched against the gray sky, the shudder of death and the sound of bones breaking. She had seen and felt it all. She had lain beneath a red and yellow quilt in a patch of sunlight, sipping ginger tea, and she had seen these things, and then she had slept peacefully without dreaming.

Beverly

Beverly lied. She told her mother she was going with Marietta and Ethel to see a movie. They did this every so often. Either they walked to the movie theater in Kelso or begged a ride from Aunt Constance and went to the Longview Theater, which was much nicer.

Today Beverly explained that they were planning to have lunch and see *The Way We Were*, which seemed safe enough to Mrs. Sherman until she heard from a friend that it was pro-Communism. Beverly swore to her mother that they would see *Paper Moon* instead, and that she wasn't going to see *The Exorcist* with Constance as a chaperone. She swore on a bible at Mrs. Sherman's insistence and in imitation of her gravely dramatic expression.

Lunch and a movie would be about three hours. That would be enough time, by Beverly's estimation. She didn't know for sure. She had never done this before, snuck off to the woods with a boy she liked.

He was new in town. His name was Oliver, a very odd name for a boy in Skillute. It sounded uppity. That was the first thing Beverly had noticed, right after she noticed Oliver's shaggy brown hair. He had the kind of hair that would make Beverly's father ask, in his bear-like, old-fashioned way, if he was a boy or a girl. Beverly was dreading this pathetic joke so much, she was afraid to invite Oliver to her house. She was also afraid that Oliver would find her home small, overcrowded, and tacky. He would see her mother's collections: a cluster of dolphin-shaped Avon bottles in the bathroom, a pile of ceramic poodles on a shelf in the hall, and the Robert Goulet albums next to the RCA stereo in the living room.

As far as Beverly was concerned Oliver had every right to be uppity. His family came from back east, as far away as New York and New England. That was almost as good as being from Europe. His mother was a Daughter of the American Revolution, a fact that Beverly found impressive. Her mother didn't know what D.A.R. stood for, and her ignorance further convinced Beverly that it must be very high toned. What her mother knew was how much property cost. She estimated at a glance that Oliver's parents occupied the most expensive house in Skillute.

"Rolling in it," Mrs. Sherman had said more than once. "That's what they are. Look at the marble lions next to their front gate. That house looks like a library, or a courthouse!"

Oliver had already completed the books on the current list at school. He seemed bored in class. He would often get a dreamy, faraway look as though he knew a much more interesting place, where he'd like to be.

Beverly's mother said she had been "itching for trouble" for a long time, ever since she turned fourteen. Beverly wasn't sure what that meant. The way she saw things, she was simply on the alert for the unusual. She bought clothes without her mother's advice, and paid Ethel's aunt to alter them for her. Ever since the Christmas when she caught her mother sewing fake Casual Corner labels into her school dresses Beverly had known that the adult world was treacherous and not very bright. Women with children were the biggest liars of all.

She wanted authentic, unique things, or nothing. She was finding that the more outlandish something seemed to the people she knew the more likely it proved to be valuable. Like caviar and fondue. Her father had never heard of fondue. He thought it was a country near Sweden. Beverly found his ignorance shocking, especially since he had served in the Navy during a world war. How could he travel all the way around the world and learn nothing?

This year, to top off the list of things that disgusted Beverly, all the boys in her class were learning to spit. It was their favorite pastime, spitting. She couldn't imagine ever being in love with or married to one of these lumbering, tongue-tied, saliva- and tobacco-spewing boys.

Oliver always nodded and watched her expression closely when she talked. He was the only boy at school who did this. The others grunted and looked past her like they were waiting for someone else to show up. They only looked at her when she walked away.

Beverly longed for a boy to fall in love with her, a boy or a man, someone who wasn't a singer or a character on a TV show. She wondered what it meant to be swept away. She had seen movies where men swept women up in their arms, but that looked made-up.

She couldn't get advice from her friends. They knew nothing about seduction. Ethel still had posters of David Soul and Michael Parks in her bedroom, and she lit candles and looked up at them like a little girl. Marietta was more grownup but in a watchful, silent way that sometimes gave Beverly a chill.

Nowadays Marietta's aunt kept her out of school whenever she felt like it. She used the girl as an assistant but didn't pay her much. The only money Marietta was allowed were tips for providing gullible people with what Delphine Dodd called her intuitions.

Of the three, Beverly decided, Ethel was the lucky one, despite her immaturity. Since her crazy mom and dad had died in a fire that almost killed Ethel too, she had been living with her dad's sister. Constance Burney ran a tailor shop in their home. She was quiet and patient, bland in her views, a teetotaler and a Republican. She never discussed politics or religion with anyone, because she said these subjects were in poor taste. She taught Ethel to sew, a trade she could use anywhere. Aunt Constance was even saving up to send her to the community college for a year of fashion and costume design. After that Ethel could probably get a job in Vancouver or Portland. She could leave Skillute if she wanted to.

Beverly sighed. She had often dreamed of her meddling, messy family going up in smoke. When she was nine years old she had written a solemn story about a nine-year-old who murdered her dull parents and loudmouthed siblings and burned their bodies in the fireplace. The heroine had eaten dainty cucumber sandwiches from a silver tray while the considerable layers of fat crackled and sizzled in the glinting fire.

She practiced a bereaved expression, just in case. She could see the black silk dress and hat she would wear to the funeral, both designed by a famous French woman. Beverly's teacher pronounced the woman's name "Shah-NEL." Beverly's mother mispronounced it "Channel." Beverly had seen the perfect black dress in a magazine next to a monthly column by Mademoiselle Chanel, who was a genius on the subject of what women ought to wear. One rule of thumb was to make sure your hemline wasn't too trendy. It was supposed to match your age. Mademoiselle Chanel said: If a man laughs when he sees a woman climbing out of a car, her skirt is too short.

Oliver held out his hand to help Beverly. They followed the ivy-covered incline and walked for a quarter of a mile until they reached a patch of cedars. The woods here were spotty, strewn with weeds and dead branches, dotted with the brittle spines of devil's club, the shrubs starting to die off.

Only a year earlier one of the big companies had come through and pulled out most of the Doug fir for timber. Now it was nothing like the place Beverly remembered. Only a slim ring of fir and cedar leaned rakishly between busy residential roads and the freeway. She recalled the silence of the place, above all. It wasn't silent here. The traffic sounds were softened but not shut out.

"Here we are," said Beverly, looking forlornly at their destination.

She felt sweaty. She brushed away the perspiration from her forehead with the back of her hand. She had once seen an actress on *Here Come the Brides* do this and she still thought it was a very feminine thing to do. She wished she had worn lace gloves.

"So this is the spot?" Oliver asked, grinning. He stood with his arms crossed and looked around at the forest, then back at Beverly.

"I think so."

"You and your friends used to play here when you were little?"

"Not exactly," said Beverly. "We kind of took an oath."

"Really?" Oliver smiled.

Now it all seemed ridiculous. How many years had it been since she had seen this place? She wasn't sure. It might have been two or three years, but it seemed like more. She remembered the fire, and saying some words they had memorized. She remembered the lipstick and the white shoestring she had stolen from her mother that day, and running from the fire.

"Do your mom and dad have hair like yours?" She asked, anxious to change the subject.

"I guess so," he told her.

"What does that mean? You know what their hair looks like."

"Not really," he said. "I'm adopted, so, you know?"

She had never met anyone who was adopted. Orphaned or abandoned to relatives, yes, but adopted by another family? That was a story she had only seen on TV, along with babies left on doorsteps or deserted and raised by wolves in the wild. She felt an overwhelming pity for Oliver that made her want to kiss him.

"That's so sad," she told him.

"Why?" He asked. "My parents are okay. My dad's rich."

"But your real mother gave you away."

Beverly winced. She hadn't meant to say this so bluntly.

"Please," said Oliver. "She was probably a junkie, or some other type of criminal. We don't talk about it. Anyway, I got lucky, believe me."

Beverly sensed the weekend traffic on the main road flashing beyond the fringe of cedars to her right: A quick, bright light in her peripheral vision.

A memory flooded her senses. She inhaled the fragrance of cedar. Underfoot she now saw the remains of wood shingles. Some of them were smashed to bits. She smelled smoke, turned, and flinched when she saw Oliver.

"Hey!" He said. "Everything okay?"

She stepped closer, placed one hand on his chest and kissed him. He laughed.

"What?" She asked.

"That's, um," he shook his head.

"Yes?"

"Did you know you were standing on one foot when you did that?"

Against all of her will, her face flushed hot pink. She had only kissed mirrors and pillows and a few doors and the back of her hand. She had kissed these objects the way she imagined romantic kisses. Now with a flash of self-loathing she realized her pose was ridiculous.

"I didn't mean it like that," Oliver told her. "It was kind of cute."

She wanted to retch.

"Very cute," he said. "It's all right."

He kissed her. His lips were dry and his breath smelled like grape bubble gum. She was about to tell him that she was joking before, but he kissed her again. This time she felt his tongue, warm and slippery, gliding between her lips. His tongue wiggled against the roof of her mouth.

He put his arms around her and pulled her close. She felt a tingling in her chest and between her legs. It crossed her mind that she might be starting her period, and she blushed again. Before she could decide what to do Oliver pressed against her and gently guided her to the ground. He lay on top of her. His sweat smelled clean like salt water.

She didn't like having her dress bunched up around her hips. Or his wet tongue stuck inside her left ear. She forgot these annoyances when he licked the palm of his hand and reached inside her panties.

"Uh!"

"It's okay," Oliver whispered in her still-wet ear.

It wasn't okay. He was slathering her, down there, with his spit, with the saliva and mucous from his mouth. So this was the part of lovemaking they left out of TV shows, the part no one was allowed to see. Whatever it was, Beverly didn't care for it, but she was too mortified to say anything until she felt Oliver's flesh as he shoved his way inside her. This burned so much that she almost cried out, but she was afraid to scream or cry. She was afraid that if she started screaming Oliver wouldn't stop. Then what could she do? At the same time she was afraid he would laugh at how pathetic and ignorant she was. He would tell everyone at school that she had never even kissed a boy before.

So she clenched her teeth and closed her eyes. She concentrated all of her strength on the darkness behind her eyelids; the quiet darkness where Oliver's grunting didn't nauseate her and the perspiration from his neck didn't swipe across her chin every time he heaved his body against hers.

A few minutes later Beverly sat up. She was sitting on the ground looking up at the trees. Oliver gave her a peck on the cheek. Then he put his hand on top of her head and stroked her hair. He smiled. In the next moment he was trudging away, taking the path they had used to reach this pitiful, balding patch of woods.

She didn't watch him go. She smoothed her dress and took a compact out of her purse. In the mirror she saw that the thin layer of lipstick she had applied that afternoon was smeared on one side.

She was sore and she didn't want to move. Her mother would worry if she didn't come back soon. She had to get home before anyone came looking for her.

She forced herself to stand, then to walk on legs that felt like they had springs instead of bones. She smoothed her hair and her dress again and took a few more steps, watching the ground to avoid stumbling. She saw a stone sticking out of the ground and stooped to pick it up, just to see if it hurt to do so.

Her fingers grasped the stone, which now appeared to be a shell. Only when Beverly held the object closer and turned it over did she realized that it was a jawbone, darkened by fire or paint. Tiny and delicate, it was also unmistakably human, with a crooked row of teeth small enough to belong to a child.

She stood in the dappled light, gazing at the strange memento. Slate in color, it was so smooth and clean it looked as though it had been polished. She gently wrapped the jawbone in a linen handkerchief and placed it inside her purse next to her compact.

The story her family concocted had to do with a bad case of mono and spending the rest of the school year studying at home. As a particular punishment she wasn't allowed to have visitors at home during her pregnancy. Mrs. Sherman called this her confinement, a term that conjured images of wild-haired women in prison chains.

Ethel and Marietta were told to stay home, to avoid risk of infection. The boredom of these months, and the fear of boredom, stayed with Beverly all of her life.

Eight and a half months later, the only thing she knew about her daughter was the first name given to her by her new parents: Lydia. It wasn't a name Beverly would have chosen. If asked, she would have suggested Gabrielle. That was Coco Chanel's real name. She never had a chance to say this, because no one asked.

The stout woman in chubby lace-up shoes who represented the adoption agency said she wasn't entitled to know either the infant's gender or name. The new parents had granted Beverly this rare privilege out of kindness. They had heard that the child's mother was young, and they felt a natural sympathy. Hearing the word "sympathy," Beverly drew her arms around her knees and stared sullenly at the TV set mounted on the wall opposite her hospital bed.

"You've got no one to blame but yourself, missy."

Her mother said this so many times that Beverly started hearing it in her sleep. During her hospital stay she comforted herself with lemon pastries delivered by candy stripers, and by imagining her mother being hit by a meteor.

She didn't think much about Oliver any more. He never spoke to her after their day together in the woods. She knew he would leave Skillute after high school and she expected he would never return. First he would go to an Ivy League college. Then his parents would marry him off to a girl from a rich family. That was how those people operated, and it made perfect sense to Beverly. If her family had been rich, she would never have wasted her time with anyone who wasn't rich. She realized now that boys like Oliver didn't fall in love with girls who behaved the way she had behaved. It all made sense, and she accepted it with bitterness.

On the day she was scheduled to vacate the hospital room she had shared with three other teenage girls, whose families usually kept them hidden behind curtains, her mother arrived early with a change of clothing. Beverly had hoped for a new dress but her mother said there was no point until she lost weight, and if she expected a reward after all the trouble she had caused, she could think again. This "little adventure" in the hospital had cost her parents most of their savings. She was lucky they didn't have to pay someone to take her "mistake" off their hands. She would spend another month confined to her room, thinking about what she had done.

Beverly would also think carefully about what she and her friends had done, and how their oath in the woods had failed. Maybe it was her fault because she had lied to Ethel and Marietta, but they had been little girls back then. She had never believed in the oath, not with her whole heart.

She knew Ethel believed, and Marietta entered into the ceremony so gravely that Beverly had almost laughed out loud while listening to her say the words.

They were silly, both of them, but they were her only friends. Throughout her pregnancy they had gone on trying to get past her mother, if only for a brief visit. Finally they had started taping cards and notes to her window. Beverly had retrieved and read them at night when her mother slept. She thought of so many replies, so many things she wanted to tell them. Yet she kept these thoughts to herself, maybe because they were the only things she could command in her parents' house, once she had disappointed them forever by "ruining" herself.

Naively she had thought only people who made love all the time had babies. Not a girl like herself. Not because of one afternoon in the woods. She was ashamed, but not because of the baby. She was ashamed to find that she was so gullible, so ignorant, so much her parents' daughter.

She had heard of other girls her age, teenagers who had to leave school because of mono. There had always been stories and rumors. Now she could only think of those young women like herself, hiding in their bedrooms. Pretending to be asleep to avoid another conversation about consequences. Being assaulted with questions they would rather die than answer. Plotting impossible escapes by night, plotting murder and other forms of spite while their fat, stupid families slept and snored throughout the house.

Marietta

Marietta was seventeen, almost eighteen. Ever since she started high school she had been responsible for more and more of Delphine's clients and their needs. Now Delphine was slowing down, aging fast and frequently ill with arthritis. Marietta was capable of taking over her aunt's business, but she wasn't sure she wanted to. She felt more than ever at the mercy of her erratic visions, or "intuitions" as Delphine called them to make them seem less frightening to the women who visited with various ailments.

Often nowadays Marietta wondered what it would be like to be an ordinary young woman. The more she learned from Delphine the more she felt burdened by the old woman's ancient profession. In particular she wished not to carry the weight of what she knew about Delphine's past.

"Back then."

Delphine began her stories this way. As though she were telling a fairy tale, or the events she was about to recount happened so long ago that they were shrouded in mystery and the people involved could be forgiven for their backwardness because they were not as educated or evolved as modern people. In truth the individuals Delphine named were intelligent enough to know what they were doing, and the events took place only a few years before Marietta was born. The proximity made all of it that much worse.

Marietta's only option was to tolerate what she knew. To damn Delphine would be to damn herself and her home. Over the years, as she learned more, she also learned to accept more.

"Back then, being poor in Skillute didn't mean getting

by. It meant starving and watching your children starve. This idea people have nowadays about community, there was nothing like that in Skillute. People looked out for their own, and no one else."

"You said yourself," Marietta reminded her aunt, whose thoughts seemed to fade a bit each day. "What's dead and gone doesn't come back, if you're careful. It's over and done."

"No. I said: As it was," Delphine corrected her. "Nothing that was real can be real *as it was*. An injured spirit sheds life but not the craving. It still wants to live."

"How?" Marietta asked.

"As something else. We break down into the smallest bits of dust and become whatever is around us. If that's purely good, we become part of the good."

"Then there's nothing to be afraid of."

Delphine shook her head.

"There's no pure good in anybody I've met. People wrestle with themselves and good doesn't always win, even in a person who wants to be good. Wickedness comes looking for a home. It's a cancer you've got to avoid, Marietta. Keep yourself clean and keep your house clean. Say your incantations every day. Once you let it in, all that's craving life in the shadows will find you. If things want to live, they find their way to the wicked."

John Colquitt was thirty-five, twice divorced, and unemployed most of the year. Why Marietta chose him she couldn't explain. All he owned was an old Chevy pickup, bleach-white, sagging in the middle where the frame had bent when he rolled it in a ditch during a four-day binge. He had worked here and there, in a factory line, planting trees, picking strawberries and wild ginger and selling it on the road in summer, any odd job that paid.

He had lined up a three-day chore clearing blackberry bushes for Delphine. It wasn't an arrangement the old woman liked. But given another season the blackberries would overwhelm the herb garden and the house and the beehive, and every square foot of Delphine's already limited property. Doing away with the pernicious plant was a job for a man. She hired the first one who came along offering his services. She told him if he wanted to be paid he had to finish up in less than a week and be gone.

It was a sweaty job and John Colquitt went shirtless a couple of times. Each time Delphine went hobbling out to the yard to speak with him. Marietta heard their voices raised and saw John make a show of putting his perspiration-soaked work shirt back on. As soon as Delphine's back was turned he made a bowing motion with a tiny flourish, like he was saying goodbye to a queen.

Delphine had been ill for a few years. She was often in pain, but she got by with her remedies and with help from Marietta. As far as the girl knew, her aunt's only real complaint was arthritis. She was dumbfounded when Delphine died in her sleep, leaving her the rundown house and its contents.

Marietta had lived with her aunt all of her life. She wasn't surprised at her meager inheritance, but she was confused by the prospect of living alone. She had her friends Ethel and Beverly, but because of the nature of her aunt's work she had never been allowed to bring people home after school. There was no one close by that she trusted completely.

The morning after the burial John Colquitt paid Marietta a visit. She had brushed her hair for a long time at dawn, and made a wish against her better judgment.

"I figure you could use a shoulder to cry on," John said, offering a rough handful of violets.

Marietta looked him over through the screen door. She knew he'd pulled the flowers up nearby, maybe even from her back yard, but she thanked him. Nobody had ever given her flowers, and she had always wondered what it was like. She broke into a smile, and this was surprising to her. It felt good.

She had to find a clean glass for the violets. John Colquitt followed her and stood nearby while she searched the kitchen cabinets for just the right one, a ruby red glass with a leaf pattern cut into it. When she tried to move past John to reach the sink, he gently touched her arm.

"You're all by yourself now," he said, taking a look around the sparsely furnished house. His hair and face smelled of aftershave; it was strong and Marietta liked it. She remembered nothing about her father except the potent fragrance from a brown bottle of cologne, a rum-scented aftershave.

"I've got coffee started, if you want some," Marietta told her future husband.

She had finally stopped going to school altogether that year. Ethel was living with her aunt and getting ready to take a few design classes at the community college. Beverly was making the most of being on the cheerleading squad her senior year in high school. The three met for lunch once in a while. She said nothing about John.

For all her friends knew, Marietta was living alone after Delphine died. They said they envied her. They said she had a nice house all to herself. Then they went home, and she was alone.

The women who came to her aunt for remedies and advice were just as happy to visit Marietta as Delphine, but now Marietta began to turn them away. Still they kept stopping by offering a gift of chocolates, silver jewelry, canned ham, a roast chicken, or a bolt of fabric. She stopped answering the door. She was going to forget all of it, the spells and remedies, the shadows and visions. She would call her intuitions dreams. She would be like everyone else from this moment on. She was afraid of what John Colquitt would think if he knew the truth about her. She did all she could to bury the past with Delphine.

She told herself this was just a natural step. After all, she had never referred to her intuitions as anything psychic. The person who knew the extent of Marietta's condition had been her aunt. It took some effort but over the years Delphine had helped her to appear normal. Marietta had learned to act as though her intuitions were simply bad moods brought on by cramps and migraine.

She occasionally wished she could talk about what she knew, but she had discovered most people didn't want that. They might say that they did, but faced with the facts they would shy away, or run away. Even Ethel and Beverly believed that her intuitions were feverish nightmares that came true a little more often than most people's, by coincidence.

People wanted to hope for silly things they probably didn't deserve. Hope was the balm they wanted to buy. They didn't want to know what could actually happen to them. Delphine had understood this. She accepted the donations women offered for harmless predictions, and she urged Marietta to keep her intuitions to herself unless they were good ones. The bad things, the terrible things, were a secret. When it became clear that Marietta's great gift was to see the terrible things, Delphine began to lie. From that point on, together they had mostly squandered the girl's gift promising homely women they would be loved by handsome men someday.

"The secret is to say that what's coming won't happen right away," Delphine explained. "They've got to be patient. You say what they have their heart set on is only going to happen once they forget all about it."

"But what if it never happens?" Marietta asked.

"Doesn't matter," Delphine told her with a grin. "See, they'll never stop pining for that one thing. So they can only blame themselves."

Marietta's problem was: whatever she saw clearly came true, and it was seldom about romance with a good-looking man. She once made the mistake of warning a teacher not to take a scheduled trip to Mexico. A week later, when a temblor demolished the hotel where the woman had reluctantly canceled her reservation, she didn't thank Marietta.

She never spoke to her again, and never looked in her direction in class.

After the winter break in her senior year Marietta had decided to leave school. She reasoned: if she felt alone in a roomful of people her age, she might as well have her freedom. Two good friends like Ethel and Beverly were enough. And Delphine had been enough of a family.

Now her friends were busy with their last days of school. Delphine was gone, and Marietta was alone.

Pretty soon John moved in. The house seemed to shrink around him. It was nothing but eight hundred square feet of oak and tin on two thousand square feet of land. There was no view, only thick woods out back and the road out front. The railroad tracks nearby were coated with rust and hadn't been used since the 1950s.

Out back between the scrap of yard and the woods Marietta kept the beehive. She could never compete with the beekeepers that rented out their hives to pollinate trees and crops. She had nursed it along in hopes of earning a little cash from the honey and from beeswax candles. This, she decided, would be better than selling her intuitions. Above all, she would need some kind of income she could admit to ordinary people.

The place needed repairs from time to time. There was running water but the electricity was dodgy, set up when the little house was built in the 1940s and never upgraded. To keep the refrigerator and freezer running all the time she had to take turns between the other appliances. Marietta had learned to wait.

Part of the roof was duct taped into place. The bungalow had rugs nailed to two of the inside walls for insulation. In winter these remnants soaked up moisture and smelled of mildew. The furniture was ruined, ornate stuff Delphine had inherited from her grandmother. There was a TV set but it only worked about half the time.

The bathroom was peeling, rusting outward from the tub drain to the walls. The yellow tiles were nearly brown, and cracked in a hundred places.

"Why don't you use some caulking on that?" John would ask after a couple of beers. "Then paint it. That'd look a lot better, and people wouldn't take you for a hick!"

He laughed when he said these things. At first Marietta laughed too. He told her she laughed too loud. He told her not to wear shorts.

Pretty soon John was taking little digs at her for the way she walked. Then it was her hair, and why didn't she wear makeup? But if John wandered into the bathroom and caught Marietta brushing her hair or looking in the mirror, he would bump her aside on his way to the toilet.

After six months, she had to admit to herself that this bully was not the family she had hoped for when she let him kiss her and undress her and spend the night. All of that had been interesting at first, and then mostly a letdown.

Washing his clothes and cooking his meals just so he could brag that he'd had better made her aware that she was biding her time. Yet she didn't know exactly what she was waiting for. She had lived poorly with her aunt. She didn't mind that, but every day it seemed like this gruff, angry man came closer to doing her real harm. She knew it was only a matter of time.

"We ought to paint this place and sell it," he said one day.

"This house is all I've got," she reminded him.

"Start by burning that beehive."

He hated everything about the place, but especially the bees. He called them a nuisance because he wouldn't admit he was afraid. He would burn the hive. She knew it. He would have burned the house down if she'd had insurance on it.

Marietta was loath to admit the bitterness of her disappointment. All of her life she had seen women who had chosen poorly, who accepted their fate because they were too embarrassed to say they were wrong. Finally she had to own up to a lapse in judgment. John had looked like a change, but nothing had changed for the better.

Marietta had weakened after her aunt died. She had spent her nights staring at the kitchen table, lost in her thoughts. When John Colquitt had come to her door that day, he had seemed like a lifeline back to the world. Now she was paying the price for weakness.

Aunt Delphine told her never to let a man take care of her. She said there was no cure for loneliness. It was a fact of life. And the only cure for boredom was to get up and do something you want to do. She said a lot of things. Like: Always keep your money stashed in a safe place. And: A smart girl would have nothing to do with men and all that mess. From the moment a man walked in, she said, the light would start to go out of you, every minute of every day, until there was none left.

The day Marietta came home after swearing that childish oath Delphine began to tell her about the girl, and the woman who bought the girl. She told the story in bits and pieces at first. She told more as Marietta was able to comprehend more. The point was to know, and to be wary, not to feel sympathy but to be armed in advance. If Marietta ever encountered what was lying in wait, she would recognize it.

Her aunt's strategy didn't work when Marietta was a child. Although she learned to be cautious, to keep at bay the darkness in the woods, the story haunted her. She felt the sorrow of the girl who had been wronged. She couldn't help it.

By the time she decided she had to get away from John Colquitt, it was too late. She was expecting a child.

At the beginning of her pregnancy Marietta would stand in front of her house late at night, while John slept off a pint of whiskey. The fruit trees were etched in shadow and the beehive was quiet. She could see stars arcing overhead. The earth turned with her on board, like a carnival ride. The rush made her dizzy. Clouds moved so quickly she could barely catch sight of them. She imagined her mouth full of sticky, sweet cotton candy. She watched constellations expanding in the endless, deep darkness: Orion, Perseus, Andromeda. Light and light and black shining light.

She knew she had been changed. Her body had been tricked into doing this work, making this baby. She knew it. She had let down her guard. Each night she lay on the bed next to her sweating husband. Every snore from John sent a wave of sour whiskey breath over her.

She let her head drop onto the pillow and heard a rusty squeak from the mattress springs. Then she entered a silence as deep as the center of the earth. There it was like a cocoon surrounding her, and she did not dream. Nothing appeared to her in this silent sleep. She lay wrapped in the quiet of death until six in the morning, when she awoke and her misery started all over again: Pregnant, living alone with John, with no place to go from here. Her intuitions were gone.

Marietta said nothing about this when she went out with her friends. They sat in a booth at Jessup's and talked about the old days of a year ago, when they were still in high school together. By this time Ethel was enrolled in two classes at community college. Beverly had finally given in to her mother's wishes and was taking an accounting course by correspondence.

Marietta kept her troubles to herself. She didn't say that she was afraid, because she couldn't tell the other women what she feared. They might not believe her, and that would be worse than facing it alone.

She felt something moving, taking her over and trying to occupy every corner of her house. Nothing was hers any more. Nothing looked or smelled like Delphine any more. Nearly every inch of her world had been touched and tainted by John Colquitt.

She saw the whole outline of her life before her. Even without an intuition, she knew everything that would ever happen if she stayed with John.

Years later, these were the things she would remember. She would tell herself that what happened was part of the natural course. She would tell her friends too, that everything had taken its rightful path. No one would question her when she said this, but that was because she would forever keep two secrets from everyone she knew.

On a Friday morning a few months into her pregnancy Marietta woke up and told John she had one of her crippling headaches. He said he thought those only happened when she had her period. She said she had never been pregnant before, didn't know what to expect, and now her migraines had come back. Anyway, she couldn't get out of bed, she told him, not for a while.

He was already drinking his coffee. He walked away, stood in the kitchen leaning against the counter, squinting from a hangover. His belly hung low beneath his unbuttoned shirt. Even from the next room Marietta could see the thick hair on his stomach, sticking out in all directions.

She wondered for the thousandth time how he had come to be here, in her house. What accident had occurred, to make these things possible? Why had she not foretold the death of her aunt and all that would follow, when the knowledge could have helped her? What was the use of such a gift as hers? She wondered. She aimed to find out.

"There's another shirt, it's clean, outside on the line."

She was struck by a powerful sense that she had said this before. Of course, she might have said it any time, on any day. Yet every detail, John's green cotton shirt with its deep front pockets draped over the wooden clothes rack in the kitchen, the smell of slightly burnt coffee grounds, the rumble of county transport trucks passing the house toward the highway to lay a new coat of tar and gravel, all of this was more familiar than a memory.

Maybe this was what her intuitions would be like from

now on. Not a picture, exactly, but a feeling, a sense of having been here before. More than that, it was as if she were repeating what she had already done. She told herself that this was because the action was already taking place, the course was set, and what would happen was already over even as it occurred to her. The event itself was out of her hands, in a way.

John's new job was one he wouldn't tell her much about. She knew he was on one of the road crews. She guessed he was getting paid in cash, off the books. Maybe it was a union job he wasn't qualified to do. It was keeping them stocked with groceries, but he was tired when he got home and in no mood for what he called her "messing around."

More often than not, mercifully as far as Marietta was concerned, he fell asleep after supper and a few shots of whiskey. Then she always washed out his shirt and left it on the line outside. On this occasion, however, she placed another shirt, cleaned the night before, on the wooden rack.

"I left another one outside on the line, so it's fresh too," she told him.

Without answering John turned to the rack in the kitchen and picked up the clean shirt. He pulled it on and buttoned it while he grumbled about what he had to do today, and how much smarter he was than the foreman, and how they ought to make him the boss if they wanted to get anything done.

"Your favorite shirt might bring you luck," she called out. "It's right outside, there, on the line."

"Let me alone," he warned, in the tone of voice that meant this was the last thing he would say.

Marietta still had a mark on her right thigh, curved and gouged in the spot where John's belt buckle sported a lump of turquoise. So she said nothing, but she smiled to herself. It was out of her hands now. He had made up his mind. She had tried to change it. He had refused, and that was that.

So she lay back in bed and pulled the sheet up to her chin in spite of the morning sunlight pouring through the eastern window. She heard him leave, heard the truck engine grind away followed by quiet. After a while there was only the solemn, steady humming of bees outside the window.

Sweltering heat filled the room in ripples and waves. Light hovered over the bed in a cloud of quivering dust motes. Then all at once, for the first time in weeks, her head flooded with pictures. She wanted to sleep, to rest and wait. She felt that this was not merely one of her intuitions. She was imagining, but also reaching out. She reminded herself that John had made his decision that day. He had chosen his fate, she told herself, and she was merely watching.

She saw the green shirt, and the yellow and black heat swelling in the air. She heard the sounds of workmen on the road. These came of their own accord like a song or a nursery rhyme that repeats and repeats no matter what you do, or like the sickening memory of a meal in the throes of nausea:

"Over and done, John Colquitt. Over and done."

She was still lying there, clutching the threadbare sheet, when the road crew foreman knocked at the front door. Marietta answered wearing her slip. It didn't matter now. John wouldn't know. The foreman had come to say he was gone.

Behind the foreman she saw John's beat-up white truck parked in the yard. Another man she'd never seen sat waiting in a second truck, newer and cleaner, "better kept" as Marietta's aunt would have said.

The foreman was mumbling. It sounded like an apology. But no, he wasn't apologizing. He was explaining how John acted up all the time. Showing off and joking around, like he'd been warned not to, like he did every day. Marietta suddenly recalled the way John had bowed to Delphine when she wasn't looking, with a sort of curtsy and a wave of one hand.

The foreman was here in person to make sure Marietta wasn't one of those wives that might make trouble. She realized, then: If she wanted she could name her price, within reason. She decided to hold her tongue and see what the foreman would offer her as a donation.

They had been laying gravel. John's primary job was to signal the driver when to release the load. He was supposed to stand clear, call a warning, check again, call out another warning, and then give the driver the signal. He knew this routine well. He'd done this dozens of times.

It was an accident that John had brought on himself. The foreman wanted to make this clear. One man on the crew swore he saw bees in the air around John's face and hands, but nobody else could say if this was true. So they had all agreed that the mishap (that was the foreman's word) was John's fault. They all saw him take a step forward after the final warning and the signal, right into the path of the truck. When the men on the ground shouted at him, he took a second step in the wrong direction. The driver didn't see him and it was too late even if he had. John was standing in his blind spot, in the very place he had said was all clear.

The driver was a good man. He knew what he was doing and swore he hadn't made the mistake that claimed John's life. This was all that the road crew saw that morning: just a man with a surprised look on his face vanishing into a torrent, buried, his mouth and eyes and nose filled with gravel, collapsing under the weight before he could shout for help. He was turned, that fast, into nothing.

Marietta knew it all before the foreman broke the news. Now John was dead and it was his own fault, nobody else's. He was careless and stupid. He drank too much and his sweat smelled like booze. Everybody knew it. Everybody knew he couldn't hold down a job for long. He messed around at work, and made dumb jokes nobody laughed at. He always got fired, except on that day, when he got himself killed.

She didn't cry. She asked the foreman if he wanted coffee.

The man blinked and seemed to relax. He touched a hand to his hat, and said no but thanks just the same.

She told the foreman she couldn't afford to bury John. He'd have to be buried by the county, if he was to be buried at all.

"And I've got no way to collect him," she said. "I can't even drive his truck."

The foreman looked at Marietta's belly, swollen inside the flimsy, yellow slip. Her violet eyes showed no sign of tears.

"We weren't legally married, or anything," she said. "I don't expect he had anybody else. He didn't have any friends that I know of. Nobody to notify except me."

The foreman glanced at the closed-in squalor of the house. Then he reached into his pocket and handed Marietta five hundred dollars.

"For your troubles, ma'am," he said. "We'll see to it, for you."

Then he turned away. She held the money and the keys to John's truck.

After the foreman left with the other guy, she put the money in a coffee can in a hole in her bedroom closet, with the ones and fives she'd been hiding. She had stopped keeping money in an herb jar after John had torn the place apart and wrecked her supplies.

She took a mason jar out of the freezer, shook it, and left it on the kitchen table for a couple of hours. Later she counted two, three, four dead bees. Six were humming for dear life. The same number that thawed out in the pocket of her husband's shirt that day.

In the late afternoon she put John's clothes into a cardboard box. After the sun went down she burned them in the yard. She took the license plates off the truck and buried those. She parked the truck out back, near the blackberry bushes. They were coming back because John hadn't pulled them up at the root. He'd been too lazy to do the job right. After a while they would cover the truck completely.

Marietta did away with every sign that John Colquitt had ever been part of her life. Except for the baby inside her, a baby she hoped would be a boy who was nothing like John. The only other thing she kept was his last name, because she liked it.

In her sixth month Marietta had a telephone installed in her house for the first time. She called her friends to let them know that John Colquitt had left town, and she'd had word from Portland that he had died in a bar fight. It was a crazy story. Maybe that was why Ethel believed it. Beverly said the man was a lazy, no-good son of a bitch and had probably run off with a woman. She assured Marietta that she was better off without him, and Marietta agreed.

Both friends pitched in to help: fetching groceries, cleaning house, and doing little repair jobs. Now that John was gone they seemed happy to visit. Beverly quickly redecorated the place in warm colors, with sturdy secondhand furniture she found in thrift shops in Longview. They accepted as a sign of their friend's independence that she declined to have one of them move in until the baby was born. They made Marietta swear that she would call them when her time came. She promised she would.

This was a lie, like the story about John, and like her assertion that she was seeing a good doctor who didn't mind making house calls. She told so many lies she wondered if she could keep them all straight. There was nothing else she could do.

During her entire pregnancy she had only one dream. It began right after John died, and once it started it came almost every night. In the dream Delphine appeared by her side, looking over her shoulder and whispering:

"She's coming now. She's almost here. Don't go outside."

In her dream Marietta walked to the front door. She looked out at the yard, softly blurred at the edges in the hazy moonlight. The road beyond was invisible, shrouded in fog.

"Did you bury it?" Delphine asked.

"Yes," she replied.

"How deep did you bury it?"

"Deep enough."

"She's coming now. She knows you."

Her time came at four a.m. three quarters of the way through her eighth month, in the middle of the week. She forced a knot of cotton cloth between her teeth to keep from screaming. She let the baby come, half hoping it would die, and then wishing like hell she had called her friends for help. She wasn't ready for this, she thought too late, and the pain cut through her.

It was only when she stopped to take a full, deep breath and the infant lay shivering on the bedclothes between her legs that she realized she was giving birth again. By the time she started to push, the twin had crowned and it came quickly, slippery as spit, chasing the path of its brother.

Marietta cut the cord to each baby with a scalpel. She dabbed them with alcohol and tied them off. She wrapped the twins in a red quilt, cleaned herself with warm water and a towel, and carefully changed clothes. Then she sponge-bathed the infants, just enough to clear the clots of afterbirth from their bluish-pink flesh.

The boy lay sleeping, breathing gently with a thin grin across his lips. Marietta placed him in the crib. She turned her attention to the girl, who wasn't moving. Marietta thought she might be dead, she was so still, and her face was set with its features tight like a fist.

Marietta moved to pick up the baby, and the infant's

eyes opened. She didn't jerk her head or look around. She stared straight up at Marietta with eyes as blue as a cornflower petal. Her brow remained furrowed but her lips formed an even line. She was watching with such intensity, Marietta's hands began to tremble.

"This is not dreaming," she said. The baby only stared at her.

Marietta sat down and tried to put her thoughts in order, but every route she took led back to Delphine's words. She considered the baby sleeping peacefully in his crib; then the second baby lying on the bed, watching. Marietta shook her head. She sat for several minutes like that, with her hands in her lap.

Then, in the stillness, she heard it. Faint at first, like an insect buzzing in another room. A fluttering noise, closer, gave way to a murmur, a voice murmuring to itself.

It was thinking. She could hear it thinking. Not the wonder and fear of a newborn, but the ruminations of someone old, the rough litany of ancient memory.

Marietta stood and without a word or another thought she went to the kitchen. She opened the cabinet doors under the sink and reached back into the mildew-scented darkness. There she found an old toolbox her aunt had kept for years, always at the ready for the many repairs needed around their outdated home.

She could hear her infant daughter starting to fuss in the bedroom. It sounded like a baby, any baby, hungry for its mother.

"You can't fool me," Marietta whispered.

She lifted out the metal toolbox and opened it. She spread a cloth on the floor and began as swiftly and quietly as possible laying aside all of its contents.

When Ethel answered her phone call and came to the rescue with Aunt Constance in tow, they found Marietta awake in bed. In her arms she cradled her newborn son. She told them she had just nursed him for the first time, without any trouble. She told them she was tired but otherwise she felt fine. She told them she had decided to name the boy Henry. Although she couldn't manage a smile, she ate a bowl of applesauce and drank a glass of water and told them she felt better than she had in months.

The Women (1979)

The space station crew gathered around a cluttered table. They were celebrating the recovery of the sickly guy with red hair, who now looked haggard and hungry. Bad jokes and plates of steaming food and cans of some mysterious liquid were passed around. Everyone was laughing. Relief made them giddy.

The man started coughing. He gagged and choked. He fell backwards onto the table, on top of the food.

"Disgusting."

"Be quiet."

"Right on top of the food!"

"Shh!"

His friends grabbed him by the shoulders and held him, trying to stop his convulsions, but he went on gagging. Everyone at the table caught him by his arms and legs and held onto him. The doctor tried to force a spoon into his mouth, to hold his tongue down. The red haired man's feet kicked in spasm, and he screamed.

"He's going to die," Beverly whispered. "Wait and see."

"Argh!"

The three women screamed and jumped, along with the other movie patrons, when the man arched his back and blood burst through his white t-shirt. His friends tried to hold him down, but he kept convulsing.

"He's hemorrhaging," the captain shouted.

"See?" Beverly said, but no one heard her.

"Argh!"

The audience screamed as another clot of blood popped from the man's chest. The man let out a wail of agony.

"Oh, that's," Ethel started to say something.

She was silenced by the man's screaming and by the shrieking of the audience all around her, when something that looked like a blood-soaked fist jumped out of the man's chest. It shot upward, tearing the man's skin and organs, and spattering everyone with blood.

The audience screamed again. Blood spurted up and out of the man, in wave after wave. One of the women slipped in the gore and fell down. A monster face with tiny, metallic teeth shot upright from inside the man and looked around while the man's hands fluttered involuntarily.

"Gaah! No!"

People were screaming louder now. Someone in the back row of the theater stood up and bolted, leaving the double doors flapping back and forth. No one turned around to look. All eyes were fixed on the monster inside the man. Coiled, perched atop his dying body in triumph, it was working its little teeth. It opened its mouth at the man's terrified friends and made a tiny growl like a baby or an animal, reveling in their fear, warning them to stand back.

The crew watched and pressed themselves against the wall to get as far from it as possible. The creature took off with a noise like a tearing zipper and flew across the room, leaving the man's body torn open, gaping on top of the table.

"Good Christ," said Ethel.

Marietta nodded silently, her face transfixed by the images on the screen. Beverly fetched a tissue from her purse, delicately blew her nose, and then whispered:

"That would never happen."

The other two looked at her in the dark. Then Ethel began to laugh.

Two hours later over neglected Cobb salads at Jessup's Diner the three young women sat in stunned silence until the waitress stopped by to ask if anything was wrong. They looked up from their booth and shook their heads no.

"We just saw that space movie about the monster," Ethel told her.

The waitress' eyes grew wide.

"Oh, boy," she said. "My sister saw that and told me all about it. I hate scary movies. She said it sure was good, though."

She was gone in the next instant, checking on other customers. It was Saturday and the place was packed.

Around here Saturday afternoon was for movies and lunch with the family. Then a barbecued supper at home, if the weather was good. A roast chicken if it rained. In either case too much food and too much beer. Sunday morning was for church service and regret. Sunday afternoons were reserved for more beer and ball games on TV. Once a month most people gathered for a potluck meal after church.

"What was that thing, anyway?" Ethel asked.

"An alien from outer space," said Beverly with a grin. "Or were you talking about the waitress?"

Outside the diner Marietta said she had to get home. Henry, her little boy, had been with a babysitter all afternoon and he was a handful. He could be loud. Instead of using words he would push his head against people when he wanted something. He took things apart too, clocks and telephones, and left them in a hundred pieces on the floor.

The only babysitter who had any patience with the boy was Bonny, a pastor's wife. Bonny refused payment for helping out, but she urged Marietta to bring Henry to Sunday services. She wanted him baptized, too, but this was more than Marietta could agree to, just to hold onto an agreeable babysitter. It was bad enough to come home and find Henry clapping his hands and laughing while

Bonny sang hymns.

"Give him our love," said Ethel.

"I'll do that," Marietta said.

They watched her cross the street at the corner ahead of them. When she was well out of earshot, Beverly said:

"I think he's a little bit retarded."

"Who?" Ethel asked.

"Marietta's boy, Henry."

"He may be slow. He isn't retarded."

"How do we know? She's never had a real doctor look at him, just some green intern over at County Hospital."

"I guess an intern knows more than we do," said Ethel.

"Does that seem right to you?"

"What?"

"Don't most children go to the doctor at least once a year?"

"Marietta's aunt taught her a lot. She's as good as a nurse."

"If that's true, why doesn't she see her aunt's clients and set up shop as a midwife?"

"I don't know," said Ethel. "I think she does well enough selling those candles and soaps and things. I don't think Delphine ever had a license, and Marietta probably hated all that stuff."

"Abortions."

"For one thing, Delphine cared for women who didn't have anybody else to turn to. Nowadays women have choices. They can drive to a clinic in the city. Why would they go to somebody's house for that? No. Marietta's right to make a living selling nice little jars of honey with ribbons on them, and scented soap. She's smart."

"She'd make a lot more money doing readings and casting spells and telling people she's a white witch."

"But she isn't."

"Oh?" Beverly asked. "Is that what you really think?"

"She's got insights, or, what does she call them?"

"Intuitions."

"Right. She's always had strong feelings about things."

"And where does that come from? See? You don't want to speculate, do you?"

"Bev, I think she does all right. She's the only one of us who doesn't have to live at home."

"Well," said Beverly. "That's true enough."

They walked on, past the movie theater. There was another line in front of the ticket booth, but now the heat of the afternoon seemed to have beaten everyone down. People fanned themselves lazily with souvenir cardboard fans handed out by a theater usher. The fans were shaped like the alien in its earliest form, when it clung to the red haired man's face.

Without consulting one another Beverly and Ethel naturally wandered into the ice cream shop and ordered double cones. They took the only vacant table, next to the window where it was too warm. They sat licking the cones, with fast-melting scoops of pistachio and vanilla threatening to run down their fingers.

A husband and wife passed the shop with their four children. One child was asleep in a stroller with its arms dangling on the sides. The oldest child, a boy with unevenly cut hair, was dragging his feet and whining that he wanted to see the monster movie. His father rolled his eyes toward the ice cream shop window and gave the women inside a look of pure, unveiled envy.

"Well, I'm keeping my word," said Ethel.

"About what?" Beverly asked.

"Not having babies. You know."

"That was nothing but a joke. A bad one."

"I'm not joking," said Ethel.

"No. I mean: what we did. It didn't work anyway."

"Why do you say that?"

Beverly looked out the window. Then she said:

"That magic stuff was a game. Marietta was showing off. Like the time she predicted that boy would break his arm, on the beach. She said she predicted it. How are we supposed to know if that's true?"

"You believed it back then."

"I did not. And the oath was just a game. I didn't even do it right."

Ethel started to speak, and Beverly interrupted:

"We could have burned down half of Skillute. It was crazy. Stupid kids."

Ethel looked at the ice cream droplets on the table between them. She watched the weekend shoppers wandering by.

"Something else happened that day," she told Beverly.

There was a pause between them. Both young women looked out the window for a moment.

"I know," said Beverly. "That was bad luck, Ethel. I'm sorry it happened."

"No. Before the fire at home, I saw something."

"Something in the woods?"

"Yeah," Ethel admitted. "We found something, but we left it there. That's not what I mean, though. I saw a face. I heard noises, at home, when I was by myself, and I saw a face at the window."

"You mean a prowler?"

Beverly's interest was piqued now.

"You think a prowler set the fire?"

"No," Ethel said. "No. I just had this feeling."

"Okay."

"I had this feeling."

"Yeah?"

"Like maybe somebody followed me home that day."

This was the first time Ethel had said the words out loud. She watched Beverly's face, measuring her reaction.

"Who do you think followed you?"

"I," Ethel began. "I don't know."

"Well, did you ever see them again?'

"No."

Beverly wiped her hands with a paper napkin and tossed the last bite of her cone into a trashcan. She said nothing.

"So, what about you?" Ethel asked. She smiled. "Are you planning on sticking to the oath? I mean, whether you believe it now or not."

Beverly took her time retrieving lipstick and a compact from her purse. She applied her lipstick with care and checked it twice before answering.

"I wouldn't have a child if you paid me."

The Women (1989)

Beverly decided to marry Rex Dempsey despite the trashy side of his family. That branch included two adult cousins who couldn't read or write. Beverly had never imagined she would end up related, however distantly, to someone who couldn't write his own name on a piece of paper. She imagined Rex must have seemed like a genius to that part of the Dempsey clan.

She was bookkeeping for a construction sub-contractor and the money wasn't good. Skillute, along with the rest of the state, was in a slump that kept getting worse. The office where Beverly worked was on the firm's latest construction site, in a trailer surrounded by a muddy field and surveyed by an aggressive murder of crows. She had to pack a lunch every day because there was no place to go on her break. She had worked at many locations. This one was the worst.

She spent her days reading balance sheets and financial statements. She avoided conversation with the dirt- and sweat-stained laborers who tramped through the trailer. The only people Beverly talked to on a regular basis were the owner of the firm and the woman who answered the telephone, an anorexic named Darla with eczema and a pixie haircut, who flirted shamelessly with any man who got within ten feet of her.

Beverly was living in a tiny apartment in Kelso. She spent more time than she wanted to with her parents. They had more room and more food than she did. In truth she was bored to death with her family. Especially her mother with her endless complaints about her colon and her lack of grandchildren and Beverly's advancing age.

The first topic was too ugly to think about and the second made Beverly laugh bitterly. As far as she could see, her mother had no right to grandchildren. If she wanted them so badly she could hound Beverly's brothers and their overweight wives. The third topic was supposed to be off limits.

"Twenty-eight isn't old," she reminded her mother.

"You're thirty-one," her mother replied. "Almost thirty-two."

"Twenty-nine."

"We're not bartering over the price of a watermelon, here, missy," her mother said. "I ought to know how old you are."

Beverly wasn't against getting married. She was tired of dating men who didn't open doors for her, and didn't compliment her on her outfit, and didn't remember to buy flowers on her birthday. She was bored with her job and her life as a single woman in a town where single meant going to the movies with her girlfriends and buying small portions of food at the grocery store. The baggers smirked at her and wished her a good weekend in a tone that said they knew she had no plans. She needed a change. Almost any change would do.

"I'm not going to spend my life playing bingo with purple-haired old ladies!" Beverly declared the day she announced her engagement.

Rex Dempsey owned a drywall business. The first time he walked into the trailer for a meeting with Beverly's boss, she took note of his height, exactly six feet, his strong jaw line, and his perfectly pressed shirts and pants. He was a man who took care of himself. What she also noticed, and this swayed her, was that he removed his hat as soon as he walked through the door, and his voice was low and deferential when he said he had an appointment.

Of course Darla was all over him, serving coffee and spilling it on his shoes. She even had the gall to ask if he was married. Rex turned to Beverly and gave a little nod when he answered:

"I've never had the pleasure, but I hope to someday."

She talked her parents into a good-sized wedding at a Methodist church where the minister wasn't picky about whether or not couples were members of the congregation. Beverly told the minister she believed in God on principle, but she didn't see any reason to make a big show out of it.

Ethel altered the wedding dress, a Chanel knock-off from a boutique in Portland, to which she added a flourish of pearls at each wrist. The skirt was lace and the bodice and sleeves were made from satin. The entire dress was ivory, a color that satisfied Beverly's mother. They had argued about whether or not white was appropriate. Beverly said that white was acceptable for a first-time bride. Her mother said it would be bad luck, and she could only blame herself if something terrible happened.

Ethel and Marietta constructed the bridal bouquet, a small cluster of dendrobium orchids cinched with ivory silk. Later they watched it sail into the hands of a scrawny young woman Beverly described as "one of my husband's hillbilly cousins."

The young woman, the cousin, had teased her hair and twisted it into a bun for the occasion. When she caught the bridal bouquet she smiled like she had won the lottery. Her joy revealed a crooked row of tobacco-stained teeth. The wedding photographer captured the moment, but later on Beverly plucked that picture out of the album and briskly tore it to shreds.

"I don't even know that girl's first name," she told Ethel. "Why would I want her ugly face in my wedding book?"

Rex and Beverly lived in a bungalow he built on two acres of wooded land he'd inherited from his father. It was cozy and pretty, but not the ostentatious home everyone expected the bride would demand.

"Oh," said Beverly. "I hate the way some people show off every penny they have, don't you? I wouldn't live in one of those hideous fake colonial things for all the money in the world."

Ethel complimented Beverly on her decision, saying:

"If I could, I'd have a nice two-bedroom with all-new fixtures and everything clean and modern. It's like a fresh start on life, isn't it?"

Marietta was pleased, too, until she heard about the two-acre lot where they were building their home. Then her smile faded and she asked:

"Are you sure you want to build there? That road doesn't even have a name, does it?"

"What difference does that make?" Beverly asked, more than a bit peeved. "We're on the general mail route. That's all that matters."

"Wouldn't you be happier living closer to town?"

"No, I would not," said Beverly. "I don't want a house next to the train station, with all that dirt and noise. Our place is set back by itself, with plenty of forest separating us from our hick neighbors, and I can hear birdsong in the morning. What could be better than that?"

Rex wasn't rich but he did all right by local standards. Beverly was delighted with their home and her emerald green lawn with its tulip beds, windmills, and wooden geese. She ran her home like an efficient business: plenty of visitor turnover, and no lingering after hours.

They didn't plan to have children. Beverly said she couldn't. Rex didn't seem to mind. The drywall business kept him busy six days a week. He did a bit of traveling around the Northwest. She handled the books for him and filed their taxes every spring.

Only once in a while they were troubled by little events. There was nothing worth reporting to the sheriff's office, just irritations that they chalked up to childish pranks. One time a skunk got into the second bedroom by way of a window Beverly was sure she had closed, although she couldn't remember if she had locked it. The bedspread and mattress were ruined. Beverly took the opportunity to talk

Rex into letting her convert the space into a storage room. She reasoned that they seldom had sleepover guests anyway, and if they ever needed a spare they had the hideaway sofa bed in the living room.

Another time someone dug up Beverly's tulip bulbs overnight. The prankster left a trail of shredded bulbs from the yard to the woods.

In the winter the plumbing would sometimes creak. It sounded like an old person groaning in her sleep. Rex had a friend make a few adjustments and the noises went away.

On two occasions Beverly baked pies and left them cooling on the small front porch, only to have them disappear. She cursed the unkempt children of her poor neighbors up the hill beyond the woods. Rex told her a hungry raccoon probably snatched the pies, but she thought this was unlikely since the culprit left no trace at all. Not a crumb.

Aside from such minor incidents Mr. and Mrs. Dempsey led a pleasant life. After the first five or six years Mrs. Sherman stopped asking if they were sure they weren't going to have children. Beverly was in her late thirties, and people finally assumed she was right about not being able to have a baby.

The Dempseys were happy together for ten years. Then one evening Rex died of a massive coronary at the supper table, right in front of Beverly.

"He loved pecan pie with fudge sauce," Beverly told her friends.

That was what Rex was eating when he got a funny look on his face and slid sideways off his chair. He landed hard on the black and white checkerboard linoleum.

"He loved my pecan pie with fudge sauce, more than anything."

Beverly handled her husband's passing better than people expected. She was a practical minded person. She had loved Rex dearly and she would miss him every minute, she said, but she liked her life, its balance and its simplicity. Because she had lived frugally, she had plenty of savings left, plus a substantial insurance policy. She would live in the same house, do her gardening, and keep all the habits she had before. She might even redecorate the place, to keep her mind off her sorrows. The enemy would be loneliness, but she could face that. Apart from Rex there were only a few people she'd ever bothered getting close to, and they were nearby. She would mourn for an appropriate amount of time, but she wouldn't grieve. It wasn't her nature.

The Women (1999)

Beverly heard the news first. She reported what she knew to Marietta over a game at the bingo hall.

Marietta played bingo now and then. Beverly played once every week. She said it kept her in touch with her neighborhood. One time Ethel teased her:

"You feel young when you beat those old people at their favorite game."

Beverly winced at that, because it was true. Ethel never mentioned it again.

Beverly went on getting dressed up, having her hair done, and then strolling into the bingo hall like a middle-aged movie star. Sometimes she wore sunglasses all day and if anyone mentioned it, she would tap her forehead and say in a flat tone:

"Macular degeneration. Pray you don't have it, too, someday."

She waited until they were settled in and the game was underway. Then she blurted to Marietta, between rounds:

"Ethel is marrying Burt Sanders. She's already moved in with him. They've shacked up and now they plan to get married by the justice of the peace. Can you beat that?"

Marietta said nothing. They were sitting opposite one another at a long folding table draped with plastic. Beverly was gripping a pink daubing pen in each hand. On the table she had lined up six of the old-fashioned bingo cards favored by the regulars and dutifully supplied by staff on request. She hawked over the cards with both arms lifted slightly at the elbows, ready for action.

Marietta regarded the women on either side of them,

sharing the table. The redhead next to Beverly squinted through narrow bifocals. Another lady, older than all of the rest, leaned over her cards with one protective arm curved around them like a schoolgirl afraid of copycats.

"N-34!" The caller shouted from the stage at the front of the room. "N-34!"

Beverly dotted two cards with her daubers. The redhead next to her grinned and pushed the bifocals up an inch on her nose. The fluorescent lights high overhead gave an occasional flicker, as if there were an electrical short or one of the lamps needed replacement.

"Bingo!" An eighty-three-year-old man at the next table yelled.

"Oh, damn it," said Beverly. "He's not even a regular. Wouldn't you know it? I was going for that toaster, too. Mine has a broken cord."

She returned her attention to Marietta.

"Did you hear what I said? Ethel's getting married, and she's moved into a house right down the road from me."

"Not that old place Joe Sanders used to live in?" Marietta asked.

"That's the one," said Beverly.

"O-12!" The caller shouted. "O-12!"

"Bingo!"

Two rows behind Marietta a woman with a brown pageboy haircut and horn-rimmed glasses on a chain around her neck got so excited she knocked her bingo card off the table. She bounced in her chair a couple of times and held up her card.

"Bingo! Right here!" The woman shouted again and waved her card in the air. "It's me! Bingo!"

"We hear you," said Beverly under her breath. Then she whispered to her tablemates: "Her prize is nothing but a tile trivet anyway. She's so excited, just because it's painted by some *artiste* from New Mexico!"

Marietta and the redhead exchanged a polite grin. Nearby an elderly woman started hacking and sneezing, and blew her nose into a pink handkerchief. It was cold season. Throughout the hall, the air was densely sweet with the scent of mentholated cough drops.

They had seen Ethel two months earlier, when she had to pack up her aunt's belongings. It turned out their house had a lien against it. Constance had put herself in debt over the years, moving her tailoring business to Skillute and starting over from scratch in a town where most women made do with a few blouses and t-shirts, a couple of pairs of slacks and a good dress for Sunday. She had trusted a local insurance broker with her investments, and lost her nest egg when the firm went out of business. The Burneys never caught up, even with both women working part-time at a fabric shop in Kelso.

"How did she meet Burt Sanders?" Marietta asked.

"I introduced them," Beverly told her. "I had Ethel to my place for supper a couple months ago, right after she closed up her aunt's house. You know how she felt about Constance passing away. Anyway, she was pretty low, so I invited her over. Burt stopped by to talk with me about a couple of odd jobs I asked him to do. It's a trial keeping my place in good condition without a man around the house."

"So you tried to cheer Ethel up and Burt happened to stop by?" Marietta asked.

"Mm-hmm."

This was a supper to which Beverly had not invited Marietta. Over the years Beverly had started putting each of her friends into a category. Marietta belonged in the lunch date and bingo category. In fairness, these had originally been the times of day when Marietta had no trouble lining up a babysitter for Henry, when he was growing up. Marietta's status had not changed, although Henry was in his early twenties now, and starting his fourth sales job in a row. He was drifting but he wasn't a child any more. Marietta was free to meet her friend any time she liked.

Ethel, maybe because she worked so many hours at home, doing alterations into the night sometimes, had become the friend in Beverly's holiday and special event category. That would change once Ethel became a common neighbor.

"Burt's a loner," said Marietta.

"What does that mean?"

"He likes to be alone, as far as I can tell. That's what people say."

"Well," Beverly said. "Who doesn't like to be alone? I do. So do you. So does Ethel."

"I've heard Burt drinks quite a bit."

"So does Ethel."

"I don't think so," Marietta said, her violet eyes fading to pale gray in the stark fluorescent light.

Beverly nodded and mimed taking a swig from a bottle. She turned her attention back to her cards when the caller on stage shouted:

"L-9!"

Beverly touched two of her cards with a pink dauber. She grinned. No one was calling a winner this time.

"L-9!"

"How do you know these things? Did Ethel talk to you?"

Beverly glared at her.

"I have eyes, Marietta. Ethel needs a man in her life. She works too hard. So I introduced her to Burt, and they hit it off. He isn't ideal. I know that. Burt may be a cracker. I haven't met a man in Skillute who isn't a cracker, but he's a man with deep feelings. He's in love with Ethel," she said. "That's better than nothing."

The redhead laughed. Beverly turned toward her and smiled. She nodded toward the redhead's cards.

"You're not doing very well today, are you?" She said.

The redhead bit her lip. She kept her eyes on her cards for the rest of the game.

"D-3!"

"I don't think Burt and Ethel have that much in common," Marietta said after a while.

"D-3!"

"Name a man and a woman who have anything in common," Beverly said. "The trick is to find somebody with a good job who doesn't get on your nerves all the time. That's what a happy marriage is."

The eighty-three-year-old man had decided to go home. He had collected his toaster and was making his way between the tables, heading for the exit.

"You have fun with that!" Beverly called after him. To the women at her table she said:

"He'll never use that thing. What the heck is an old man, living alone, supposed to do with a four-slice toaster?"

"You think Burt and Ethel will be happy?" Marietta suggested.

Beverly wasn't listening.

"J-12!"

Beverly jabbed one of her cards with the dauber and flashed a big smile.

"Right here!" She shouted. "Bingo!"

Part Two

Ethel

Ethel never told anyone what happened the day she and Beverly and Marietta sneaked into the woods to take an oath against having babies. As far as Ethel knew, no one suspected what the girls had done. It was a silly game that got scary, but no harm done, she told herself. No real harm. Marietta had a son, if any proof were needed. Obviously they were not doomed to be childless, unless they wanted to be.

Yet it stayed with Ethel, the afternoon and the oath and what happened after that. She had tried to convince herself, over the years, that she had been dreaming when she heard scratching on the walls. Or maybe it was a squirrel or raccoon looking for a way inside, a path to food and away from the storm. Or maybe Beverly was right when she said it was a prowler. These were reasonable explanations, but they didn't account for the charred jawbone Ethel and Marietta had found, or the sense of dread Ethel had carried home with her that day. No matter how she tried she could never shake the feeling that something was following her, just out of sight.

When she was a girl Ethel had made up her mind not to get married. She knew some of the people in her hometown would make jokes at her expense. They would call her an old maid, and speculate about what was wrong with her. That prospect wasn't any worse than the things people had said about her all along while she was growing up: the mouse, the orphan girl with glasses, whose shiftless parents died from smoking cigarettes in bed. It was pitiful and dumb. It didn't make a good story, even in hindsight.

Her parents' death was commonly considered an example of bad living. Stupid people doing stupid things and getting what they deserved for it.

"You might change your mind about getting married, when you meet the right man," Beverly teased Ethel, when they were young. She must have said this a hundred times.

"Might, but won't," Ethel always replied.

Lonely as she was, she shied away from anyone who took an interest in her. A look that lingered more than a second would cause her to become self-conscious. The idea of being with another person for the rest of her life gave her a chill. She could remember the voices of her parents climbing, shrill and hateful, into the night.

Shirley would end most fights with a shriek of disgust. Then she would stomp off into the woods to smoke and ignore her middle-aged husband and the daughter she didn't want. The more often Shirley had followed that trail away into the shadows and the night, the more she had seemed to resent having to return to their trailer home with its dust bunnies, its grimy sink, and its corners filled with crumbs.

"Why am I cleaning up after you all? I've got better things to do with my time!"

"Name one of those things, sugar," her husband would ask, and then the vodka would flow until they were either screaming at one another or grunting and crying out behind the locked door of their bedroom.

Ethel wanted nothing more than quiet, a clean house, music on the radio, an uninterrupted TV show, weekends free from confusion and terror. She found these things with her aunt. She returned Constance's kindness by being polite, neat and grateful. She was never a problem. She never stayed out late. She completed her homework and her household chores on time and without complaining. She followed instructions and learned to assist Constance in her meticulous work.

Clients routinely stopped by for a fitting or to drop off

a bag of clothes for alterations. Ethel greeted them and offered them coffee and a magazine if they wanted to wait. She lingered nearby in case they needed anything. She wore her best dresses to show them what a fine seamstress they had employed. Constance never asked her to do these things. She took it upon herself to behave impeccably.

All of this made sense to her and seemed to come naturally, when she was a girl. It only dawned on her many years later that she was trying too hard. In her mother's absence she was still trying to win favor. As an adult she looked back at her child self and felt a wave of sadness and pity, although she didn't recall indulging in self-pity when she was little. Only with the maternal instinct of a grown woman could she think:

"If I knew myself as a child, now, I would love me. Why didn't she?"

There was some distance and strength in this recognition but no release, no real joy. What she was admitting above all was that Shirley had failed her in every possible way. Ethel spent half a lifetime absolving and ignoring her mother's persistent cruelties. Now that she was old enough to care for a child, she realized with a shiver that her mother was a heartless bitch. Distance, yes. Maybe even wisdom. But what could she draw upon, for tenderness? Aunt Constance, yes, but Constance was not her blood mother, her source of life, the woman whose love she had first learned to seek, whose love she could never stop seeking, no matter how old she became or how much she changed in other ways.

Time and again she caught herself thanking waitresses until they grew weary of her and stopped meeting her gaze. She over-tipped and said thanks again on her way out.

A saleswoman with kind eyes talked her into buying a full makeup kit she never used. It was so expensive she couldn't bring herself to throw it away until years later, when the mascara and foundation had dried up in the bottles and the powder broke into solid bits like clay.

At a yard sale she let an elderly woman sell her a hideous sweater, an off-white thing with bits of sparkling ribbon in the weave and large, unflattering shoulder pads. The woman had hauled it out of a box and insisted she try it on. She had placed it on Ethel's skinny shoulders and gently smoothed the arms and back until Ethel was lulled into a state that felt hypnotic. When the woman saw she had made a sale, she upped the price to ten dollars. Ethel gave her twelve and took the sweater home, where she immediately stuffed it into the trashcan and then cried for half an hour.

She tried, over the years, to imagine herself as an infant in her mother's arms. Her photos had been destroyed in the fire. So she scrambled through the few remaining family pictures, the ones Constance had received now and then.

Ethel turned the photos this way and that and studied her expression. Was she happy at three years of age? Was she smiling at one and a half, in her hand-me-down clothes, standing in front of a three-foot-tall aluminum Christmas tree? Yes, her lips were smiling, vaguely, but her eyes were fixed on someone outside the frame. Her eyes revealed uncertainty and trouble as early as one year, as early as ten months. It was a revelation, then, the day her aunt located a birth announcement buried in a box of old greeting cards.

Constance opened the soft cover and handed Ethel the photograph taken at the hospital soon after she was born: Ethel Rosalie Burney, seven pounds, two ounces, and her birth date was listed. Here was the proof: A newborn face, plump and round, eyes closed but her whole face was smiling. Happy, she was happy to be alive and in the world.

According to family legend, Shirley was heavily sedated and unconscious for the first twenty-four hours of Ethel's life. So here was proof of happiness, joy, before Shirley got her hands on her and began to teach her without a doubt that she was not wanted.

The first time she met Burt Sanders, Ethel felt at ease. Not untroubled, not free from a grain of doubt. The worry was permanent, she knew. Talking with Burt, laughing with him over the foolish things they both did and said, laughing sometimes for no reason, seeing the quiet and unfaltering acceptance in his eyes, was as close as she thought she would ever come to peace and joy. That was reason enough to marry him when he asked.

Burt

Burt Sanders was pleased with himself, for a change. Bumping along the no-name road in his truck, avoiding the worst of the potholes, he hoped Ethel would be in a good mood when he reached home. It was too much to expect her to be happy. That would only come with more time and patience.

This area from the freeway to the forked road that led to Burt's house was full of remnants. There were houses partially built during the last boom and left to rot after the crash that followed. In the past couple of years real estate reps from Portland and Seattle had repaired a lot of run-down houses, replacing all the fixtures and the roofing, finally selling them for a decent profit as second homes.

Nobody lived on these lots. They weren't homes. They were investments. Young people earning money in the city could eventually cash in their retirement portfolios and settle here, but more likely they would sell the houses and retire to some place more interesting. Burt imagined his life might have been like theirs, if he had studied computer programming the way he wanted when he was in his twenties. He might have moved to Seattle to go to school, if he had sold his dad's house and put Skillute behind him. He might have been one of those geeky guys who worked at a software firm and made a ton of money.

Burt laughed. These were idle fantasies. He was too old for the world at large. The one time he had spent a couple of weeks in the city people had made fun of the way he talked, the chaotic traffic drove him crazy and all the women he saw had weird hair and pierced noses. It was like a cartoon.

Skillute had dwindled while Seattle was beginning to thrive again. Small local companies had gone under, if they hadn't sold out in time. Big companies had been through layoff after layoff. The best timber, the boom period, the motels that dotted the highway and catered to people taking family road trips, that was long gone. There were roads plowed up for miles, ending nowhere or gradually narrowing to footpaths. There were all ages and sizes of fir and cedar, clusters of hemlock trees, devil's club in patches scattered between the cultivated lawns with their Japanese maples and tulip beds. The land was dotted with abandoned cabins, trailers and sheds, even a few remaining outhouses and run-off trenches. In some spots railroad grades were cut thirty feet deep through hills now exposed as shelf upon shelf of many-colored earth, with roots sticking out of the dirt walls like fingers in the sullen rain.

Burt was used to the rain, of course. He'd lived in the Northwest his whole life. For a few years he'd lived with his mom in Tacoma. He had only moved back to Skillute when his father died. Secretly he had hoped the old man was sitting on a bag of gold or a hundred shares of Microsoft. No such luck. Joe Sanders left him a ramshackle house badly in need of repair, on an acre of land that wasn't fit for much.

Most of the town appeared to be collapsing. Well, you couldn't even call it a town. A couple of intersections with a dozen or so retail shops, a boat building company and a train station. What was that? He didn't think of it as a community, exactly, since people never congregated for anything outside of church. Despite their reputation for being closed-mouthed and diligent, however, the locals sure did like to gossip. They did it at particular times, over supper, after church, and especially at the bingo hall, as though keeping it segregated from the main portion of their lives made it less hateful and made them better people.

Skillute was a pretty messed-up place, Burt realized. He hadn't missed it during the years in Tacoma after his parents split up. He had stayed on after his dad died because he could offer Ethel a home where she had friends and clients. Having to relocate would have been the final straw for someone as fragile as she was. She was good at giving the appearance of strength, probably always had to wear a mask, thanks to her crazy parents. Burt could see how much of the time she was just getting by. He could see the effort it took for her to do the simplest things. It made him angry, made him wish her parents were alive so he could punch both of them right in the face.

Once he had settled in, Skillute felt uncomfortably familiar but not intolerable. The social options beyond his marriage were limited, to say the least. He didn't like church, so his chances of making friends were even lower than they might have been.

At least no one pestered him to shoot things any more. His father had hunted deer, elk, and grouse all his life. Burt hated shooting animals. His one recent attempt at being a hunter had landed him on his backside in a ditch full of elk droppings in a town whose name he couldn't remember, somewhere in Montana. And that was the highlight of the trip. By the time he dragged his weary soul back home three days later he had sworn off hunting, microbrews, and any human being with the nickname "Mudflap."

Ethel had laughed at that story. At least it was worth something.

"You gave it a good try," she said. "Now maybe they'll leave you alone."

She was wrong about that. Every time Burt ran into Mudflap at a convenience store or buying lumber at Rudy's, the guy slapped him on the back and asked when Burt wanted to hit that Elk Slide again. He laughed good-naturedly enough, and he always had a decent word of advice for Burt about practical matters like roofing repairs. He didn't seem to mean any harm, with his lame jokes and corny songs. Burt kind of liked the guy. As long as they didn't talk politics or religion or football they got along pretty well.

Now Mudflap had done Burt another good turn by telling him about a site a few miles from his house, where a road crew was punching through a new route to the freeway. There had been a lot of reconstruction between here and Mount St. Helens when Burt was young: New bridges and roads, reclamation of the land around Spirit Lake, the dredging of the Cowlitz River. Not a lot of change since then. Just more commuters than anybody ever dreamed possible.

The county had finally gotten around to sending a crew, charged with the task of logging what was left of a couple acres of public woodland. The area was small, just a bit of timber that had been stranded when the highway was first constructed. Now it was an obstacle to building a new I-5 on-ramp. Not an urgent job, but one that had to be done to accommodate future expansion. The crew had no interest in the timber they were clearing. They were stacking most of it along the side of the road as they worked.

"That'll make some decent firewood for winter," Mudflap told Burt. "And all you got to do is load it up and haul it home."

Mudflap had made it sound like a newfound treasure. A lot of the fir was unusable, but there were some good scraps. Burt had loaded the bed of his truck with anything that seemed worth the effort. This included a stack of old cedar shingles. Most were broken. They couldn't be used for the roof, but they were dry enough to take home for general repairs and kindling.

Ethel

On the drive home from the doctor's office, Ethel pulled over at a Chevron station and asked for a key to the women's washroom. The instant the door clicked shut behind her, the scent of industrial cleaning agent hit her nostrils and she erupted in tears.

In the shoddy mirror under a row of throbbing fluorescent lights, she looked old. The color she'd started putting on her hair had grown out an inch and a half, revealing gray roots etched above the over-saturated brown. Her glasses were round and wire-rimmed. They reinforced a quizzical expression that she disliked intensely. She kept meaning to replace the frames, but she had put it off. It seemed like a luxury. Now she could forget about new glasses. She wouldn't be able to afford them.

How had she accomplished such a ridiculous feat? That was her first question. Never mind the conversation she would have with Burt, who was now laid off from the mill ("last in, first out"), unemployed and forced to pick up handy work all over Skillute and Kelso. The only asset they had was the ratty two-bedroom house Burt inherited from his dad. It wasn't even worth fixing up to sell. It would have cost less to scrap the whole place and start over, but they would never get the chance, not in a million years. She still wondered if she had married Burt because she loved him or because it was easy to marry him and more comfortable to be with him than to be alone.

At forty-three years of age Ethel had never conceived, never had a close call or skipped a period. She was careful on the rare occasions when she needed to be.

Then one day Burt had come home with wood scraps and hardware store supplies, and announced that he was going to fix up the garage and use it as a workroom. The damn thing leaked and had mice in every corner. Cleaning it out and plugging the holes would take time, but he was determined. This was the start of a new era, he said.

Burt never got around to fixing the garage. That was the day they had opened a bottle of red wine. A storm kicked up that afternoon and kept them indoors. They spent the rest of the day at home, first in bed, then eating dinner, then back in bed. They made love three times and she wasn't careful. Maybe it was the wine, or the mood, or the sheer unlikelihood that anything would happen.

By the time she made an appointment to see a GP in Longview, she had missed two periods. When she asked the doctor if she could be menopausal, he grinned and said:

"Not until after the baby comes."

In the gas station bathroom she washed her face and hands, and dried off with paper towels. She noticed with dismay that her blouse, skirt, shoes and sweater were brown, to one degree or another: Copper, beige, khaki, and taupe.

She felt trapped inside herself. It was as if she had learned nothing about life or clothes or anything in the time she had been alive. She had gone on half expecting a startling event, a calling, a sea change, until her hair turned gray and four decades had flashed by, and she was still standing in the same spot. She tailored clothes to earn money, but ever since Constance died she had stopped taking time for herself. In her heart she had drifted back to the girl she once was, whose decent clothes were reserved for school, and who didn't know how to dress.

Her mother used to snort with laughter and say:

"Little Ethel ought to be a model. She likes to wear four shades of the same color all at once, and three of 'em go together!"

It was a line that never failed to get a laugh out of some-body. Even the truck drivers and car salesmen Shirley brought home laughed at her jokes.

Ethel was about seven when she first realized some of these men, the ones who were from other towns, had been told by Shirley that Ethel was her little sister. Sometimes her mother regarded her with the contempt of a sibling and resorted to fighting, elbows and claws, for food and TV shows and space. Then she would say:

"Little sister, what's wrong with you? Get our guest a beer. Bring another chair from the kitchen. Go buy me some Marlboros. "

Ethel slapped the mirror at the Chevron station. The impact cracked the surface and cut a thin, crimson line across her wrist.

"Shit!"

She ran a paper towel under the tap and touched it to her arm. The cut wasn't deep.

She looked in the mirror at the heavy gray and brown hair hanging over her shoulders. She studied the jagged tearstains on her cheeks, and then wiped them away. No use standing around crying about it.

She noted the late afternoon light failing outside. She wouldn't make it home before dark. Burt would wonder what happened to her. He was sweet to be concerned, but what could happen to her in Skillute? Did getting knocked-up by her husband in middle age count as a misadventure? If so, it was her first.

"Miss Knocks'll get you!" She told her reflection with a bitter laugh.

With startling clarity she could recall every moment of that day in the forest when she and her friends were little girls. She remembered the blackened jawbone protrud-ing from the dirt, the fire and smoke, running home in the fierce rain, the face at the window, waking up coughing and staring up into the sky.

Ethel had long since stopped believing in either gods

or monsters. She was now convinced that what she had seen was a hallucination, born out of fear. That was a little girl's fear. As she grew up she learned to be afraid of real things, actual things, like wild animals and women who hated their children.

She looked into her bloodshot eyes in the gas station mirror and said: "Not like my mother. I am not like my mother. I'm not."

How could she be? She had none of her mother's pretty looks, her mean streak, or her hillbilly glamour. Her mother had hitched a ride west, across the state, and teased her way into a dead-end marriage in Skillute. A former stripper, a thin blonde known for narrow, chiseled blue eyes and a cruel sense of humor. She had slim hips, pretty ankles, and crooked front teeth. She was popular with married men and hated by their wives. Everywhere she went other women recoiled from her. Not that she took the blame for their broken marriages.

"If she had done what a wife ought to do, and put out once in a while, he wouldn't have gone with me in the first place. Crazy bitch!"

Shirley had died and Constance had raised Ethel with kindness and generosity, and not grudgingly. She had never lost her temper, never put her needs ahead of Ethel's. Yet something was missing, and in the absence she remembered only Shirley.

Shirley seemed to be with her, taunting her more as the years went by, and especially since Constance had passed away. Sometimes Ethel was haunted by the words her mother had spoken a few days before she died.

"When you have babies, if anybody marries you, then you see if you're any better of a mom than I am. You'll see how it is."

Ethel didn't want to see. The last thing she wanted was to feel her mother sneaking back to life from some place buried inside her.

Once Ethel had chased a neighbor's cat with the garden

hose, when no one was looking. She hadn't meant to do it. The cat climbed into their yard several times a week and relieved itself under the rose bushes. Constance paid Ethel to clean up the droppings. On this particular day, though, she was tired and ready for supper. She let out a heavy sigh when she spotted the tabby hopping from the fence to the lawn to do its usual business. Then she picked up the hose, turned the water on full blast, and hit the cat with a shocking spray just as it started to poop. The cat sprang up in the air and tore across the grass with Ethel in pursuit, blasting it two, three, four, five more times and soaking the tabby's fur. It never came back to their yard, and later Ethel felt a wave of shame when she remembered the terror in its eyes and its indignation at being soaked with water and forced to flee. Yet in that moment, while she was breathing heavily and chasing the animal, she had laughed triumphantly.

More than anything, Ethel did not want to know what she would do to a child that provoked her. Yet, now, after all her years of caution, here she was.

She could ask Marietta for help. Surely Marietta knew how, or at least she knew someone, maybe a friend of her late aunt, someone who could do away with the child. She couldn't imagine asking her doctor for advice. The way he had smirked at her after the examination, his smug derision seemed to seal her fate. Yet if she wanted she could drive to Portland and go to a clinic. No one had to know.

She looked at her reflection and knew that she was going to keep the baby. Not out of love. She realized this wasn't love. It was pride and vanity, and something more. Standing before the mirror in the gas station Ethel had this wild thought: She could have a baby, if she wanted one.

The fact surprised her and she held onto it, turning it this way and that in the light. She decided she enjoyed being like other women in this regard. She had never felt normal before; ordinary and drab, yes, but not normal. Now she did, and she found it comforting. She could have a child, and no one could stop her. In fact, no one would dream of telling her not to do it. She felt a little surge of power for the second time in her life, and she liked it.

There wasn't much going on in Skillute that month. The news of Ethel's pregnancy traveled like a flash flood along the two branches of the nameless road where she and Burt lived. Everyone had an opinion on the subject:

Ethel was past a decent age for motherhood and Burt was no saint and they both ought to know better.

A baby was a blessing no matter what. However damaged or disabled and however much of a burden the child might turn out to be, it came from the Lord and it deserved to be tolerated.

Nothing good would come of it. Ethel would pay the price. The strain might ruin her health. Might even kill her. Anything could happen.

The baby was doomed. It would never grow to full term. And if it did, it would be sickly and miserable all of its days.

The whole thing was vanity, showing off like a high school girl who's knocked up, looking for sympathy and gifts and to be the center of attention. Except Ethel wasn't a girl. This baby wasn't her fault, exactly, but it made her look like a foolish, old woman.

A few others expressed a backhanded hope that things would turn out all right. Then they all waited for the next round of news, which couldn't come soon enough.

Ethel gave birth to a baby girl whose eyes and lips and skin were so remarkably fine, several nosy people speculated about whether Burt could be the real father. Ethel was a good person and all, but she wasn't known for her physical attributes. How did two such homely people come to make a perfect child?

It was an easy birth, which surprised Ethel. The infant was delivered in record time without a mark on her. She didn't cry, and only fussed when she wanted something. She slept soundly in her crib, which she seemed to prefer to being held, and she wore an expression of perfect calm.

She was blond. When she opened her eyes, they were as blue as the sky. That was normal, the nurses told Ethel. The color might change. They were wrong. The baby had bright blue eyes, and from the start she appeared to watch the people around her with great concentration. She didn't tremble with effort when she moved her hands and feet. From early on, much earlier than anyone expected, she lay perfectly still and simply reached out toward whatever she wanted.

Ethel named her Connie Sara, after her aunt and Burt's mother. The baby's name was the only tribute she could afford. She felt that she owed Constance something even now; a nod, a gesture.

When the baby was born Burt was overcome with relief and joy. He had spent months drumming up odd jobs and applying for full-time work. He hadn't yet managed to find anything steady, but he had saved enough money so the hospital bill only set them back a few months. The first time he looked into his newborn daughter's eyes he said he didn't care how hard he had to work, it was all worth it.

In awe and in honor of his baby girl he got stinking drunk the night of her birth. With Mudflap's help he collected a batch of the leftover cedar shingles lying in his garage, nailed them together two at a time and tagged them with the words "Connie Sara Way" in white paint. Then the two men marched around late into the night, nailing the signs to tree trunks and fence posts up and down the unnamed road in a small but raucous celebration.

The gesture was a source of amusement to most people, who expected Burt to pull down the signs once he sobered up. But he never took them down, although plenty of people complained.

The New Mother

The baby didn't like Ethel's milk, so Ethel stopped breast-feeding and put her on formula. She wasn't interested when people tried to get her attention with baby talk or toys. The stuffed animals in her crib lay untouched.

On the advice of parenting experts from books and TV, Ethel took care not to over-stimulate her with too much eye contact, but she found that Connie Sara didn't grow either tired or over-stimulated. She didn't fuss or whimper. In fact she would sometimes watch Ethel's face so intently that Ethel grew uncomfortable and finally turned away.

This was embarrassing enough, and she couldn't explain it. She wondered about it, and soon it got worse. She found she couldn't make herself turn and look at the baby again, once she had turned away. Sometimes she had to wait for more than an hour for Burt to come home. Then she would sneak out of the room and return, breaking whatever delicate tension she felt was between the baby and herself, and starting over.

She had never been superstitious, so she felt ashamed every time she found herself unable to look. She tried, and tried, but the thought that she might turn her head or re-enter the baby's room and find her still staring, still making eye contact, still *waiting* for her, made Ethel feel sick to her stomach.

She was sure it was a case of nerves. The doctor had warned her: postpartum reactions were difficult to predict in a woman her age especially if she had never given birth before. This particular symptom would surely fade away with time if she didn't make too much of it.

Marietta and Beverly

Beverly bought gifts for the baby. First she offered toys. When the baby showed no interest in playthings she switched to beautifully made clothes and booties.

Marietta was home sick with a cold when Connie Sara was born. She came to visit a week later but she didn't stay long. She said she was still a bit under the weather and ought to rest up. In fact she had been feeling poorly for a while, generally slowing down. She was now reconsidering her son and daughter-in-law's offer, to have her move in with them.

"Henry's right across the road and over one house," Ethel said.

"That's right."

"Why does he want you to move now?"

"Oh, he's been trying to talk me into it for a while. He doesn't like me living by myself any more."

"We'll be neighbors," said Ethel. "And Beverly's only a couple of miles away. Isn't that funny?"

Marietta smiled. She promised to visit again soon.

Beverly and Marietta held their tongues on the subject of Ethel's baby until they met for lunch at Jessup's a couple of weeks later. Both noted that Ethel had seemed at first exhilarated by motherhood, then weary. This reverse in the usual order of things caused concern between her friends.

Beverly glanced around to make sure they were far enough from the other diners not to be overheard. Then she said:

"This is the reason women don't have babies at our age.

Thank goodness."

"My aunt knew quite a few women who had babies when they were over forty. It's not that uncommon. I don't think age is the reason Ethel acts the way she does."

This drew Beverly's full attention. She leaned forward in the booth and rested both elbows on the table between them.

"What do you think it is, then?"

Marietta sipped her coffee. She looked at Beverly, and said nothing.

"Come on," said Beverly. "What's on your mind?"

She waited. And waited.

"Do you remember Ethel's mother?" Marietta asked.

"No. Wait. Didn't she make Ethel go outside and stand in the rain one time? What am I thinking of?"

"We were sleeping over at Ethel's house. We only did that twice, and that was the last time."

"That's right!" Beverly said. "I remember. She came home drunk!"

"And woke us up."

"Ethel's dad. Where was he?"

"Working. He was always working."

"That's right. I used to think Ethel made him up. Like an invisible friend."

Marietta considered this.

"Might as well have," she said.

Both women were silent for a minute. Then Beverly asked, again:

"What is it you think is bothering Ethel? If it isn't just being tired."

"My aunt knew Shirley," Marietta said. "She came to our house. She was one of the women Aunt Delphine helped."

"She was pregnant?"

Marietta nodded.

"Nobody else knew?" Beverly asked.

"No. The reason I say this is, I remember Shirley very well. And what I remember is how she would look at me with those ice cold eyes of hers."

Beverly caught herself staring and snapped out of it. She grinned.

"That baby girl." She said. "Oh no, you're right. I hadn't noticed until you said that. It's the spitting image of her!"

Beverly let loose a rough, snorting laugh and then clapped a hand to her mouth. She lowered her voice to say:

"Well, that's a shame. Poor Ethel."

Marietta nodded.

"You know," said Beverly. "Rex looked exactly like his granddaddy when he was young. And I resemble my great aunt Ida, more than my mother, which is the only reason I ever get down on my knees and give thanks to God."

Marietta shook her head.

"It isn't the resemblance I'm talking about," she said. "I think that's a mask."

"A mask?"

"A familiar face. It hides more than it shows, that way."

The waitress stopped by to pour another round of coffee. Beverly and Marietta were silent until she left.

"I don't know what you're telling me, Marietta. Ethel's baby looks like Ethel's mother, but it's, what? A mask? You mean, like a disguise? What does that mean?"

Marietta pursed her lips and shook her head.

"Have you seen something?" Beverly asked. "Did you have a dream about the baby?"

"No," said Marietta. "No. But every time I see her, I can feel something, it's strong and it's deep."

Beverly looked out the window at intermittent traffic heading toward the new freeway entrance. The clink of silver and coffee cups filled the diner.

"I'm sorry," she said. "But I think Ethel is too old to look after a baby. That's all there is to it. She's worn out because she made a mistake. It's one thing to believe life is precious and good. It's a different thing altogether to have a baby and raise it while your friends go through the change of life."

"You might be right. Maybe that's all it is," Marietta said in the even tone she employed to reassure Henry and her friends, after she'd gone too far and spooked them. "You're probably right."

"Well," Beverly said. "Time will tell. So I guess we'll have to wait and see how it all turns out."

Ethel

Things were all right while Burt was at home. Even when he wasn't in the same room with Ethel he kept up a steady stream of noise in the background: whistling, humming, playing the radio, or hammering away at this project or that in the garage. She knew he was there. And he was good with the baby, always happy to carry her around wherever he happened to be in the house.

When Burt was at work or running an errand the stillness of the house crept in around her. At the sewing machine, she felt like she was being watched. Not by one person but by something that followed every move she made. It felt as if the house itself were alive and waiting for her to do the wrong thing. She caught herself tiptoeing in the hall and in the kitchen, even when the baby was awake. She realized she was avoiding turning on lights unless she had to. She began to whisper to herself, and couldn't make herself stop the habit.

Connie Sara didn't sleep in short cycles as the parenting books warned. She fell asleep around ten o'clock and woke at seven every day. When Ethel confided this to the mothers she knew, they expressed envy and astonishment, but Ethel didn't feel lucky. She didn't sleep well. She had anticipated a more complicated sleep and feeding cycle. Her mind was ready for things that never occurred. She stayed up late to check on Connie Sara until she realized there was no reason to. The baby slept soundly. Ethel slept less and less. If the wind caused a branch to tremble outside, she woke up.

She began to pay closer attention to the women she met

who were nursing infants. Their babies fussed when they were hungry and nuzzled against them when they were held. Connie Sara didn't do these things, yet in all physical respects she was normal, the doctor said.

"She sleeps all night and doesn't like breast milk," he said. "Count your blessings."

After that Ethel felt ungrateful. Her child was perfect and beautiful. She ought to celebrate. She ought to brag. She ought to take a million photos, but she never took one. Burt recorded all the big moments in their daughter's life and placed the pictures in a photo album that Ethel never opened.

She visited the doctor three times to complain about things most mothers would have loved. She had free time to watch TV, to sew, to have a glass of wine. Yet some nights she didn't sleep at all. She would sit at the kitchen table sipping chamomile tea from a bright green ceramic cup. She would stare out the screened window at the blue-black night sky. Everyone in Skillute was in bed. Her daughter slept. Her husband snored away in bed, alone. She knew she should feel free, this time was hers, but she never shook the sense that she wasn't alone.

She had set aside time for the baby, let her clients know she wouldn't be available for a couple of months. Now she felt silly calling customers and inviting them back, saying no, her baby didn't need her after all. Beyond the basics, diaper changes and bottle-feeding and bathing, it was true: her child barely needed her.

In the absence of larger concerns, she began to resent small things. Rinsing out the baby's cloth diapers in the toilet. Dunking them in the cold water. The movement, the predictability of it was nauseatingly familiar after the first hundred times. Abruptly she switched to disposable diapers and told Burt she was doing it for Connie Sara's health because disposables were less likely to cause a rash.

She began to dread checking the water temperature before Connie Sara's bath. Filling the bottle with formula.

Opening the shampoo, or the canister of baby powder. Folding the baby's clothes. Placing them neatly in the chest of drawers. Lining up the drawers evenly in their tracks when she closed them. The repetition grated on her nerves. Each necessary movement seemed to take longer each time she performed it.

More than ever, when she was alone with the infant, who never slept during the day, she would feel a foreign presence in the room and turn to find Connie Sara watching her. At first she told herself this was natural. Why wouldn't a newborn look in the direction of its mother, its source of life and love and food?

After a while this reasonable attitude wore away. No matter where the baby lay in relation to her, when Ethel turned to check, Connie Sara was staring directly at her. Not with obvious affection or mirth, not with satisfaction, she decided, but with a cold expression that said Ethel wasn't up to this job. She was playing mommy with none of the proper instincts. She wasn't even interested in it. She would fail. Sooner or later she would make a mess of things.

Her pregnancy had been surprisingly easy. She had come to expect that the baby would lift her spirits for good. She had longed to feel joy. She couldn't recall the last time she had felt free, the last time she had seen her life as other than a burden.

Now she realized that the child was a burden, too. Her few needs were mundane and boring. Her gaze made Ethel uncomfortable. She had changed Ethel's life, but not for the better.

Ethel would put up with the tingling sensation, the feeling of being observed and judged, as long as possible. Then she would have to jump up and start tidying the room, washing clothes, sweeping the front porch, anything to have a real purpose and to escape having to look into her daughter's eyes.

No matter how tiresome she found it to care for the

baby, Ethel couldn't bring herself to hire a sitter. Marietta offered to sit for free. She was now living with her son Henry and his wife. Close enough to walk over in an emergency. Close enough to provide relief when it was needed. Yet Ethel couldn't ask for help. She searched her conscience to explain why. It didn't make sense. Marietta had raised a child of her own. She knew more about caring for a baby than Ethel did. Surely it wasn't that she didn't trust her friend. Why was she uneasy about leaving a friend alone with her child? From this a host of questions came to mind and overwhelmed Ethel.

Why did Marietta move in with Henry and his well-to-do wife when she always said she was happy in her own little house, a house she now kept boarded up with a barbed wire fence running all the way around the yard? She never sold off that property. She claimed she was saving it for one of her distant relatives as a retirement gift, but no one had ever heard her mention such a relative before. Now she lived close enough to Burt and Ethel to justify weekly or even daily visits, yet they hardly ever saw her. When they did she never failed to ask if they wanted a night off, saying she would be glad to watch the baby. The child. The baby.

That was the thing. That was the thing nagging at Ethel all along. Marietta never called the baby by her name. Why not?

Ethel felt a flush of shame, mulling over these questions. Beverly and Marietta were her best friends in the world, for all intents and purposes her only friends. She owed them so much. Yet she had this sinking sensation in her heart whenever Marietta brought over a loaf of her daughter-in-law's fresh baked bread or carrot cake, smiled gently, and said for the umpteenth time:

"I'll be glad to sit with the baby any time you and Burt need a night off."

Ethel longed to leave the house with her husband for a few hours, but what would a sitter (even a best friend) make of Connie Sara's peculiarities? What would happen while she was away? Maybe nothing would happen, and this would prove Ethel was simply unfit to be a mother. Unfit, maybe even crazy.

Why was Marietta so keen to be alone with the baby, while Beverly showed no special interest after the initial gift offerings? Ethel couldn't bear to find out, so she went on caring for the infant without help.

When she couldn't stand it any longer, any time she thought one more hour trapped in the cocoon of her home would drive her to violence and insanity, Burt was there. He had no qualms about Connie Sara. He was happy to feed her, change her, or hold her in his arms while watching a ball game with Mudflap. Sometimes he would simply stand next to her crib talking to her, not baby talk but long, serious, one-sided conversations about life, about Skillute, about how work was going.

With Burt the baby seemed different. Not only more cheerful, more animated, more natural in her movements and expressions but also genuinely contented and secure. For Burt the baby laughed. She would roll over onto her stomach and then pull herself up holding onto the bars of her crib, and laugh triumphantly when he praised her. She giggled at his attempts at peek-a-boo and an old half-remembered lullaby. Burt was the one who noticed when she started teething, and he spent hours trying to elicit her first word.

With her father the baby was happy and normal. Rather than reassure Ethel, this made things seem worse. How could she explain to Burt how she felt when she was alone with his beloved daughter?

In less time than Ethel thought possible, Connie Sara learned to crawl and to climb. Now she would climb out of her playpen and drag herself around the house, following Ethel from room to room while she worked. Wherever Ethel settled for a moment's peace, at her sewing machine or at the kitchen table, she would hear a sort of shushing noise, and grunts of physical effort, and soon the baby was a few feet away, on the floor, staring at her. The moment Ethel was visible the child would stop and rest there watching her. If she moved to another room, it would start all over again.

She told herself: to a baby this must be an innocent game. She follows because she can crawl, and because she likes to see her mother.

Nothing helped. Her most reasonable explanation was crippled by panic, by a feeling that she was being pursued. She couldn't run away. She couldn't hide. She knew, because she had tried.

One morning while Burt was miles away helping Mudflap paint the fence around his house, Ethel reached what she thought was the breaking point. Her impulse, to reach out and kick Connie Sara away, frightened her so badly that she left the baby on the floor in the kitchen and walked briskly down the hall. There she opened the linen closet as quietly as she could and climbed inside, gently pulling the door shut.

She stood in the pitch dark, barely breathing, with the scent of clean sheets all around her. Outside there seemed to be a lull, a heavy pause, as though the baby were genuinely unaware that she had gone. Maybe she didn't care. Maybe this would be the way to break her of the habit of following.

A thin noise came from the kitchen, halfway between a sigh and a voice calling. Connie Sara couldn't talk at this age, didn't know a single word yet. Was Ethel losing her hearing, or her grip on reality? She could have sworn she heard the words "find you." No. She was listening too hard, imagining actual words when all that she could hear was this sound that was more like an absence of sound. Then she did hear it, coming after her.

At the gentle tread of stubby knees and chubby hands navigating the hallway, Ethel felt her stomach tighten. It was coming. Why did she think "it?" Her child, her adventurous child was coming to find her. That was all. Yet the closer the thudding of knees and hands, the closer Ethel came to screaming out loud.

What was she afraid of? What could possibly happen to her? She was a grown woman safe in her own home with a harmless baby that loved her. Wasn't she? Didn't the baby love her? She couldn't tell. Connie Sara didn't reach for her, or cling, or cry when she left the room. She simply came after her.

Thinking this, Ethel realized that there was silence outside the door. The crawling sound had stopped, she didn't notice when. She couldn't make herself open the door. It was ridiculous! She had to open the door. She had to make sure nothing was wrong. Anything could happen once a child was mobile; she could climb on furniture and fall, or discover a pin or a tack on the floor, and put it in her mouth. With a shudder of self-loathing Ethel realized that for a split second she had experienced relief thinking these things. She also realized that she couldn't stay in the linen closet until Burt came home.

With more resignation than courage, she gripped the doorknob and turned it. She forced herself to open the door and look down. There was Connie Sara, and the child met her gaze without smiling and without a sound.

Brusquely Ethel seized the baby, scooped her up and carried her to her crib. She lay her down on her back then yanked up the crib's barred side panel, locking it into place.

"Stay there," she said, noting that her voice had descended to a husky whisper.

"Stay."

She looked at Connie Sara's face. No expression, none of the delight she had seen in other people's babies when they first began to speak.

"What did you say?" Ethel asked.

Now the child was silent. She would not speak again, if she had spoken. Ethel went to the kitchen to prepare chamomile tea to calm her nerves.

What would people think of a mother who hid from her baby? How could she describe the dark and hateful glee in her daughter's eyes, or her stubbornly blank face? It sounded crazy to say her daughter was after her. Didn't it?

"After me," Ethel said, and blushed.

Mother and Daughter

Burt blamed the pre-school for the first accident. Wasn't it their fault, for allowing young children to play on dangerous equipment? He called a consumer agency to get the manufacturer's rating and found out the makers of the carousel were being sued by a family in the Midwest. The news confirmed his suspicion. He told Ethel they should consider filing a complaint or a lawsuit, he wasn't sure which. He was sure that what happened was not their daughter's fault. He took the information about the carousel to the head of the pre-school and argued on behalf of his child, and won. That first time, she was allowed to stay in school.

Ethel had to promise to have a serious talk with Connie Sara about safety and supervision. Since none of the other children had seen what happened, it was officially recorded as an accident.

The smaller girl, Jane, had a dislocated shoulder, but she wouldn't say whether or not Connie Sara had pulled her off the carousel. There were other children everywhere but they said they didn't notice the two girls until Jane started screaming and fell from the carousel onto the sand. Then they all stood around and gawked at the shrieking girl until the teacher and the school nurse came running.

Ethel was uncertain what to do. Burt insisted that they give their daughter the benefit of the doubt. He still thought the child was a small miracle. So what else could Ethel do? She had to tell herself and her friends that Connie Sara was going through a phase, although she knew this wasn't the whole story.

She suspected the problem was inherited, a streak of something harsh and aggressive running through her family. That was the answer. It had to be, because no one in Burt's family had ever been mean. His father liked to hunt but he had always cleaned, cooked, and eaten what he killed. He had put food on the table. He didn't hunt for the hell of it. He didn't hunt to prove anything. He certainly didn't hunt in order to harm animals.

Ethel's mother Shirley had been too rough with her. Now she had to struggle constantly not to be rough with Connie Sara, not to yank her by the arm when she refused to budge in the checkout line at the grocery store, not to push her when she didn't want to get out of the car, not to slap her face when she said smart things.

There was a strain of pure spite in the women of Ethel's family. That was what she came to believe while she was raising her daughter. This angry drive, this energy might be used properly to achieve many things, but more often it was misused. It all depended on how it was directed.

Ethel held on to this belief while she had her talk with Connie Sara. She convinced herself that she could set aside the troubles between them and help the child onto a better path.

"It's good to watch out for the other children. They're not strong like you," Ethel began over breakfast a couple of days after the accident.

They were alone. Burt had gone to Longview on a work assignment, stopping on his way out the door to kiss Connie Sara on the forehead and tell her to listen to what her mother had to say. The girl munched away, working steadily on her second bowl of cereal.

Ethel told her to remember that her strength didn't make her grown up. There were times when only a grown-up could figure out the right thing to do. She reminded Connie Sara that she might hurt someone without meaning to, and then she would be sad, wouldn't she? The whole family would be sad. The county might even decide Burt and Ethel were bad parents, and take her away from them. At this, the girl looked up but said nothing.

Ethel told her that children would stop being friends with her if they were afraid of her. When she had finished explaining how some children are tough and some are gentle, and the tough ones have to be kind to the gentle ones, the girl looked at her through vagrant strands of blond hair and said:

"If they're weak, they should stay home where they won't get hurt."

Connie Sara blinked, and went on eating. Ethel was struck for the millionth time by the resemblance. Her mother's eyes and her hair color had skipped a generation. For Ethel, not even a glancing blow, but her daughter was the spitting image of Shirley. She had her eyes exactly: small slivers of blue ice with a sly expression. Her eyes seemed to tease and laugh even when she was serious.

After she dropped the girl off at pre-school for the morning, Ethel returned home and tidied up. She washed the breakfast dishes and put them away. She settled in front of her sewing machine with a fresh cup of coffee and a spool of the yellow rickrack she was adding to a new skirt for Connie Sara.

Now that the child was away for part of every weekday, she had some time to herself, and she was grateful. She sometimes thought if she had been forced to spend another month stuck in the house with Connie Sara, she might have done something awful. Fortunately that was over. She would do anything to keep the girl in pre-school. Again she ran through a list of reasonable arguments she could offer in favor of keeping her daughter among children her age.

Kids were often defiant, even mean. It was part of growing up and facing the world without the protection of their parents. All of the parenting books said so. Soon Connie Sara would move on to another phase and become more generous.

Even as Ethel thought these things a thin, cruel voice

in her head told her she was lying. Her lie was selfish and dangerous to other children. There was something wrong with the girl. There always had been. The cruel voice said she had missed her chance to do what was right. She had been stronger than the baby, but she wasn't stronger than the girl.

By the time she had started pre-school Connie Sara seemed remarkably resilient in body and in will. She was slender, with no awkwardness or baby fat. She was tall for her age and was constantly moving, with an athletic rather than nervous energy. She had delicate features: pale blue eyes that shifted to a metallic gray with lapses in sunlight, a fair complexion, and an abundance of unruly blond hair. She was hearty and tomboyish. By mid-spring she had a bit of suntan, far ahead of the boys who played outdoors in any weather.

Ethel told friends that her daughter was just a tomboy, but she felt afraid. What she knew frightened her, and she was sure there were things she didn't know. There were secrets, now that the child could roam free outdoors and get into trouble.

Ethel made rules and the girl ignored them. That much was obvious. With Burt she was pretending, preening, and playing with his emotions. With Ethel she was openly defiant.

Connie Sara climbed trees, tall oaks mainly, and used trellises and drainpipes to scale neighbors' homes, often in the middle of the night. She would survey the dark patches of forest and the freeway from rooftops.

She stole a boy's knife, called it a gift, and whittled her own slingshot from a block of wood supplied by Burt, who was amused by the odd request and then too amazed by her accomplishment to consider punishing her. Later, alone in the meadow behind the Sanders' house, Connie Sara spent hours perfecting her aim at squirrels and blackbirds. In the evening she would lay low in the weeds and hunt feral cats for practice.

A Special Talent

Across the road from the Sanders family lived a retired mill worker named Jim Jasper. Years ago when Mrs. Jasper was alive, the family had kept a blind goat named Hank after their favorite singer, Hank Williams. They liked the name so much they also called their son Hank. With light-hearted humor and without intending any harm, Mr. and Mrs. Jasper had kept track of these three by calling them Hank-the-singer, Hank-the-goat, and Hank-the-boy.

Unknown to his parents, for years Hank-the-boy led a train of classmates and cousins all the way to school. Down the hill they ran, and across a meadow, shouting at the boy's back:

"Hey, sing that song again, Hank! Beh-eh-eh!"

When he was fifteen, Hank ran away from home and his parents never heard of him again. It broke his mother's heart, but she accepted the loss. He wasn't the first person to disappear from Skillute without a word. It was the kind of place that inspired clean breaks, when they finally occurred.

For a long time Hank-the-boy's former classmates would sometimes pay tribute to him after a long night of drinking. Stumbling home in the moonlight, they would stop by the rusty back gate that led to the Jasper ranch house, throw their heads back, and bleat the first bars of "Your Cheatin' Heart."

After his wife died of cancer Jim Jasper lived alone for a while. He grew a beard and people said he drank whiskey in the middle of the day.

The same year Burt took over his dad's old property

across the road, Jasper bought a pit-bull and named it Kojak. He kept Kojak on a chain in the yard most of the time. The dog had everything he needed: a plywood house, a ceramic water bowl, and a food dish.

Jasper fed the dog scraps of steak and wild rabbit. Whenever he went to town he took Kojak along on a leash with a muzzle. The dog rode in the cab beside him without the muzzle, smiling and slobbering out the window. He was a good-natured animal and his master loved him like a child.

Eventually Kojak began to slow down a bit. He was still in fine condition but he wouldn't live forever, so Jasper took him to a breeding farm and when the litter was born he adopted the strongest and smartest puppy and named him Baretta. Now the two dogs shared the yard, Kojak on his chain and Baretta in a small pen.

Soon after the puppy arrived Connie Sara began sneaking across the road to Jim Jasper's house. She had been strictly forbidden to go there. She was told that the dogs were dangerous and if she got hurt on Jasper's property it would be her own fault. Secretly she took bits of cat fur and rabbit skin late at night and tormented Kojak with the scent. Or she would pelt Baretta with small, sharp rocks until Kojak's barking woke Jasper. Then the girl would run away.

Naturally the pit-bulls came to hate her, to hate the sight and the scent of her. But then most animals were agitated by Connie Sara's presence. She paid them back with contempt and cruelty whenever possible. The only animals she liked enough not to injure were the screech owls that swooped down from the night sky and snatched their prey out of the tall grass.

By the summer before she started first grade she had developed an interest that worried her parents at first. When she killed a bird or a rodent with her slingshot, she would bring it home and ask Burt to skin it. He did so reluctantly. After watching Burt use the techniques his father had taught him for cleaning his kill, Connie Sara announced that she wanted to skin and stuff the animals she hunted.

When Burt's buddies heard about this, they chuckled and told Burt he was raising himself a little Skillute native, for sure. Their amusement made Burt think he had overreacted. After assurances from his friends that their sons were practiced hunters by the age of eight or ten, and at least one other child his daughter's age had taken up taxidermy and showed a talent for it, he decided it wasn't such a strange request. This was just a part of the life he and Ethel had chosen by staying on in their hometown. If Burt couldn't be the hunter and fisherman his friends and neighbors were, at least his child would fit in.

Soon the girl could clean a carcass without help. She kept stray bones and beaks, talons and claws in her room. Occasionally she took these items to school as show-and-tell projects.

Once she trapped and killed a fox. She brought the pelt to class, and told everyone she was going to sew it to the collar of a winter coat. She would have, if Ethel had not thrown the pelt away in disgust. When she turned it over in her rubber-gloved hands and bundled it into a plastic bag, she wondered how the child had gotten out of the house with it, without letting anyone know what she was up to. She checked inside the girl's backpack, and when she found spiky red hairs stuck in the zipper she threw the backpack away, as well. She said nothing to Burt. He always found a way to excuse or defend the girl, and this had caused enough arguments between them.

Connie Sara was six and a half years old the day Ethel stepped outside to hang sheets on the laundry line and discovered all the blooms from her fuchsia had been shredded and scattered on the ground around the bush. Among the torn flowers she discovered the bodies of hummingbirds that been returning to the bush for some time. All had been crushed and left to die. A few had struggled from beneath the flowers and perished in the grass.

When Burt got home, Ethel was crying. Try as she might, she couldn't describe what had occurred. She only begged him to go outside and see for himself.

Without another word Burt raked up all of the refuse and carried it to the trash. Later he asked Ethel if he ought to punish the girl, but he also told her he didn't believe Connie Sara was responsible. Ethel could only shake her head and say:

"No, please, no. If you do, something worse will happen."

Beverly

However Ethel wanted to put it, "adventurous" or "just a tomboy," the girl was vicious. She had a smug, mean smile. She bossed her parents around, especially Ethel. It was embarrassing, Beverly felt, and it was the reason Ethel and Burt's friends had drifted away.

If the Sanders family invited anyone over for a barbecue their guests had to eat whatever Connie Sara wanted that day. Nobody was allowed to do otherwise or the girl would throw a tantrum and ruin things. If people came over to watch a ball game or a TV show they were subject to the whims of Connie Sara, who might decide at any moment to change the channel, and that was that.

The sickening thing was that Burt and Ethel went along with these demands. Not with the indulgent smile of proud parents but with an embarrassed shrug, as if they were afraid to do otherwise, as if to say:

"We don't mean to treat our friends this way, but what can we do?"

Beverly knew what she would have done, if that girl belonged to her. She had seen parents who took charge and parents who didn't, and she had seen the consequences. What kids needed and wanted, even if they didn't realize it, was a firm hand. They needed to know what time to get out of bed in the morning, and when to be home.

More often than she could recall Beverly had glanced out the kitchen window to see Miss Smart Mouth prancing around at the edge of her lawn, playing outdoors more than a mile from home, even after dark. The first time it happened, Beverly called Burt and told him to come pick the girl up. He claimed she was sound asleep in her room.

"Burt Sanders," Beverly had told him. "I was looking out my window ten seconds ago."

By the time she said this and turned to look again, the girl was gone. Beverly figured she must have run home as soon as she knew she'd been spotted.

On certain nights even now Beverly looked up and caught a glimpse of Connie Sara messing around near the tulip beds, or chasing a kitten, or gathering sticks and stones. Beverly shouted at her to get home. She didn't bother calling Burt and Ethel any more because they always said she was wrong: their little girl was in their back yard, or sleeping, or watching TV. Then there were the times when they didn't answer the phone at all.

They never punished the girl for a single thing. All they did was make excuses. They said she didn't fit in because she was so much brighter than the other children. That was a hoot! Or they said she was naturally over-aggressive. It was a purely physical fact and what could they do?

That excuse was almost confirmed by the principal at her elementary school. First he recommended home schooling. Then he insisted on it. When Burt and Ethel procrastinated the principal expelled Connie Sara. He didn't call it a special problem, or say she couldn't fit in with children who weren't as gifted as she was. He called it a safety issue.

She was dangerous, that's all. She couldn't play with other children for long before they got hurt. Nobody would say it quite that way, but it was true. They could call it a safety issue to be polite, but the girl was a danger to everyone she met.

"They'll pay the price," Beverly told Marietta over a lunch of tuna casserole and iced tea.

Marietta didn't have to ask, "Who's that?" They talked about the girl so often.

"Burt and Ethel are raising a criminal. Mark my word."

It was Sunday afternoon. They were eating in Beverly's

kitchen with its shiny counters and checkerboard linoleum floor. Marietta had her back to the window and Beverly sat opposite so she could enjoy the view. Sometimes a breeze swept across her front yard and set the miniature windmills spinning.

"I think they're paying the price already," Marietta said.

"Well, that's their own fault," Beverly told her. "They made their bed. But that's no reason for the rest of us to suffer. If they had any respect for my state of mind, at least that would be something."

In conversation Beverly routinely found moments to remind people that she was a widow. Since she was also a sensitive woman, she pointed out, it was more than a hardship for her to cope with problems and childish pranks. Ever since Ethel was forced to home school her daughter, the girl had become a real nuisance.

First there had been the piles of weeds, clusters of dandelion and grass on Beverly's doorstep. Then the lock on the shed where she put the day's trash had been broken, and garbage spilled out onto the ground. Beverly had to get one of the Dempsey cousins to come down the hill and fire a shotgun to scare off a coyote that wandered into the yard, attracted by the scent.

Then there was the tulip bed. Beverly had long since banned Connie Sara from setting foot on her property. Of course, the girl still made frequent nighttime appearances in the forest along the edge of the yard, and Beverly was considering sharing her grievances with the sheriff.

The breaking point had come this very morning. The sky was smoke-gray and the ground was still damp from the overnight rain. Beverly was pouring herself a cup of coffee. She was thinking of the times when she and Rex used to drink their coffee and eat Sunday breakfast in bed.

They had married for love, she told her friends, and because she was broadminded enough to overlook his family. She sent cards to the cousins every Christmas and attended a few baptisms. Other than that she had as little to do with the Dempsey family as possible, socially. They were the kind of people she hired to do repairs around the house.

For their part the Dempseys minded their own business. They lived in rundown trailers and cabins up in the hills and ridges behind Beverly's home, and in the woods along the road that led to Burt and Ethel's house. It had crossed Beverly's mind that one of the Dempsey kids was also playing pranks on her. But she felt deeply, no, she knew in her gut that it was Connie Sara, all of it.

Marietta was the only person she knew who never contradicted the assumption. In fact Marietta believed everything Beverly told her about the girl, and this was one reason they had grown closer in recent years.

That Sunday, early in the morning, Beverly had taken a sip of coffee and gazed out the kitchen window. At first the tulip bed nearest to the house seemed larger than it had been the day before. A closer look revealed the edges spreading out over the grass on all sides. The earth had been dug up again.

"That little bitch!" Beverly said. In the next second she slammed her coffee cup down on the table and went striding outside in her nightgown and robe.

The closer she got the more of a mess she saw. Tulips and dirt were thrown in all directions. This was worse than vandalism; worse than pulling up weeds and leaving them on her doorstep; worse than knocking over the garbage; this was a hateful disregard for all that was beautiful and alive.

Beverly was livid. She would call the sheriff, and report that girl. She would tell him the local gossip that no one had informed him about. She might even go with him to Ethel's house, to confront her and get the truth. She was turning these possibilities over in her mind when she saw something protruding from the ground where the tulip bed had been.

She picked up a stick and pushed at the dirt. Where it

separated she could see a wide, flat tongue and the jaw-bone of a small animal. It appeared to be broken sideways. She thought maybe it belonged to a raccoon but even torn and bloodied it clearly wasn't the right shape.

Looking more closely she realized it was a puppy, Jim Jasper's pit-bull puppy, Baretta. It was still sticky with blood. Bits of fur remained, but most of the skin had been torn back from the skull.

She remembered the memento she had stashed in her purse all those years ago, after she met Oliver in the woods. The small jawbone with its row of childlike teeth, charred black from fire or some chemical reaction, lay wrapped in a silk handkerchief in the bottom drawer of her dresser. Once in a while she took it out and looked at it. These were the only times when she remembered her child, her lost child. Sometimes, holding the little jaw in her hand, she would sit on the edge of her bed and weep.

Recently she had hired a private detective to locate her daughter. There was no one else she wanted to mention in her will. Someday she would leave a few things to friends, but she wanted her daughter to have whatever would be left of her savings. The house would be hers to sell or claim. Putting her affairs in order would bring Beverly peace of mind, she had decided. She didn't want to worry about these things. She wanted to take care of it and then forget about it forever.

She had been thinking of this only the day before. She had held the delicate memento in both hands and looked out the front window at the rain spattering her tulips.

In a sickening flash Beverly had decided not to call the sheriff after all. This latest prank was beyond his limited abilities. How could he help? This was rank, worse than criminal. And how could she let the sheriff break the news? Better to let Jim Jasper think the puppy had run off. It would break his heart, wondering if the animal had suffered. Of course it had. Why else would the girl have done it the way she had? She liked causing pain. She must.

The girl was evil, probably a serial killer. Something decisive needed to be done. For that she had to speak honestly, bluntly, with a friend who knew the girl as well as she did. Beverly called Marietta and invited her over for lunch that afternoon.

"She has to be locked up for good. Her parents are afraid of her, that's why this has gone on for so long. If they had any respect for my state of mind, they would take my advice and find out what that little monster's been up to," Beverly told her friend.

"I don't think it's about respecting you, Bev," Marietta told her. "They've got no choice. They think the girl belongs to them. They have to look after their child."

It crossed Beverly's mind that Marietta was also talking about her feelings for Henry, the son she never wanted but loved despite his failures in school and at a long series of jobs before he announced his "calling" to be a preacher. Now he was the pastor of a church he had invented, a church hardly anyone attended. Marietta lived with Henry and his homely wife in a house that was much too big for them.

"If she were my child," Beverly said. "She would've turned out in a different way, that's all."

"Isn't that what people always say?" Marietta asked.

Beverly turned away to clean her plate in the sink. When she came back to the table she cleared her throat.

"What I'm thinking is that I'll contact social services for the county and have them interview Burt and Ethel. If the girl's as dangerous as I think she is, they'll take her away. It might do her some good to be in foster care, but I doubt it. I think she needs to be in the county hospital."

"She wouldn't like foster parents that tried to make her do what they wanted," Marietta said. "Listen, you can't punish Burt and Ethel. They don't know what they're keeping in their house. It isn't what they think it is."

This last was said with more gravity than usual. Beverly perked up.

"You mean you agree with me, she's psychotic?" She asked.

She was fond of this kind of talk, analyzing people to figure out what made them tick. She followed several TV shows that specialized in solving people's mental problems in front of a studio audience.

Marietta looked at her for a while in silence. Then she folded the linen napkin in her hand and set it on top of her plate.

"If I tell you what it is." She stopped.

Beverly waited.

"I've held my tongue. I always thought I could get close enough to solve the problem without hurting Ethel any more than she's been hurt already. If I tell you what I think it is," Marietta said. "Do you promise to go by what I say, and do what I ask? Because it might sound like a bad thing to do."

This was even better than Beverly had expected. This was the kind of high drama and mystery she loved, on the rare occasions when Marietta allowed her into her private thoughts, and the world of her intuitions. Beverly nodded, thrilled to be making a pact of so much importance, and wondering what she was getting herself into.

Winston

Along this part of the road Doug fir had once grown in abundance. Now the grass was littered with tree stumps and snags. Just beyond the last house the broken asphalt gave way in stages to gravel and dirt. Further on there was some alder springing up in the gullies and Western hemlock scattered at the outskirts of the remaining forest, but even these grew as if it were an effort. They seemed stunted, unable to find the right spot in which to thrive.

This was where the boy and his schoolmates were never supposed to go. Only the poorest families lived beyond the junction, where the road split. On one side right before the intersection was the big brick house that belonged to Pastor Colquitt and his wife. That was the good side. The other branch curved downhill to this place, the corner of nowhere.

Old Man Jasper lived here, and he would chase kids away with his shotgun. Across the road from his place Connie Sara Sanders lived with her parents in a drafty old house with a good-sized garage that Burt Sanders kept trying to remodel into a workroom. You couldn't tell much by looking at the place from outside. The walls had sunk and settled with the years. The back of the garage and most of the patio were overgrown with moss. The outside walls needed paint. On this particular gray afternoon there was only one light shining inside, at the kitchen window.

The boy was here because he had lied to his mother. And today's lie was a whopper: He said he was helping his classmates, two boys whose family his mother approved of, and would like to impress. He said they were building a kite for a competition in Long Beach. They were meeting at another friend's house, and he would walk there and back. He would have done worse than lie to his mother, to stay in favor with Connie Sara.

The boy had red hair. His name was Winston, but his mother often embarrassed him by calling him Winnie. She also embarrassed him by showing her friends the glass jar in which she saved the golden red curls from his first haircut.

"A woman would kill to have hair like this," she cooed, clutching the jar with one hand and touching its surface gently with the other. Her lady friends always nodded and agreed: They would kill to have those long, loose, silken curls that caught the light in the living room and made the boy wince with discomfort.

Winston crossed his arms over his chest. He made an effort at not looking scared, but the smirk uncurled from his lips when he said:

"I don't believe the part about the witch."

"Are you calling me a liar?" Connie Sara asked.

Winston considered the seriousness of this charge, and said:

"No, but I'm saying you might be wrong. You might think she's a witch, and she might not be. Sometimes it's hard to tell."

They sat in the brittle fluorescent light of the Sanders' kitchen, drawing pictures with crayons and butcher paper. The sound of Connie Sara's father Burt snoring out a great guffaw in the bedroom down the hall startled Winston. Her mother was at the grocery store. Connie Sara leaned close and whispered:

"What a baby you are. No wonder your mama calls you Winnie. I don't care if you believe it. There's a witch living in the woods, and she's got somebody in a dungeon that she beats and pokes at with a stick. At midnight, if you go walking by the place I'm talking about, you can hear a poor little girl calling for her mama. But you don't care. Nobody cares."

Winston kept his arms crossed, and stared straight into Connie Sara's sky-blue eyes. He was afraid of what she had said, but more afraid of what she might say about him to the boys he knew at school. They made fun of him because he'd been held back a year. They said he was slow, but the truth was that his mother thought he needed an extra year to mature. The boys didn't care about the reason. They loved any excuse to taunt him. Especially Troy, who thought Winston was a crybaby and sometimes followed him home, pitching rocks at the back of his legs.

"Hey, Winnie!" Troy would call out when there were no grownups in sight. "What's that on the back of your pants? Hey, Winnie the Poop!"

Winston was afraid of the boys' bathroom, because there was no door on the last stall. That's where Troy and three other boys had ganged up on him, teasing him with vague threats until he burst into tears. Once Troy was satisfied with his victim's panic and tears, he had left Winston alone in the stall. But the next day, afraid to use the toilet, Winston held it until he was about to explode. In fact, he did explode, just enough to make a small mess in his underpants. He was standing on the playground near Shelly Miller, who kept sniffing the air and shrieking:

"What's that smell? Holy macaroni! Can you smell that?"

Pretty soon everyone knew where the smell came from, and Winston had a nickname. He wondered every day: Would people know about this, even if he moved to another town? When he was a man, would it still be like this? Did grownups call each other names? Were they allowed to do that?

Luckily, this had happened a couple of months after Connie Sara left school. She and Winston had been in the same class for half a year. Then her parents took her out for home schooling. The teacher said she played too rough with the smaller kids. Somebody got hurt on the playground, and nobody wanted to talk about it, but they all said it wasn't the first time, and they all blamed Burt and Ethel Sanders.

Winston knew better than to show his friend a sign of weakness. The more he brushed off her smart remarks, the more she sought him out. She was the only person his age who ever did that, the only one who invited him to her house on the weekend and asked him to join a club. She was also the only person he had ever known who lived on a road that was named after her.

Together they had built a fort out of plywood against a maple, but the first storm of the season tore it down. Even without the fort, they had sworn an oath of loyalty, and they'd eaten a handful of dried crimson berries from a devil's club plant, which made Winston gag. Eating the berries was part of the oath, so he did his best. His mother hated devil's club, its spindly thorns catching any clothes or skin that came near it. Whenever she found it in the yard she would dig it up and throw it in the trash. He thought of this while trying to choke down the berries.

Winston and Connie Sara were blood scouts, now. So here he was, killing a cloudy Saturday afternoon, against his mother's orders.

He wasn't even sure why his mother didn't like the Sanders family. She made little remarks to her friends: Burt and Ethel were too old to have a child, the house they lived in was a rat-trap, but nothing that explained why he was forbidden to see Connie Sara after she stopped coming to school. He wasn't small or weak like the kid who got hurt at school. He could fend for himself against a girl, especially one who was a year younger than he was.

"You do believe me, don't you?"

"I don't know," he said. He needed more time to think it over. "Where exactly does this witch live, anyhow?"

"Nowhere," said Connie Sara. "Nowhere that most people can see. Her house is painted like the woods, so it's invisible. That's how come nobody else knows about it."

A rumble of thunder rolled across the darkening valley. On this gravel and dirt road leading to where Connie Sara lived, the useless pastures were overrun with blackberries in the summer. In front of the Sanders' house, year-round, a disassembled tractor lay rusting on the grass. From the side, its parts looked like a pre-historic bird fossil.

"How can she have a dungeon, if there's no house?"

Winston was pleased with this question. He crossed his arms again.

"I didn't say 'no house.' I said it's invisible. It's disguised. The dungeon is buried down in the ground," she told him. "And the little girl is real. You can hear her crying late at night."

"Well," he pondered. He swallowed and thought it over again. "Who do you think it might be, the little girl? Who does this witch keep in the dungeon?"

Connie Sara got up and closed the kitchen door. The sound of her father's snoring faded away. With the door shut, a tiny shift in the air pressure flattened their voices. Connie Sara sat down, leaned in with her hands clasped together on the tabletop, and said:

"She's got little Tracy down there in the dungeon."

Winston felt a cold rush at the name. Tracy Carson had been gone almost a year, lost walking home from school. She'd gotten into a fight with another girl. Nobody remembered how it started. Tracy wandered off and nobody ever found her. The sheriff and his deputies and Tracy's mother had finally given up combing the woods and the nearby junkyard, posting pictures of the missing first grader.

"My mom said she got kidnapped by her dad, over the customs." Winston knew this was the wrong word, but couldn't remember the right one.

"Well. Maybe she doesn't know what she's talking about. Was your mom right about toadstools?" Connie Sara asked.

Winston's mother had warned him off eating things he found in the woods. When she discovered a few truffles in the pocket of his jeans, she force-fed him a large, store-bought mushroom coated in castor oil, until he threw up. Then one day Connie Sara teased and dared him into splitting a toadstool with her. He'd found, to his amazement, that his mother was dead wrong. He didn't get sick at all.

"Was your mom right about the creek?"

Everybody knew the putrid creek that dribbled down from the Kelso lumber mill was polluted. To make sure Winston stayed away from it, his mother told him it was radioactive and anyone who played in it would lose the parts of his body that touched the water. Connie Sara had shown him that his mother was an outright liar, the day they stripped down to their underpants and shirts and went wading in the sludge. It took three baths to kill the awful stench of his legs and feet, but Winston had learned another lesson that day.

And it wasn't the last. She had always been right. In school she had predicted which kids would get sick before it happened:

"That one's weak, and her mama treats her like a baby."

Sure enough, the child she pointed out would go home sick before the end of the week. In every way, Connie Sara had proven that she knew more about the world than Winston's parents did. She had made his mother's fears and coddling seem silly.

"Aim for the body, the broad part," Connie Sara had whispered. "A little bit lower."

Winston had taken aim. He felt the polished pine handle of the slingshot clenched in his fist. He heard the rough twang of rubber that sent the rock shooting through the air. The robin never made a sound.

They ran to the spot and gazed down into the wet leaves where the robin had fallen. Its feathers were damp, and its chest was crushed in. While Winston watched, the robin gave a shiver, a spasm that lasted a second, and that was it. Yet the two children went on watching until they were sure nothing else would happen.

"You see, now?" Connie Sara said.

Winston nodded.

"Winnie," his mother must have said a thousand times. "God loves all creatures, but they can't all go to heaven with us. Only birds go to heaven."

At this point she often paused in her embroidery to admire the tall cage full of hopping, chirping finches in the corner of the living room. Winston, when he was a toddler, had loved this story. He would watch his mother's rapt expression as she described the afterlife of birds:

"Every one will be part of the celestial choir, Winnie. Can you imagine: Millions of birds, in all colors of the earth, singing in harmony? They fly straight up into God's hand, the moment they die. You can actually see the fluttering of their wings in the sky when that happens. They leave their bodies and become pure spirit!"

Now, at last, Winston knew why his father made a face every time he heard this tale about the birds. It was a lie. If not, then it was the stupidest thing anyone had ever said. And why would she tell such a lie to her only son? What else was she telling him that would prove to be wrong and make him look like a loser?

"It all comes down to one thing, Winnie," the girl said. "Do you want to be a hero and a blood scout in the Devil's Club, or just a crybaby?"

"I'm not a crybaby," he said. And he recalled the times Troy had followed him to the very edge of his front yard:

"Whiney Winnie the Poop! Yeah, get your fat butt into that house, or I'll kick it in!"

Connie Sara came up with the plan, but Winston agreed every step of the way. She told him the only method for sneaking up on a witch, and avoiding the same fate as little Tracy, was to travel by night when they wouldn't be expected. This seemed reasonable enough. And since Winston had snuck out of his house on two other occasions to go exploring in the woods after dark, he was sure he could handle the unexpected. On one of those nights he was startled by an owl, and almost wet his pants. But he had gotten home all right. He had slept deeply and, for once, dreamed of nothing he could remember. It was a wonderful feeling.

They agreed that they would each bring their own

flashlight, and meet at the giant fir tree where the meadow and the forest met the dirt trail leading from Connie Sara's backdoor. This meant that Winston would have to travel twice the distance Connie Sara had to cover, but this fact appealed to him.

"I've hiked seven and a half miles down and back up a canyon with my dad, last summer," he told her.

"That's pretty good," she said. She tucked a strand of her hair behind one ear and Winston felt a surge of pride.

"That's right," he said, to confirm it.

"Well, then," she said. "This ought to be easy for you. I found the place by accident the first time. Going back there on purpose is going to be hard. I just hope I don't get too scared and run off."

"You won't run off," he assured her. "And we won't get lost. You can count on me. I never get lost."

On the designated night, Winston dropped to the ground outside his bedroom window. His sneakers wobbled when he landed, but he righted himself without making a sound. He crept in the shadows, whisking weeds and wildflowers that grew along the side of the house. Everyone in his family was sleeping. He might have walked out the front door without attracting any attention, but slipping out through the window was much more exciting.

He carried a pillowcase slung over one shoulder. Inside were a flashlight and a rope. He was proud of this second item, which Connie Sara had neglected to mention. If they were going to form a rescue team, they would need a rope to lift young Tracy from her underground prison cell. That much was clear to him, if not to Connie Sara. But then, he had seen more action adventure movies than she had, so he knew these things.

Once they had completed their quest and returned the missing child to her grateful, weeping mother they would appear on TV, at least on the news, and maybe on their own show. Winston figured: if this kind of thing, young girls being kidnapped and tortured by witches, could happen here in Skillute, then there must be places all over the world where heroes were needed. He (and maybe Connie Sara) could travel to those places, and save other kids, all expenses paid by television fans and parents. This required the kind of courage and know-how that Troy would never have. After a while he would ask Winston if they could be buddies, and that would be okay as long as Troy was his sidekick and did what Winston said.

He was picturing himself aboard a huge private plane, sipping grape soda and eating popcorn, when Connie Sara reached out from behind a fir tree and grabbed him by his shirt.

"What!"

"Shh!" She warned. "That way," she whispered, and nodded toward the woods. "That's the path we have to take, to keep away from animal traps."

"Traps?"

"Shh!"

She didn't speak again, only pointed the way with her flashlight and pushed him ahead of her. The flashlight revealed a barbed wire fence, the old fashioned kind. Farmers who were serious about keeping people off their property put up stronger barriers, with coiled, barbed wire at the top and bottom. Some even used electrical wire. Fortunately this fence was made of four strands of barbed wire stretched between wooden posts. They could make it through.

Winston pinched one of the middle strands and lifted it carefully. It crossed his mind to offer Connie Sara the first passage, but this seemed like the kind of gesture guaranteed to make her mad. So he pulled the middle strands of wire as far apart as needed and gingerly climbed between them. Connie Sara followed. At the last second one of the strands popped back into place, catching her hair and skewing it out of its pigtail.

Once they were past the fence, Winston stumbled along a dirt route so narrow it was nothing but a footpath scuffed up between the trees. He took hold of leaves and branches along the way and pulled himself forward, up inclines and around swollen roots protruding from the earth like the knuckles of giant fingers. As he approached a big-leaf maple, he caught hold of a licorice fern sticking out from its mossy trunk. He pulled himself forward with all his might. As he did, his right hand stripped the fern bare, leaving a slender, jagged cut across his palm. It stung so bad his eyes watered, but he didn't complain.

When they had been walking for a while Winston began to have the feeling that they were traveling in a wide circle, but he couldn't prove it. He wished he had brought his dad's compass. He wanted to tell Connie Sara, but then he thought: maybe this was part of her plan to sneak up on the witch. Or maybe it was a test.

If he hesitated for more than a second, the sharp point of Connie Sara's index finger would jab him between the shoulder blades until he moved on. By the time she stopped prodding him and they reached a clearing, he was out of breath and his shirt clung damply to his skin.

"This is it," she whispered.

Winston opened the pillowcase and withdrew the rope, which was thin and bristly. It was pilfered from his father's garage, where it had hung on a nail for as long as he could remember, so he didn't think it would be missed before Tracy was rescued and he returned in glory. Now he noticed for the first time that the rope had a worn spot, almost a break, and he cursed himself for not checking it more carefully before stuffing it, still coiled, into the pillowcase.

Connie Sara pushed leaves and twigs aside on the ground, until Winston could see a mottled sheet of old wood so green and mossy it looked like part of the forest floor. She picked up one corner and motioned for Winston to do the same. They lifted the wood aside, revealing a deep, narrow, impenetrably dark hole in the ground. At once the air around them filled with two sensations: icy cold and a stench so foul Winston dropped his flashlight and covered his mouth and nose with both hands.

"Aw!" He moaned through the fingers he held against his face like a muzzle. He spoke from behind his hand. "What is that? It's awful!"

He pinched his nose and tried not to gag. Connie Sara was watching him carefully. She seemed not to be bothered by the foul smell emanating from the hole in the earth, so he tried to take his hands from his face. But he could only breathe in once before a current of nausea shot through him. He clapped one hand back over his face and stood shivering in the midnight air.

"Where does it come from?" He mumbled.

"There used to an outhouse here," she told him.

"I thought we were going to the witch house," he said.

"I said we had to get Tracy out of the dungeon. This is it."

"Where's the house?"

"A couple of miles away. No trees there any more. Once upon a time there was a cottage there, with a roof made out of cedar. It burned down."

Winston's eyes smarted and he blinked at her.

"Who burned it down?"

He was trying to speak normally, trying not to shiver. The effort made his knees and his neck stiff. He was afraid because of the hole in the ground, and because he was so far from home, but also because he now remembered that Connie Sara had said the witch house was invisible, not that it had burned down.

"Who did it?" He asked again.

Connie Sara smiled.

"I did," she told him.

Winston studied her face.

"I set it on fire," she said. She laughed lightly.

Winston found he couldn't move. So he tried the only answer that might make sense to him.

"Did you do it to kill the witch?" He asked.

He was sucking in short bursts of air between his

fingers, but it was agony to breathe in the stench flowing upward from underground. Connie Sara was pointing her flashlight toward the hole. She had draped the coil of rope over her shoulder. She stood watching him. Waiting.

"Go on," she said. "Take a look down there. Get closer, so you can hear Tracy."

The cold, the clouds obscuring the moon, and the rush of rotten air from the ancient latrine combined to make him shiver so hard his teeth made a chipping sound like a woodpecker. Sweat trickled from his scalp, collecting strands of his red hair in little tapers at his temples. He didn't swallow for fear of throwing up. High up in a canopy leaves rustled and an owl gave a careless hoot.

With a sudden resolve to get this over and get home, whether they found young Tracy or not, Winston took Connie Sara's flashlight and turned it toward the ground. The beam swept across green leaves and scarlet berries, a small, bright cluster of devil's club near the hole. With a swift, smooth, arcing motion he directed the beam of amber light into the center. Last of all he took his gaze from Connie Sara's face, followed the light beam and squinted down into the foul-smelling earth.

The inner sides of the pit were soft mounds and dimples. He couldn't tell if they were mostly dirt or dung. Roots had burst forth in several places and trapped a few leaves that fell into the hole when the wooden cover was removed.

By aiming the light beam and staring straight down through a tangle of roots about five feet from the surface where he stood, Winston could see more clearly. There was a larger mound, caked in mud and slime. It reminded Winston of a half-digested mouse he had once seen when his uncle cut open a snake he killed in the yard.

Winston scanned the shape with the flashlight. He had the uncomfortable feeling that he was staring into a great, open mouth and this was its tongue. Then he reached its top end, near the surface. Tilted upward, in a grimace of pain, was the rotting face of a little girl.

Winston heard himself scream. The flashlight tossed a wide arc of amber into the air to be extinguished when the underbrush consumed it. Winston stepped back from the hole and the ruined body, slick with dirt and worms. He bumped into Connie Sara and felt the sharp pressure of her fingers on his back, shoving him forward, pushing him toward the gaping hole and the rotten corpse of little Tracy. Her hands took hold of his shoulders and forced him downward.

The dread that engulfed him was worse than the day Troy and his friends had cornered him in the bathroom stall. That day he was afraid, and humiliated by his fear, but he knew with absolute certainty that Troy wouldn't kill him. Whatever Troy did to him, he would be alive when it was over. This was different, and he knew it. He panicked. He swung wildly at Connie Sara, connecting with her jaw, knocking her to the ground.

At once Winston was in motion, running, hurtling away from Connie Sara. He fell with his full weight onto one side, righted himself with flailing arms and legs, and ran again. His feet skidded until he found traction, then they pounded the earth. He ran to a drumbeat in his chest, thinking only of distance.

He tried with all his might to scream again but now, just like in his nightmares, no words would come. His throat was dry, caving in on him. The barbed wire fence was in the other direction, he thought, but he wasn't sure any more. While he tried to get his bearings, he kept moving, and suddenly he was shocked to find himself sliding uncontrollably down a bank into the wide trunk of an oak tree, which he hit full-on with both hands.

Something popped in his left arm, and a burning pain ran up his side. He scrambled to his feet, crying, and kept running. Covered in dirt and sweat, he fell again, tumbled and rolled, hit the ground, and shook his aching head. His arm throbbed with pain.

Worse than the hurt and confusion, he could hear

Connie Sara running after him. She was up there, above the bank he had slid down. She had found the flashlight. He saw the beam bounce up and into the trees overhead. She was looking for him. That meant she wasn't sure where he was, and he had a chance.

He hunched over and ran, and soon he found he was on a wide dirt path. It was one of the routes cut years ago by loggers to haul timber out of the forest to the main road, where they would transport it to the lumber mill. He knew this, and knowing gave him a glimmer of hope. He ran on, with the dirt walls rising at sharp angles on either side of him, until the rubber toe of one sneaker caught a twig and sent him tumbling head over heels.

Sitting there with the wind knocked out of him, Winston looked up at the dirt wall to his left. He could see devil's club sprouting from the red-brown soil. While he tried to catch his breath, a narrow beam of light cut through the trees above him. Connie Sara knew how to track a wild animal, especially an injured one. She was coming for him.

He scuffled along on the ground. He thought of an injured crab one of his cousins had tormented at the beach last summer, the crab scrambling in circles, trying in vain to escape its enemy.

He looked up once more at the maple-shaped leaves and crimson berries growing inexplicably from the dirt wall, and decided it must be a sign. Here was the only hiding place he could find.

He pulled himself up against the dirt wall of the truck path, scrambled back and forth and found a shelf, a pocket or a tunnel, maybe a vein from an old mine that had been left there when the makeshift road was plowed. The ledge inside the dirt wall was just wide enough for him. He shoved his way in, and found that he fit.

By the time Connie Sara reached the edge of the hill directly above him, he was entirely concealed. The light flashed down, slowly scanned the dirt and swept up the wall on the opposite side.

"Winnie!"

He heard her slow, keening voice and his heart turned over. All he wanted was to hear his mother calling that name, instead of this high, cold sound in the night air.

"Winnie, oh, Winnie the Poop. Where are you?"

How could she know? How could she know? His blood felt electric, pounding in his temples. He tried not to make any noise breathing. The pain in his arm and side made tears run down his face, but he bit his lip and held back until the light above swept up, and down, up and down, and away. He waited. Yes. Yes! She was moving away. She had given up on this part of the woods. She was going away.

Slowly and in pain, Winston started to shift his weight again, to climb out of the shelf. He would have to look around, and it would take him some time to figure out how to get home from here. But he thought he recognized this path from long ago, a walk in the woods with his father, who had warned him not to climb inside caverns and dirt shelves like this one.

Wouldn't his dad be amazed when he learned that Winston had saved himself by doing the very thing he was told not to do? Wouldn't he be proud, instead of angry?

His mother would kiss his face and hold him in her arms. She wouldn't be mad that he had sneaked out at night, or that he had trusted the terrible girl she warned him not to play with. She would only be happy to see him safe. And he would never leave her side again. He wouldn't make fun of her. He would listen to her stories about the birds that go to heaven.

Winston pressed down and out with both feet for leverage, preparing to hoist himself free. As he did so the damp earth gave way, ever so gently, all around him, filling his eyes and nose and mouth, muffling all the sounds of the night and quietly surrounding him with darkness.

Marietta and Beverly

"Do you promise to go by what I say, and do what I ask? Because it might sound like a bad thing to do."

This was the fourth time they had met since Beverly discovered Baretta's remains in her tulip bed. Marietta was easing her into it, she said. There were things Beverly needed to know that she might not like or approve of.

"How bad?" Beverly asked.

"It's a terrible thing, Bev. An awful thing."

"Well," said Beverly. "Tell me what it is, and I'll see if I can do it."

"That's just it," said Marietta. "If I tell you the rest of what I know, then you've got to do what I ask. If you hear it, you won't be safe unless you do exactly what I say, no matter how it strikes you."

Beverly took a minute to consider this. She looked at her hands, and then she looked at Marietta.

"How long have we known each other?" She asked.

"Since we were little girls. Since the first day of school we've been friends, you and Ethel and me."

"Why?" Beverly asked. "Have you ever wondered that? Different as we are, the three of us, how is it that we decided that day to be best friends, and we've never been otherwise?"

"That's not really true," said Marietta. "About best friends. We let you down. We let you have a baby by yourself, and all we did was write you notes about who said what at school."

Beverly shook her head. Then she asked:

"How did you know?"

"Because I saw your baby in a dream. I never told Ethel."

Beverly said nothing. The two women watched one another closely. Marietta reached across the table and took Beverly's hand.

"Listen to me. Your daughter isn't part of this, because she got away. She's safe, because you gave her away. You don't have to regret that."

"My family made me do that, they said I couldn't have a baby."

"You let her go. You saved her life when you decided to do that, before she was even born."

"How do you see these things? How?"

"I don't know. It comes to me. It isn't what I want to see, Bev. It just comes to me."

Beverly was silent for a while. She took a tissue from a box on the counter top and blew her nose. At last she said:

"What if my daughter, somehow, comes back here?"

"Why would she do that? She doesn't know you at all, does she?"

"No. But if she did, what would happen?"

"Nothing. I think nothing would happen."

"How can you say that for sure?"

"After we do what we're going to do, this will be over."

Beverly laughed, a bitter little sound. She touched the tissue to her nose and then said:

"Over and done?"

"Yes," said Marietta.

"Well, what is it? What is it you have to tell me?" Beverly asked.

"It's a story my aunt told me. Not all at once but gradually, over the years, like a bedtime story that never ends."

"All right, then. Let's hear it."

"The whole thing started here," said Marietta.

"In Skillute."

"On this property. Right where we are right now."

"There was nothing here before," said Beverly.

She watched the windmills on the lawn. One of the

wooden geese had fallen over.

"Are you sure about that?" Marietta asked. "Think back."

Beverly shook her head no, then stopped. Recognition came into her eyes.

"The first time Rex brought me to see the lot?"

"What did you see?"

"Steps," Beverly said. "There was a set of three steps in the grass, not leading anywhere, just standing alone. What was that?"

"There was once another house here, a cabin, on the spot where this house stands. Another family lived here, and they weren't very happy to leave."

Delphine

The Dempseys were among the families that migrated west from the Dust Bowl during the Great Depression. They loaded up what little they owned and moved to the coast, where they logged and fished for a living and worked in the canneries and sawmills.

There were three brothers and their wives with two-dozen children between them. They couldn't make ends meet, so they squatted wherever people would let them and camped as long as they were tolerated. This went on for years.

Eventually two of the brothers rented homes. The third brother moved with his wife and kids into an old miner's cabin on a backwoods road that wasn't important enough to have a name. He must have figured nobody would notice his family there.

That third brother and his wife had eleven children. Three died, one from typhus, one from a hunting accident, and one just stopped breathing in its crib. Their last daughter was born when the Dempseys were almost forty. The whole clan was broke, barely getting by, and the kids would do any odd job for cash. It was hand-to-mouth and had been for a good twenty years.

There was also at that time a midwife in town. She was known to both deliver babies and set women free of babies.

Not the Dempsey women. They didn't believe that way, although they knew of the midwife. She cooked remedies and cast harmless spells and told homely women they would find happiness with a handsome man. She earned a tiny income. Her added means of getting by was to broker deals for neighbors. She would match a lonely man with a pig farm to a man with an aging daughter he wanted to marry off. She would put a carpenter in touch with a handyman so they could trade favors, and then she got a little work from both of them when she needed it.

One spring she worked a deal she came to regret. She tried to take it back after a while, but it was too late. This is how it happened.

Not long after the Second World War the interstate highway came to Longview and Kelso, and finally to Skillute. Up until then the place was just a nameless cluster of farms and houses, a couple of small ranches and a few paper mills owned by Weyerhaeuser. There were logging camps and companies hauling timber away to the mills and to the coast for shipment.

Most people were excited by the prospect of the highway, looking for new jobs to come. Quite a few people did get work. But a lot of the good-paying jobs went to men who were brought in to oversee construction of the freeway. One of these men was William Knox, who had managed several road-building projects for the government back east.

William Robert Knox was a no-nonsense man. He was educated as an engineer and was admired in his line of business. He brought with him his wife, Harriet, who was from a well-to-do family and had been to college. They settled down in a very pretty cottage that had been built for the duration of William's job. The state estimated the work here would take about five years.

Harriet was raised to country club life, and she had already made a compromise. This wasn't the kind of place she had her heart set on when she married. Also she had disappointed William by not being able to give him a child. They had tried and been let down, so now she had a little failure to bear. You have to understand: She was a woman who wasn't accustomed to failure and disappointment.

There were other wives who settled here temporarily while their men worked at building the Interstate. These were educated women who probably would have found the spot hopeless if they hadn't gotten together with each other. They stayed busy playing bridge and taking train trips to Portland and down to California, playing golf and throwing cocktail parties. In the winter they planned ski trips and spent the holidays together.

These women were refined, but they weren't nice. They were a vicious bunch by all accounts and they believed in sticking with people who had the same advantages they had. They made only one exception to their habit of mingling with their own kind.

Harriet had a bad miscarriage the first year after she and William moved here, and maybe that changed her. One thing is sure: it caused her to swear off her family doctor. From then on she relied on and confided in the local midwife, who came to be accepted by some of Harriet's friends as a healer and a reliable adviser, and was shunned by others as a witch.

"Witch" was nothing but a word they used for women who were poor white trash and knew how to make herbal medicines. They didn't include her in their social lives, but as time went on more of them decided she was harmless and her cures were possibly therapeutic. She got to know a few of these well-to-do women, and maybe she was flattered by being let into their circle as a consultant. She also went on tending to the poor, those who couldn't afford a doctor, but she started to look on these poor people with a different attitude. Maybe she got above her place. She began to think how she might help one of these families. That wish, to do good things, might have been vanity on her part, since she was no better than the people she wanted to help.

On the midwife's say-so Harriet Knox got to know of a family that was poorer than most. This branch of the Dempsey family was still living in a two-room cabin with a tin roof but no indoor toilet. They lived off what they could raise in their yard, which wasn't much. The road they lived on didn't have a name and wasn't traveled much. Their last child was a girl named Flora, age twelve when Harriet Knox first heard about her.

Flora was undernourished and small for her age. The midwife made a good case for the girl as a general help around the house, and Harriet agreed. With a fifty-dollar tip in her pocket, the midwife spoke with the girl's parents and sweet-talked them a little. She told them what an educated woman Harriet Knox was, and that she could afford to pay them well. They agreed to let the girl move into the Knox house, in exchange for a one-time payment of one hundred dollars. That was a lot to people in their situation back then. Having one less child to feed would help, too. Mrs. Dempsey wasn't thrilled with the idea of Flora moving in with strangers, but the rest of the family wore her down.

It was understood that Flora would do whatever work Harriet needed her to do indoors, and keep her company during the long hauls when her husband camped at various work sites up and down the coast. To make this more natural and avoid embarrassing questions, it was also agreed that for the time being the girl would go by the name of her patrons and be known as Flora Knox.

From the start Flora was angry about having to leave the only home she knew. She didn't take to Harriet and her snobby friends, who made fun of the way she talked. Mostly the girl kept to her chores and her room. The idea Harriet and the midwife had, that the girl would benefit from being with people of a higher class, didn't impress Flora. She made it clear that she didn't care to be improved.

As time went on, problems developed between Flora and her patron. To the outside world they seemed close enough. People noted how Harriet would take the girl shopping and would spare no expense to make her look less like a tomboy and more like a young lady. Flora went on climbing trees and she ruined every dress she had. Harriet tried to teach her to read but Flora could never get the hang of it. She was surly with the piano teacher Harriet hired, so that didn't work out either.

No matter how much time her substitute mother spent on her education, Flora wasn't happy. She got in fights with other children, and she made claims against Mrs. Knox. No one would listen to her stories about Harriet locking her in the cupboard, or starving her for days. Harriet was seen as a refined and respected woman. She gave the appearance of wanting a child of her own more than anything in the world, and that alone went a long way. Always has, still does.

When Flora turned out to be a disappointment to her, Harriet stopped taking a personal interest and gave her more work to do around the house. If the girl slacked off on her chores, Harriet had William punish her when he came home. That's when the real trouble started, with petty acts of spite between the woman and the girl.

Flora got a reputation for defiance and back-talking, which would try anyone's patience but infuriated Harriet, who felt she had given up the whole world to stay at her husband's side. Now her lady friends were settling down to motherhood and Harriet had fewer distractions to keep her happy. After each flurry of excitement, and the baby shower that followed, she would describe to the midwife how letdown she felt, not having a baby of her own. She said she was heartbroken, although she didn't look it. The midwife judged she was terribly bored. And now the girl she had rescued from meager circumstances wouldn't mind her any more.

No matter how many times Harriet locked the girl in the woodshed for lying or for running away back home, no matter how many times her real father hauled her back to the Knox house, no matter how much William beat the girl with his belt when he came home for a quiet rest after a two-week stint of road work, Flora was defiant. She was one of those children that won't break. Every beating only fed her stubbornness.

All of this worry took its toll on the marriage. William got to see a side of his wife she had kept hidden before. He was ashamed of himself for punishing the girl on nothing more than Harriet's say-so. He began to side with Flora against Harriet, which made things worse.

It was after Harriet and Flora had formed a deep, lasting hostility that Harriet noticed signs of a different kind of betrayal. The girl was fourteen by then, and had been menstruating for over a year, when her period stopped. Naturally Harriet consulted the midwife, who assured the angry woman that any number of reasons could be to blame, and it was most likely because of how she had been brought up by the Dempseys. The girl was scarred from years of malnutrition. That was the best explanation.

The midwife was lying, playing for time. She could never get the girl away from Harriet long enough to give her a remedy, even if the girl had cooperated. All she could do was wait, and cast her spells, and hope for a miscarriage by accident.

Flora started to show in her fourth month. William was away in Portland, the first time Harriet noticed the girl's belly. That day she beat the girl black and blue and demanded to know the name of the boy she'd been sneaking off with. But the girl said, and she never changed her claim, that the baby would rightly be named Knox after its father.

Around the same time the company William worked for offered him a permanent job on the west coast. He would manage operations in Oregon, Washington, and Idaho. It meant staying put in the Northwest, instead of moving back east. This was a big step up for a self-made man who had paid his own way through college. He accepted the new job without first consulting his wife. He also told his employers he was satisfied with a home base in Skillute, turning down their offer of a house closer to Portland, where his wife might have been much happier.

Harriet was livid when she found out, but she pretended to her lady friends that it was her idea to stay in this backwoods corner of Washington. She was too proud to let other women know how little her husband thought of her feelings. She didn't complain in front of anyone except the midwife. Seeing how things stood, with her marriage in the balance, she didn't dare accuse her husband of doing the things Flora claimed. Her hold on William had weakened that much during the time they had lived here. He spent more time away from home, and Harriet spent more time with the midwife, who consulted her cards and oracles to determine what the woman ought to do next.

Of course by this time the midwife had seen her mistake clearly enough and she was in favor of sending the girl back to the Dempsey family. She assured Harriet that this was what the oracles instructed. It was also the sensible thing to do. The girl was ruined, she said, and was obviously lying to hurt the reputation of her benefactor's husband, and not worthy of the goodness Harriet had shown. The midwife all but pleaded with her to send the girl back to her family to take her chances.

Nothing would persuade Mrs. Knox once she decided on her course. She would wait until the baby was born, she said, and adopt it as her own. This was the only fair compensation for what she had been through. She was owed a child, and she would collect on the debt. Then Flora would be sent away and could fend for herself.

Harriet said: "If the girl is so smart, she can make her way in the world. I'm done with that ungrateful monster, but she owes me for taking her under my wing."

On the night when Flora gave birth, only Harriet and the midwife tended to her. The baby was underweight and malnourished. At first they didn't believe it was alive. The midwife would claim all of her days that it was stillborn.

The two women fought. Seeing all that had occurred because of her vanity, the midwife's conscience shamed her and she argued with Harriet about what they had done. While they fought over whether or not to call the doctor, Flora bled out. She was so small, and the birth was even harder than they expected.

Now this is the part that Harriet denied. The part no one would believe.

The very second after Flora died, her child took its first breath and cried out. The midwife dropped to her knees at the sight of the baby she had pronounced dead, now alive and screaming for its mama. She said it was a demon, something come through the baby to be born again.

Harriet pushed this idea aside. She said the midwife was a superstitious fool, and would be in a world of trouble if anybody else heard the story. Harriet was greedy for a child of her own. She took the baby in her arms and claimed it. From that moment on her life was changed.

Nobody was much concerned back then with how Flora had lived or what happened to her. Children from poor families were expected to be sickly and were likely to die early. The story told by Mr. and Mrs. Knox was good enough. They were respectable people. Also, William had the right to hire and fire the men who worked on the roads. There wasn't anybody who would cross him. If he said his wife had given birth to a fine beautiful baby girl, congratulations and gifts poured in and no one argued, although several people knew the real story. One of them was the midwife, who now felt she had made a terrible mistake, an unforgivable act, guiding Harriet to Flora Dempsey's family.

Around this time one of the foremen working for Knox and his crew bought the land Flora's family had been living on for years. The Dempseys had been staying there dependent on the kindness of their neighbors and the authorities, you see. Despite their cabin and their vegetable patch, they were still nothing but squatters. That kind of thing was tolerated right after the Depression but things were different now. New people arrived every month and looked around and decided to stay as long as the jobs held out at the lumber mills and the pulp mills. These were people who wanted to buy land and settle down.

Flora's family was the poorest and the least educated of the Dempsey clan. With no paying work and no prospects, they drifted up the hill into the woods to hide out. They lived in tents and later in trailer homes. Meanwhile the land they once lived on was sold. It became the property of the foreman and his family, until they moved up to Canada. That's when they sold it to another branch of the Dempsey family. While Flora's parents were just hanging on and hoping for the best, their in-laws had made sacrifices and saved what they could. They had bought a couple of acres here and there, scattered around Skillute. So when timber finally got to be scarce and the big companies went poking around for any privately owned scrap they could still get, the family earned a handsome profit.

But all of this happened over the course of the next decade. By then Harriet Knox was all but forgotten, although her spiteful neighbors started to call every little thing that they didn't like the fault of "Miss Knocks." Miss Knocks made the rain that ruined the company picnic. Miss Knocks was looking down from the treetops when a logger was injured and lost an arm.

It was superstition, blaming a hateful woman (whose real name was barely remembered) for everything bad that happened in Skillute. What people didn't know was that something was alive in the woods, but it didn't come from Harriet Knox. In fact it was Harriet's sworn enemy and it wouldn't die until it was satisfied.

The Knox household was considerably quieter after Flora died. You see, no one confirmed her death. Harriet told people she had stolen some jewelry and had run off. Everything known about the girl confirmed that she was the kind that might do such a thing. She was hard to handle and she had run away so many times.

Keeping quiet cost those who knew Mr. and Mrs. Knox some of their peace of mind. Avoiding William and Harriet socially made matters a lot simpler. No one snubbed them or insulted them outright, but they were never invited to get-togethers or parties any more. People smiled and said hello on the rare occasions when Harriet went into Longview to shop. Everyone was cordial. But no one called on the Knox family after Flora disappeared. Harriet was marked. Even her educated friends thought so. There had been something wrong with her all along, and now they could all see it.

Most of those uppity women took their babies and toddlers and moved on to bigger towns, when their husbands were promoted or saved up enough to relocate. People said that Harriet went stir-crazy living alone with her baby in that beautiful cottage with its silk drapes and cobblestone walks and cedar shingles. All she did was walk from one room to another, and from the front door to the woods and back. Her husband spent all of his time working, so he never noticed something that his wife couldn't help but see every day.

There was something wrong with the child Harriet pretended was her own. Not a physical infirmity, because she seemed remarkably strong, given the terrible circumstances of her birth. The stronger and quicker the girl (named Ella) became, the more Harriet seemed to sink down into herself, turning away from any activity outside her home. Only once in a blue moon she could be seen in Longview, with Ella pulling her along and arguing with her whenever she hesitated to buy things the girl wanted. More than once the girl used rough language and called Harriet names in public. One time she struck Harriet, slapped her right across the mouth, and the woman said nothing. "Little hellion" is what the neighbors called Ella.

They called her much worse things the night she set fire to the Knox house. Everyone said it was probably one of Ella's pranks that had gone wrong. The girl herself was trapped by the smoke and flames, and died in the house along with her adopted mother.

William Knox hired some of his men to salvage what they could. It wasn't much, and the men weren't very conscientious. They hauled most of the burnt timber off into the woods and dumped it there in a stand of old growth fir and cedar.

Marietta and Beverly

Beverly left the kitchen. Marietta could hear her rummaging through a drawer in her bedroom. In a minute she returned with a linen handkerchief, which she placed on the table in front of Marietta, who lifted the corners delicately and looked inside. Then she looked at Beverly and said:

"How long have you had this?"

"All of my life, at least since the day I got pregnant."

"Bev."

"What do you think?"

Marietta shook her head. She sat back and looked at Beverly with a weary smile.

"She wants it back, you know."

"I can," Beverly had trouble saying the words. "I can see that, now. I understand. I'll bury it."

"That part of the woods is gone now, paved over."

"I'll bury it in another spot, and you can cast a spell. There has to be a way to get rid of it."

"No," said Marietta. "This is exactly what we need. You see? If this is something she wants, then this is what we can use to catch her."

Marietta

Sitting alone in her room, in the house she shared with Henry and his wife Alicia, Marietta had formed a plan, one just subtle enough not to raise suspicion. It would take place on the following day. It relied upon two things: the girl's arrogance, and her desire to reclaim the memento Beverly had taken all those years ago. If the girl wanted the relic badly enough she would pursue it, and if she were as sure of herself as she seemed to be, she wouldn't expect anybody to trick her. It was almost certain to work. It had to work.

Another child had gone missing. That made two children in less than a year. The first was almost sure to have been snatched by her father, according to the sheriff and local gossip. But Marietta thought it was possible that the girl's father was long gone and had forgotten all about his first wife and his daughter, Tracy. He might be happily remarried, settled in another town with a new name and a fresh start and a second family. Nobody knew.

The more recent one, a boy named Winston, had disappeared from his bed in the middle of the night. A search party had given up after three days without a real clue. Now the stories were making their way from one household to another: the boy was abused and had run away to escape his mother, who was unbalanced; the boy had been abducted by a pedophile who was traveling through Skillute; he had been out playing late at night when he was taken by aliens who wanted him for their experiments on human DNA. The longer he was missing the more outlandish the speculation became.

Marietta's intuitions gave her no information she could use to help locate the children. Only her knowledge of Connie Sara told her that the girl was responsible, and that she was too clever to be caught. The two missing children would never be found.

In the quiet evening, she sometimes thought of John Colquitt, and how she had wanted him to die. Maybe she wished it, and maybe she allowed the conditions that made it come about, but she had no guarantee that he would die. Things happened and she could foresee only a fraction of those things, and urge them along. There were so many accidents, so many possibilities. She couldn't account for those, or for changes of heart. The man had possessed freewill. He might have acted differently toward Marietta, or he might not have been such a loudmouth at work, and that could have changed everything.

People could have changes of heart. She never had, about John Colquitt. She remained pleased with his absence, more so as she got older. She tried to say this to Henry once, when he was a boy. He had pestered her all day to tell him about his daddy, and she was ashamed by how easily she dashed his fantasy.

"I wasn't sad when they told me he was dead," she told Henry. "He wasn't a good man."

The boy had looked at her. He went on looking at her, saying nothing, until she told him to stop. Then he started locking his bedroom door at night, and he did this until he was in high school. She couldn't understand it.

Henry was twenty-five when he said:

"You know I'm praying for you, don't you, mother?"

That was how Marietta saw that Henry was nothing to do with her. He was a plain person, who tried to do good works. She took note of his sweet nature and she was certain: He was nothing to do with her. He had come about and had grown up as he did only because Marietta had rid herself of John Colquitt when she had the chance. When Marietta had given birth all alone in the house where she remained after Delphine and John died, she had taken no chances.

Knowing all that Delphine had told her about Flora and the Knox family, Marietta had weighed the possibilities. She had gazed down at her twins: Henry lost in slumber, and the other one, the girl her aunt had warned her about. The girl who would come back any way she could. The hateful thing Delphine had kept at bay with her potions and rituals and warnings had come to make itself at home with Marietta. It had lived off of her, had taken its blood from her and its flesh.

That time it had chosen Marietta, but luckily she had recognized it and she had known that she had no choice. It stared back at her with its hungry expression. It looked so smug, because it didn't know that she knew the truth. Later it screamed with fury, but no one heard it.

In the weeks that followed she overfed Henry until he was sick, and then pumped the milk he wouldn't take into a bottle. She had so much milk she had to throw some of it away every day. This was a constant reminder of what she had done.

She had placed the infant in a metal toolbox and burned it in the yard, just as she had burned John's possessions. She had to let it go, just as she'd had to let John go. The flames licked the box clean inside and out, and it was over. She left the bones and ashes in the toolbox and buried it in the ground next to John's truck, under the blackberry bushes. Years later when she moved in with Henry she had a fence built around that bit of land, to keep away trespassers.

All of it was necessary. All of it was a sacrifice she had to make. Otherwise, Henry would never have been the man that he was. Given his nature, he wouldn't have survived. She had done Henry a good turn, eliminating the dangers from his life. If the twin had lived, it would have killed Henry one day, out of spite. If John had lived, Henry might have been like him, or he might have been much worse when John was done with him.

Marietta noted with pleasure that the adult Henry was nothing like John Colquitt and nothing like her. For one thing, Henry would never have entertained the idea, or even the hint of an idea, of killing a child.

Kojak

Marietta told her daughter-in-law she had one of her sick headaches. This brought a guarantee that she wouldn't be disturbed. She prepared a cup of ginger tea and retired to her bed.

The night before, she had broken the teeth off the blackened jawbone with a pair of pliers. Then she waited.

The first tooth she placed in the tree that the girl climbed almost every afternoon at the same time. The girl would climb up to get a good look around and scout for prey.

The second tooth Marietta placed in the grass near the tree, where the last of the day's light would strike it like a black pearl. Each one after that she placed a few yards away, a gleaming treasure to be gathered and gathered until the girl reached the dusty spot across the road where Marietta wanted her to be.

Marietta drank the ginger tea and lay down on her bed. It was time now and she couldn't force it to happen. She could only wait and see what the girl would do, as she had waited to see what John would do. She lay still. Her joints ached and her face felt swollen. Blanking her mind, she let her jaw go slack again and again, but soon the grinding of teeth, soon the whimper, and the necessary evil she had allowed.

Her mind raced over tracks in dust, lit sidewise with a falling sun. Claws thick as talons, black against the ground. Dirt damp with drops of saliva. Quiet when the light fell down, and the master slept, and it knew because the master made sleep noises. She had crept along and put her

162

hands on the dog, and he let her pet him.

Her. Hands patting. Her again. Rumble and clink.

"Good boy," said Marietta. "It's all right now. Stay. Good boy."

She had gone quickly, just as she heard the screen door to Burt and Ethel's house slam shut. Now she heard it again in her mind.

In the quiet she listened with her thoughts. Vaguely it came to her, then closer:

Rumble and clink. Chain rattling. Rumble and clink.

Her. Warm sound. Hum sound. Gone.

Dark comes in. Fences. Trees. No rabbit yet. Up is dark, blank and dark.

That. Salt. Dirt. That coming. Rocks and sticks. Smell that. Salt. That comes.

"Look at you, Kojak, ugly stupid thing. You'll die soon, and get buried right here."

Patting ground. That. Picking ground. That smell. Salt. Saliva.

The girl looking up from her handful of broken, blackened teeth, collected across yard and road and yard again. Hate in her mean eyes.

Mouth wet. Salt. That.

Marietta rolled over and worked her tongue against the roof of her mouth. Saw the very air, the night starting, a star cutting the sky. Mouth unhinged, body yearning to lunge, to run, regardless of the chain, the clink, the snap to come. Sinews expanding.

Run! Leap!

The girl's hateful eyes narrowing on the animal, sneering and waiting for the metallic snap that will never come.

Clink and rumble. Roll of chain. Rumble of chain falling on dirt. Free! Free!

The girl screaming, falling, hateful, obscene screaming, spittle from her mouth, her eyes giving in to fear, and fear giving way to pain.

That falls. Now!

Sinews tearing. A slobbering sound. The girl shrieking.

Blood metal and salt. Meat. Teeth warm in flesh. Tearing. Bones bright in the meat.

Screaming every vile thing, and begging, begging, cursing the animal to damnation. Jasper's front door flung wide open and his eyes searching, not believing, and shock dawning slowly across his face. Disappearing back into the house with the girl's screams shattering the night.

Rip and pull. Blood muzzle. Blood meat. Licking. Salt skin tearing.

Blood soaking into his fur. Sopping with gore. Blood on his claws and eyes and tongue. Hearing but not hearing his master shouting his name, only once, before the sky-breaking shot.

In the Clearing

Ethel and Burt stood side by side at the grave. They watched the small white coffin being lowered into the earth. They didn't touch, not even to hold hands. They didn't weep.

Ethel knew her husband was broken. Everything was gone. The years of being afraid had cleaned them out. They had nothing more to offer one another. They hadn't been close in so long. It didn't matter any more.

While Henry's voice droned on about a hereafter Ethel didn't believe in, a swift, cold breeze struck her. She turned her head away from the cemetery and saw a patch of filtered light nearby.

Ethel's first thought was that her daughter Connie Sara had returned and was standing in the clearing. She wore the yellow silk skirt and the embroidered blouse Ethel had sewn, but they were streaked with dirt and blood. Her hair hung in wet strands across her shoulders.

In the dappled light between them Ethel could see the girl's eyes. They were darker than she remembered. The familiar, sullen expression was Connie Sara's, and the delicate circles beneath her eyes. There were no wounds on her face and throat, where the animal had torn her, but her skin was impossibly pale, slick and resistant to the rain that had soaked her clothes.

Ethel couldn't tell if the bruised lips were drawn into a smile or a grimace but she knew that whatever stood before her, staring with stark blue eyes and holding its arms outstretched, was not her child. It had never belonged to her. It had never come from her, but had only passed through her.

What she couldn't say, what she couldn't comprehend, were the bits of blackened teeth and fractured jawbone found on the ground around her daughter's body. She didn't want to know how or why this had come to be. This thing from her childhood had returned and she didn't want to know more. There was no possible answer that she could live with.

She held her arms tight across her chest and took a deep breath. She looked away from the thing standing nearby in the light.

"Over and done," she said.

Then she turned and started walking. She walked down the graveled path to her car. Without speaking to anyone, and while Burt watched her with a stricken, pathetic resignation, she started the engine and backed out of the parking spot along the path. By the time she reached the first freeway entrance, in Kelso, she was doing fifty-five miles an hour, and she didn't care where she was going.

Beverly

Beverly had told a lie. Now she was paying for it in a form Rex would have called "sweat equity." She had pulled every piece of furniture in the house away from its usual spot, to run a vacuum cleaner over the linoleum and carpet. She had dusted the drapes, valances and blinds. She had wiped down the counters and walls, dozens of knick-knacks, even the poker and shovel hanging by the fireplace. This was ordinarily her least favorite task. She disliked the metallic click and grate of the tools when they struck one another.

She washed all of the windows in the house, even the glass and aluminum security door. That was another nasty job. In fact, she couldn't recall the last time she'd wiped down the security door. It was a chore that she avoided with a wide range of excuses. But the cold, gritty water she squeezed from the sponge into the sink after the awful task was done gave her a click of satisfaction. Here was real, visible scum removed from her home and washed down the drain.

Late in the afternoon, she paused to admire how much she was accomplishing. The moment she sat down, she felt a wave of irritation as distinct as nausea. She had to keep moving. She plumped the sofa cushions, forcing her imagination back to the goal: A clean house, a sparkling house. That was the best she could do. Everything else was beyond her control, now.

Did the living room need a bright color scheme, instead of alternating beige and olive drab? Now that she thought about it, she also questioned turquoise in a bedroom with only one window, near the ceiling, over the mahogany headboard. The house was too small and confining for the color combinations Beverly had fallen in love with at the paint store last year.

The bungalow was L-shaped, cradled on two sides by the woods. A kitchen window faced the yard and the road. The living room window faced only the yard with its tulip beds, Japanese maple, and wooden geese. A half-mile on the road snaked, then straightened, and finally split in two directions, but this wasn't visible from Beverly's house. She had the benefit of being in the thickest part of the remaining forest. Here cedar and hemlock trees grew in abundance and the road was dark as midnight on winter afternoons. At least seven months out of the year a gray dome of clouds mimicked the sky. Even now, in the spring, drizzle fell on the entire valley more than half the week.

Several times since Rex died Beverly had considered a move south to Oregon, or even California. She had never been to California. Rex had disapproved of the state on principle, and since he'd been gone Beverly had not been bold enough to travel alone. Her sense of California came from TV and magazines, but she realized the place couldn't be nearly as glamorous or as exciting as it seemed.

The house that had once felt snug now threatened to smother its only occupant. The place needed more work to open it out, maybe a bay window or a skylight. She also wanted to take the advice of a sales clerk who recommended a combination of canary, bright white, and bamboo. Maybe a bit of cranberry trim. That would be a real project, though. She would have to hire her husband's illiterate cousins to come over and help again.

On second thought, it wasn't worth it. It just wasn't. It would cost too much. And the memory of Rodney and Darrell Dempsey traipsing around all day in their scratched-up work boots and overalls gave her a chill.

Beverly had lied about her reason for skipping the memorial; she wasn't sick at all. Now, instead of relaxing in front of the TV as she had planned, she was cleaning her house top-to-bottom on a Saturday. Sweat equity.

Rex would have laughed:

"I swear, Bev! The fifteen things you'll do, just to get out of the one thing you don't want to do!"

Deep-voiced, a broad-shouldered man with backbone, not like the shiftless Dempsey cousins, Rex had been a good man. She couldn't stop thinking about him, all day. Wouldn't he have laughed at her for avoiding a simple memorial service? Or would he have told her to go, for the sake of her old friends Ethel and Marietta? What would he say if he knew the real reason she didn't want to face Ethel today?

Anyway, it didn't matter what Rex would have thought. That part of her life was over. Now she was a respectable widow with a decent nest egg. If she had been honest about it, this was how she had always imagined herself: living alone in a nice home that was easy to care for, filling her days with exactly the magazines and TV shows and phone calls and games she wanted. She didn't have to do one thing she didn't feel like doing. She never answered the phone when her bedridden mother called to complain about this or that pain, or some new medication the doctor had prescribed.

Beverly had even done away with her message machine after Rex died. That was the day she stopped pretending to care how her mother was doing. She had relished the moment when she unplugged the machine for good, knowing she would never again come home to find the droning, whining voice of her mother waiting for her.

Beverly had lied. She said she wasn't feeling well. The truth was that she couldn't risk the memorial. She couldn't face the sickly-sweet damp of Henry Colquitt's homemade chapel, which was nothing but a white trailer with Astroturf around the outside, or the painted white pine coffin festooned with silver crucifixes and pink silk ribbons. It was too much. One of Beverly's friends might have detected a smile teasing the corners of her lips. Anything might set her off, from the rose-scented candles, to the ivory shag carpet and blond wood benches from IKEA.

Once she started, she wouldn't be able to stop. She might laugh out loud. And everyone would know that she felt more than relief. She wasn't just glad to be free of Connie Sara. She was giddy with a pure, awful kind of joy.

Her face flushed at the idea. Despicable. Terrible. Laughing at the demise of a child. It was a horrible death, horrible. She made up her mind to shut it out, and she did. She turned her mind to something good, or she would if she could think of something good. But there it was, again! She caught herself smiling. She stood in the living room and laughed for a minute, to clear her head. Delirium!

When she looked out the window she expected to see Connie Sara on the lawn, dancing around, up to no good. She was so used to it, she had to remind herself the girl would never do that again. She was as free of the girl as she was free of her own mother's complaints, more so, because the girl was dead.

Beverly slapped a stubborn cushion into place on the recliner. She moved a glass figure, a green lady with a parasol, slightly away from the lamp that overshadowed its charm.

No one else would say so, but surely most of her friends and neighbors on Connie Sara Way felt the same way. The people who lived along this road were quiet cowards. They had never dared to cross the girl, no matter what she did, no matter what they suspected she had done. They called it minding their own business. Well, the girl hadn't torn up their tulip bed and left dead things planted in it. Or maybe she had, and they were just afraid to say so. Or maybe they didn't realize all the terrible things that girl had gotten up to, or the things she would have done if she had grown up.

Beverly had crossed the girl. Beverly and Marietta, of all the people who knew Connie Sara, had understood what had to be done. That was all. They had done what was necessary.

Anyway, in truth, Marietta was the one who came up with the idea of luring the girl to her demise. Marietta didn't hate the girl the way Beverly did, but she was the first to say the girl was bad. Something was wrong with her. She wasn't sick. She didn't deserve pity. Someone had to stop her. Marietta swore there was something inside Connie Sara that was evil. She had sworn it, during those long conversations in Beverly's kitchen.

They had planned every step, but it was Marietta's idea, if it came down to that and anyone needed to know. Marietta had set things in motion. Beverly was happy to help by providing the bait, but it all came about because of Marietta, who somehow had the nerve to go to the memorial today straight-faced, nothing but an old friend to the dumbstruck parents. This part seemed heartless to Beverly, although if both women had deserted Ethel in her moment of grief, suspicions would have been aroused. She could see that. If Beverly didn't go, Marietta had to go.

Who would say they were wrong? Well, most people, but most people didn't understand how bad the girl was.

When they had decided, and Marietta had explained what she was going to do, it seemed simple. As it turned out, there was nothing simple about it. The girl was mauled and her face and throat were torn open. She had seizures, and then she lingered for two days in a coma. Beverly had feared that she would wake up and accuse them. Marietta said this wasn't the worst of their problems, but Beverly didn't completely understand why.

"If it's living inside of Connie Sara, I think we're safe if it dies with her," Marietta had said. "But if it gets loose before she dies, that's what we've got to worry about."

The whole business was a mess. It shouldn't have happened in the first place. Burt and Ethel should never have had a child. It was crazy, at their age, vain and reckless, and crazy. None of it should have happened.

More than at any time since he died, Beverly wished Rex had been there when Connie Sara pulled her pranks. He would have stopped all the nonsense before it got going. If he'd caught the girl leaving dandelions on their doorstep or pouring trash on the lawn, he wouldn't have gone to see Ethel about it. He wouldn't put up with it, and he wouldn't set a trap and then lie about it. No sir. Right on the spot, that first time, he would've taken off his belt and done what the girl's father ought to have done. Then maybe all of this would have turned out better. One good hiding might have knocked out of her whatever was bad, before it got worse. Then there wouldn't be anyone to blame for anything.

Again, though, if anyone was to blame, it was Burt and Ethel, but now that their daughter was dead Beverly was beginning to feel sorry for them. They seemed like they had been under a spell ever since Connie Sara was born. Ethel knew there was something wrong, but she wouldn't talk about it. She and Burt had tried to pretend the girl was special and smart, but they spent less time with friends and neighbors as the years passed. At home, just the three of them, they might be able to act like a family. Everyone else who visited the Sanders house knew the place was strange. Even Rex would have said they were weird.

By now Rex would have pulled down all those tacky, hand-painted signs, Burt's drunken handiwork claiming the road, naming it for Connie Sara like a birthright. They were nothing but an eyesore.

Idle dreaming, that was all she could handle at the moment. Rex was long gone. And now Ethel's only child, the only one she would ever have, was dead.

Beverly had heard the gossip and the bad jokes: people wanted to get a look, to make sure the girl was really gone. Well, they were mostly superstitious hicks living up in the woods, pitiful kids and their beat-up young wives, out of work and living off their families. They wouldn't know what to expect at a formal gathering. The casket would be closed. She was sure of that. There wasn't a mortician anywhere who could have repaired the girl enough to make her presentable at the memorial.

It was terrible, but it had to be done. Now Beverly could breathe easier. Now her daughter would be safe. Her neighbors and friends were safe, all because of what she and Marietta had done. That was something. That was the thing to remember.

She finished wiping down the living room lamps. For a minute she stood still, breathing hard. Beads of perspiration trickled between her breasts. The white cotton blouse and black knit pants clung to her skin. She itched all over.

Outside the living room window the first drops of a downpour plopped onto a row of premature tulips, forcing their stems flat in the cool air. It had rained hard that afternoon then let up completely. Now a second storm was rolling in.

Beverly arched her back and listened to the plunk-plunk on the roof. She thought she heard raindrops hitting the back door, too. But there wasn't enough of a breeze yet, for that. She fanned herself by flapping the front of her blouse.

At the end of the short hallway, past the turquoise bedroom on her left and a shapeless laundry nook full of odds and ends on her right, she studied the back door. No need to clean that. The wood paneling was in decent shape. A spyglass at eye-level afforded a narrow view of the back yard, with its Japanese maple and its catalpa, and on into the woods.

Beverly was gazing through the spyglass when she heard tapping at the front door. She smoothed her blouse and went to the living room, expecting to find the rain-soaked Pastor Colquitt on her doorstep with a morbid re-play of the day's memorial and a plea to attend his regular Sunday service. Such impromptu visits made Marietta's son Henry unpopular around town, especially among his neighbors on Connie Sara Way.

Beverly looked out the glass and aluminum door. No one was there.

Now she heard tapping at the *back* of the house. Tapping, louder than the plunk-plunk of raindrops. Knocking. Someone was clearly knocking on the back door. That damn girl, she thought, and then remembered that the damn girl was dead and gone.

Beverly returned to the spyglass. With her fingers splayed, flat against the door, she leaned carefully forward.

No sooner had her eye focused on the yard than she heard knocking at the front door again! It was ridiculous!

The rain was starting to come down like mad. In this torrent, anyone dashing from one end of the house to the other, outside, would fall down; but there was no sign of anyone, no matter how fast Beverly charged from door to door.

It had to be kids playing pranks, probably more of the Dempsey boys, some of the pathetic cousins from those little trailers up in the woods. They drank whiskey, all of them, and they played cards late into the night sometimes.

She would look up into the woods and see the amber lights of kerosene lamps, because most of them didn't have electricity. There were five or six trailers and vans parked on one piece of land. The grownups kept pretty quiet except during hunting season, but the kids were bored. The kids got into trouble. Not like Connie Sara, just the usual kind of trouble, stealing cigarettes at Misty Mart. Dumb stuff.

Beverly took a detour into the kitchen. She knelt on the checkerboard floor and opened a cabinet under the sink. She grabbed the first thing handy, a can of foaming cleanser. That would give them a surprise!

She shook the can hard and strode toward the front door, ready for action. Then she looked up, and froze. The stimulated contents of the can crept out the nozzle like drool and ran down onto the carpet. She dropped the can.

On the opposite side of the glass and aluminum door someone was watching her intently, facing the door, so close to the glass that Beverly couldn't make out any features, only the outline of a head, shoulders, and arms.

"Hello?" She said.

The person didn't answer or move.

Beverly thought: Halloween pranks in the spring! Stupid kids!

But she didn't laugh.

"Is that Darrell Joe Dempsey?" She asked.

"Rodney Junior?" She said. "You better answer me."

Not a sound. She tried to move, but she couldn't force herself to go forward. She wanted to slam the wooden door shut against the security door and lock it, but she couldn't.

Whoever it was grabbed the handle and shook it hard. The door made a tin, shuddering noise. Beverly thought it was coming off the hinges.

She stayed frozen. As suddenly as the shaking had begun, it stopped. The figure outside let go of the handle, drew back, and spat a wad of phlegm at the glass. The mess stuck and dripped down leaving a slug trail.

Startled by the smacking, fluid sound, Beverly lurched forward and slammed the front door over the glass and aluminum one. She slid the deadbolt into place. Immediately she heard knocking at the back of the house again.

She crept to the back door. The breath felt sharp in her chest. She flicked through a mental inventory of latches, bolts, and locks. She knew that all the window shutters were open but there was no way to secure them without going outside, and she was not going outside, not for anything. All her nerve had buckled when she heard that metallic rattle. She finally noticed the telephone on the kitchen wall, and dialed a number before she realized there was no tone. The line was dead.

The knocking was gone. The rain was gone, too. Not like the storm had subsided, but like the sound of the world outside had been muffled or quilted over. As if the clouds overhead had hunkered down until they covered only the house. Nothing spoke or moved.

Beverly's heart beat hard, and she swallowed dryly. She was listening with her whole body, stiff, aching. Faintly, she heard another sound: Scratching or scraping across the side of the house.

She opened the bedroom door and looked in. Outside the narrow window near the ceiling, the only thing visible was a cluster of dark clouds. Rivulets of water coursed down the glass.

Maybe it was over. Hope flickered inside her ribs and it hurt, like something broken trying to fly.

She heard the scraping again. This time it seemed softer, more muffled. She crept to the living room and looked at the door, the ceiling, and the window.

She turned toward the fireplace. And while she stared at the dry, cold center of brickwork, a thin stream of soot fell gently down, followed by another. With a scratching and grunting noise, something heaved its way down through the chimney, forcing out another quick stream of soot.

Beverly couldn't close the flue without reaching her arm up inside the chimney. Instead she upended the coffee table and pushed it against the fireplace opening. She grabbed cushions and heaved them against the coffee table. Whatever was climbing down into her house through the chimney was making progress, and grunting with a gleeful lunacy. She pushed as hard as she could and slid the recliner over onto its side, behind the coffee table.

She tossed every framed photo and lamp and cushion she could get her hands on into a pile on top of the recliner. If only she could block the fireplace long enough to get out the front door, and run for the car in the driveway.

She shoved the sofa hard against the armchair and the TV set, and a disk in her lower back twisted. The pain shot through her left leg and kidneys. She heard herself whimper, and felt warm liquid soaking her black knit pants. The smell was sharp like bleach. She slipped and felt a crack at her wrist as she hit the floor. Searing pain cut across her arm.

She looked up and watched helplessly as a foot, then a leg, thin as bone and coated in soot, thrust out of the chimney and braced on the edge of the upended coffee table. The foot was bare, with toes that tapered into square, blackened nails as thick as talons.

Part Three

Lydia

Lydia had been making nice about the scenery for miles and she was sick of it. She gazed out the window of the Toyota at the same view she had studied for the past twenty minutes of the trip. Dark green, knotted walls of Western red cedar and hemlock trees lined both sides of the otherwise desolate road.

For several miles before they reached this stretch of vegetation she had amused herself by reading misspelled signs out loud. A peeling, rundown pool hall advertised an upcoming "turment." A pizza joint that looked more like an abandoned abortion clinic identified itself as a "famly restaurnt." Some of the signs gave her a chill, but this little game at least took her mind off the number of American flags she had seen on the way down.

They had long ago lost reception on the Seattle stations. Now there was nothing but religious talk shows and country music. At every dial stop, it seemed, some yokel was holding forth about the end of the world and how the next Democratic candidate would play a part in it. Lydia turned off the radio.

Her husband Greg was driving at a steady clip and he was in one of his moods, jolly as hell and pumped up on juvenile energy. Nothing she told him would shut him up. Like a precocious kid Greg kept pointing out milestones he had heard about from friends. Lydia found all of them trivial and irritating: a billboard featuring Jesus catching a football, with a bible quote of the month in a bubble over his head; a rusted-out paper mill and its collapsed company logo; a "world famous" bait and tackle shop that had gone out of business.

Lydia only cared about one milestone as they sped further and further away from it. An hour ago they had passed through Olympia and then quickly left behind anything she considered urban, civilized, or noteworthy. Now they were in the country, far from teashops, galleries, cafes, 24-hour Indian food, artists' studios and vintage clothing stores.

"You can make this whatever you want it to be," Greg said in a voice as merry as a cartoon soundtrack.

They both routinely mocked what they called "the chirpy lingo of wellness." These were mostly catch phrases their friends brought back from workshops and retreats: Yoga, meditation, healing minerals, shamanism, spirit guides, abundance, positive thinking, and living in the present. Ever since 9/11 the language had taken on an ever-greater urgency until now, seven years later, it was insufferable.

One of their closest friends, a woman whose intelligence they had always respected, had made a pilgrimage to Ground Zero in 2003 to touch the dirt and say a healing prayer. She hadn't known anyone who died on 9/11, but she said the trip was the most spiritual quest of her life. She brought back a vial of debris and kept it on the mantel in her home on Queen Anne among her vacation mementos. It reminded Lydia of souvenir shops that sold tiny bottles of ash from Mount St. Helens.

"Keep the woo-woo to yourself, okay?" Lydia told her husband, who pretended to pout.

She was doubly irritated because earlier in the day she had broken her resolution and referred to yet another stranger as "fat." She had been doing this compulsively since the start of her second trimester. She caught herself looking around for people heavier than she was, to mock. She felt ashamed. Yet she couldn't seem to stop. And what did it prove? That she, a bit more than five months into gestation, was slimmer than an obese boy scout, a thyroid mom at a bus stop, or an alcoholic in Seward Park?

Forest and clouds knitted together in the same pearl-gray shroud. It was late June and the sky kept shifting wildly, sliding back and forth on the scale between slate and silver. Clouds gathered and dispersed. Rain came and went with only a few minutes' warning. The landscape took on the desolate colors of the sky. In this part of the state nature looked green up close and far away, yet industrial and deserted from a middle distance. The hills overflowed with trees and emerald shrubs but if you looked more closely you could see blight everywhere, pollution creeping through it all like a trickling stream.

Lydia was half-convinced that Greg was driving them to a remote place where no intelligent humans existed, a land where they would have their minds wiped clean. Then they would be stuck, unable to return. But why imagine? The reality was heinous enough. They were heading to a small town nowhere close to a beach. Buried in the scraps of forest, back roads, taverns, churches, and ditches of this non-world there was a place known to its almost certainly inbred residents as Skillute, Washington.

Crazy as it sounded now, all of this had seemed lucky a few weeks earlier. Everything had happened so quickly and had clicked into place at the perfect, desperate moment.

On bad days the whole world appeared to be coming apart at the seams. The game design studio where Greg had worked for six years had finally gone under, following three rounds of lay-offs in one year. The company president had tried and failed to sell off the business after the disastrous release of a game that wasn't ready for the market.

With Lydia still working part-time in her first trimester, they had tried everything. She took as many copy editing assignments as she could handle, then developed migraines and had to stop. Greg applied for a new job at every small studio in the city. Then he applied at Microsoft, Wizards, ArenaNet and a dozen more companies. Then he used all of his contacts and applied out of state: San Francisco, Baltimore, Austin, and Southern California. Some places weren't hiring and some were just impossible to get into as their owners tightened their belts and waited for further disasters to occur.

They spent the condo down payment they had saved, to pay for rent and groceries, so they lost their chance at the only property they might have been able to afford in the city. They heard horror stories from friends who had settled for buying repossessed homes. For the time being, renting made more sense. So they hunkered down in their apartment.

Greg's resume looked good. He always made it to the interview stage if there was an actual job available, but so did fifty other applicants. Most of these were ten years younger than Greg and willing to work for less pay. Maybe a sob story about expecting a child would have put him over the top in the '90s. Not now. On the few occasions when he mentioned Lydia's pregnancy, people looked at him as if they thought he was crazy.

"Bad timing," their expression said. "What were you thinking?" That was the extent of the sympathy he encountered.

Unemployed, running out of savings and medical benefits and the goodwill of friends who were only slightly better off, Greg and Lydia had received a letter from a law firm. They were convinced that the apartment manager had figured out Greg was unemployed and was trying to evict them on some previously unmentioned technicality. The thick envelope sat on the kitchen counter for two days before one of them had the nerve to open and read it. Then they were astonished.

The letter explained that Lydia was inheriting a few thousand dollars in cash and a house on a small piece of land, courtesy of a woman she had never met, someone named Beverly Dempsey.

Greg was ecstatic. He did a little end-zone dance on the

living room rug, in the center of the apartment.

"Don't you think it's strange?" Lydia asked.

"Yes," Greg admitted. "Strange and fucking awesome!"

"No," she said. "I mean sure, it's great to inherit something, but this is too much to think about right now."

Greg considered this. He sat on the sofa next to Lydia and put one arm around her shoulders.

"Sorry, babe," he told her. "Sorry. I was just looking at the benefits. It's obvious who this woman must be."

"Don't say it," she warned. "I don't want to deal with it. I know we have to claim the money and the house, but I don't want to deal with this right now. Does that make sense?"

"Yeah. I know. You have enough going on. But."

"I know, I know."

"We need to be practical right now."

"I told you: I know. I get it. Just shut up about it, just for a couple of days, okay?"

When Lydia was ready, they talked it over and came to a decision. The deal was: They would ignore the attorney's suggestion that they hire a real estate agent. They would go to Skillute, tidy up the house, sell its contents, and then sell the house itself. Cut out the middleman and take all the profits. Between that and the cash account, they could make it until Greg was working full-time again.

They vowed not to waste a single dime. They would clean up and sell off this property for whatever they could get. Then they would load up the car and drive straight back to the city. No questions asked.

Today, listening to Greg go on and on in his fake tourist guide voice about the scenery and the history of timber companies and unfounded leftwing assumptions about blue-collar people, Lydia wondered how she'd been tricked into such a stupid plan. She was dreading every minute of the next two months. Greg was the one who thought driving down to Hooterville would be a cool adventure. They should have handed the house over to a broker, but Greg was afraid they wouldn't get full value for it, and he didn't want to pay someone to do what they could do just as well. Now Lydia wasn't sure she cared about the full value.

The attorneys said they were not at liberty to discuss anything about this Beverly Dempsey. Here she had left her house and her savings account to Lydia, and she wasn't even allowed to ask if the woman was her biological mother. Fifteen, even ten years earlier she might have been curious. Now she was having a child of her own. She had resolved the questions that had mattered to her when she was younger. She had decided who she was and what she would do with her life when she married Greg. Now suddenly she had to take a giant step backward and deal with this woman she had never met.

Courtesy of the law firm, they had photos of the house's exterior. Greg saw nothing wrong with the chubby front porch, nothing but a landing really, painted in slick layers of crimson with a metal railing. He had no problem with the ornate green trellis, the wrought iron lawn furniture painted creamy white like cake frosting, the collection of windmills and wooden geese. Lydia wondered how she had spent their marriage ignoring and overriding Greg's taste, or lack of taste. He seemed to possess a superhuman ability to immerse himself in his surroundings, no matter how ugly.

After a lot of thought she decided it wasn't the house itself or even its location that rubbed her the wrong way. The thing that irritated her about their plan was that it was all they had. They were out of options, and the feeling of being at the mercy of fate and circumstance grated on her nerves every day.

It was unsettling to realize that all of their future plans now depended on reselling a tiny house they had never seen in person. They had pitched it to everyone they knew who might consider it an investment, or a second home for retirement. They strained relations with a few friends who stared incredulously and asked if they had taken a look at the stock market lately. So they had no prospects. Add to this the fact that neither of them knew anyone in Skillute, or Longview, or anywhere south of Alki Beach, and Lydia had to wonder if they were making a huge mistake.

She held on until the last minute to the fantasy that her doctor wouldn't let her go. At first she hoped he would say she was too far along to travel by car all the way to Skillute but as he so rudely put it, she was as strong as a horse. Then she imagined they would be miles from a qualified interim doctor. That would be it. A month or possibly two without prenatal care was impossible. Her doctor would simply say no. Yet he stunned Lydia with the news that two highly rated physicians were located near her new home.

"It won't be my home. We're not staying," she said.

"You're one lucky girl," her doctor told her.

"Did I explain that this town is in the middle of no-where?" She asked.

"Nonsense," he told her. "Plenty of people your age have bought houses in Longview and Kelso. Skillute is probably the same. This is a lucky break for you and your husband. Congratulations."

She didn't feel lucky. In a moment of paranoia Lydia wondered if the doctor was aware that she and Greg couldn't afford their medical insurance much longer un-less they sold the house she inherited. Maybe he was just breaking away from this deadbeat patient. But wasn't his job to care for her until the baby was born? Yes, she told herself. He was a doctor. That was his job. She was being silly to think otherwise.

She didn't want to give in to another crazy idea. She'd faced enough of those lately.

The shadows of fir trees cast the Toyota in semi-dark-ness. They seemed to fold in from both sides of the road and then arc together gently toward the right.

"Not as bad as you imagined, is it?" Greg asked.

"Warm and cloudy?" said Lydia. "Yeah. Nice."

"Honey," he said. "At least it isn't raining."

With this true statement, her panic started all over again. Greg didn't understand why she felt the way she did, and neither did she. Nothing they said to one another made any difference at the moment.

How could she say that she had barely been able to cope with being pregnant, and now the thought of living in the country alone with her husband and baby in what was almost certainly the former home of a woman who had given her up for adoption made Lydia want to hurl herself from the car onto the asphalt? No, this was not a thought she could share with Greg, who was already guilt-ridden about not having a job. Not a good and healthy thought. Not a tell-all, sharing thought.

Breathe, she told herself. Breathe. Be still and think of the center. Yet here came the analytical copy editor in her head, armed with a hundred questions: The center of what? Herself? Where was her center, now that she was housing a whole, new, second person inside her skin? What was she, other than a canvas, a tent around this other person? How could she have a center of her own? Every organ in her body was accommodating this other being. It was living off of her diet, her protein, her carbs, her fat, and the vitamins she took every day. It was sucking up the minerals in her bones so that she had to take supplements to save herself from depletion and exhaustion.

Every day these questions interrupted Lydia's meditation, cut short her stretching exercises, made her stare at the ceiling and talk to herself. Middle-aged people she knew, and even friends her own age, who were skittering toward middle age, talked incessantly about centering, being centered, tapping the center, finding the central place. This was not strange to them, this feeling that there was a center, that there must be one.

"Jesus!" Greg shouted.

The car jerked to the right, then slid and squealed sideways out of the lane, spitting gravel. Lydia looked up at the line of dark, blank trees rushing toward the car. She screamed.

A final shriek of brakes followed and there was a sort of lunging and landing on the shocks a couple of times. Then everything stopped. All noise stopped and the dust devil surrounding the car went slowly spinning away.

When the dust settled, they were sitting perfectly still in the Toyota, on the shoulder of the road close to the line of trees, but not pressed against them as Lydia had expected. She slid one hand across her swollen abdomen and waited for the sign: there it came, the solid kick that told her the baby was untouched, just barely aware of things threatening Lydia's very life. She was merely the protective jacket, a vehicle whose purpose was to do the one thing she hated most: sit still and wait.

She found her voice:

"What the *hell* is wrong with you?"

"Sorry, babe! Sorry!" Greg sputtered.

"Shut up!" She said.

"I am so sorry," he went on. "Honey. Is everything okay?"

He was looking at it. Not at her, but at the belly that housed his child.

"Why the hell did you do that?"

"There was an animal," Greg tried to explain. "An animal ran out in front of us! Didn't you see it?"

She shook her head. After all she had accepted, all the changes she had taken on in the past few months, this was too much. If Greg panicked at the sight of a small animal, what else might he do, to endanger their lives?

She climbed slowly out of the car. She almost slid underneath it; the right side was jacked up several inches, next to the tall line of Douglas firs obliterating the light for fifty yards in either direction.

"Watch out!" Greg called and scrambled after her. "Here I come, babe."

They edged along next to the car, Lydia shuffling, balancing around her belly, and Greg chasing after her, his arms outstretched. Lydia steadied herself against the side of the car and made her way to the back bumper. There, a few feet from the trunk, in the dust, lay the long body of a rabbit, stretched out as if it were sunbathing, toes pointed downward as she'd seen cats point their feet while napping. Only a thin, scarlet line running down the underbelly told her that it was damaged. Otherwise its shape and its fur showed no sign of injury.

Greg reached the spot and looked down. Both Lydia and Greg followed one, two, three drops of blood leading away, until their line of sight included, on the far side of the road, a small pile of entrails, heat gently rising into the warm air.

Lydia felt her cheeks flush. She turned away before Greg could say another word. She climbed back along the tilted car. Her suede loafers kept sliding, crunching fir needles and leaves underfoot. She opened the passenger side door, slid in, and pulled it shut after her. She sat shivering while Greg tried to recover from the dry heaves that had him doubled over like a sick child behind the car.

Greg was right. She should have waited for him outside. Less than two miles from their destination he had insisted he needed a Coke to settle his stomach. Restless boredom made Lydia follow him into the three-aisle convenience store called Misty Mart. As if the two flags over the front door were not enough, the customer entrance signal played a tinny rendition of the first bars of "God Bless America."

Lydia and Greg stood in line holding cans of Coke. They had to wait and listen to store manager Misty Court debating her daughter Kristy about their favorite TV show, one that featured a former child star.

Misty was ringing up a pile of candies and fruit bars purchased by the woman ahead of them. While Misty and Kristy chattered on, the woman glanced back over her shoulder at Lydia, who caught a glimpse of violet eyes, sharp as an animal's, followed by a polite grin. The woman had lank, black hair without any gray, although she must have been in her fifties.

"She ought to just go back to her family. It's where she

belongs. And anyway, her family's got more money than she ever made starring on *Seven's the Limit*."

"But I read, since she wrote that book about her life, you know what, her own mother's never spoken to her again?"

"Oh, like that's a bad thing!"

The girl, Kristy, giggled, the self-conscious, prolonged giggle of a teenager broadcasting how much she knew about the world. The word "thing" she had flattened to a nasal "thang." Lydia couldn't tell if it was the local accent, or if the girl was making fun of people who had an accent.

"Shut up, you little monster," her mother told her and laughed, "or I'll get that bullwhip down off the wall."

Lydia looked up and wasn't surprised at all to find that there was, in fact, a dusty, coiled bullwhip made from snakeskin hanging above the cash register.

More giggling. Kristy Court was red in the face, sputtering words through the clear plastic braces on her teeth.

"Like you know how to use one!"

"I know things you don't know I know, little girl."

Her mother vamped. This caused a new explosion of giggles. The violet-eyed woman who bought the candy and fruit bars chimed in this time, and warned them as she edged out the front door:

"You two better behave or you'll scare off our new neighbors."

Lydia wondered what had tipped the woman off. Clearly, she and Greg were from Seattle or Portland ("not from around here") but what made her think they were moving in? They weren't hauling anything. Their suitcases and laptops were stashed in the trunk of the car. Everything else they owned was in storage.

Misty gave her daughter an affectionate nudge. The girl moved away from the counter and wandered aimlessly down the aisle where cosmetics and hair products were on display. As she walked she picked at her wispy perm with claw-like, manicured nails.

"What you got, dear?" Misty asked Greg, who handed

her a six-pack of Coke and then added the six-pack Lydia was carrying.

"I bet you're the couple moving into Beverly's house," she said.

"Um, yeah. That would be us," Greg said. "I'm Greg Hewitt and this is my wife, Lydia."

"Welcome," Misty said, with a wink to Kristy who was peeking over the aisle to get a better look. "I'm Misty, and you can just ignore my rude daughter."

"Mom!" Kristy wailed and ducked her head down.

Misty told Greg: "I was sorry to hear about Beverly. Not that we were close, but she seemed like a good person."

"Oh," he said. "We never met. Actually the house belongs to my wife."

"Well, my condolences. We all liked Beverly. That was sad, her passing away when she was by herself."

"We didn't know her," Lydia said.

Then came the inevitable. Misty noticed Lydia's protruding belly.

"Oh, honey! Congratulations! When are you due?"

Lydia wanted to answer. She tried with all her might, but no words would come. She glared at the woman, at her matching plum lipstick and nails, her haystack of hair exactly like her daughter's except shot through with lowlights to balance the gray.

"We're a little more than halfway there," Greg mumbled, covering for Lydia, blushing at her rudeness.

Misty addressed Greg in a more sympathetic tone, as though they were talking about a disobedient child in her presence:

"I was the same way, both times I was pregnant! Don't expect the laundry to get done and the dinner made, with those hormones going crazy. New mamas reserve the right to be a little bit bitchy."

Misty winked at Greg. If Lydia had owned a gun, she would have killed the woman right there. She knew the feeling was insane and wrong, and she didn't care.

Back in the car Greg sipped his drink. Lydia popped the top on a Coke and started slugging it down.

"Isn't that a lot of caffeine for you?" Greg asked. "Lydia?"

For an answer, she tilted the can and gulped until a trickle of the foamy drink ran down her chin. She wiped it away with the back of her hand.

"What's wrong now?" He asked.

Lydia shook her head and stared out the window. She didn't know what was wrong, or why she had taken an immediate dislike to Misty Court and her teenage daughter with the awful perm. But she didn't plan to shop at Misty Mart, no matter how far she had to drive to reach the next store.

As they approached the turn-off to their new home, she saw the first road sign, hand-painted and nailed to a tree trunk. She made a contemptuous noise halfway between laughter and spitting.

"Nice. They can't afford real street signs?"

Greg took the next right turn, and they started up the driveway to the house.

"Homemade signs are quaint," he said.

"Sure. Maybe there's a class I can take. Quilting and sign making," she said.

"Okay," he told her. "I know: everybody is stupid, and nobody knows how to dress or how to do their hair, or how to decorate their house or their yard. And they laugh at goofy things and have crazy superstitions. They go to church and name their kids after *American Idol* winners. Okay? But we're here, and we're not staying long. So how about making the best of it? How would that be, huh?"

Before she could answer, he closed the driver's side door and began to survey the front lawn with his hands on his hips, taking in the quickly brightening and darkening grass, the Japanese maple, and the flowerbeds. She could see it, in his stance, in his gaze: He liked it here.

The minute he had learned about the house in Skillute, Greg had started calculating the future, talking incessantly about selling the place and getting out of debt. This was his break. He was clearly planning to make the most of it. When they inherited a home they had never seen, when it just seemed to fall into their laps, Greg was excited by the possibility of starting over. Unlike her husband in more ways than she had dreamed of when they first married, Lydia's first thought was that a woman they didn't even know, who might be her mother, had died in the house they were about to occupy.

"So you're sure it's okay for us to sell the furniture?" Lydia asked as soon as Greg opened the front door. The two of them peered into the musty beige and green living room.

"According to the lawyers, it's all yours. No other claims, no relatives wanting mementos," he said. "In fact, this is good. Yeah. We can throw a yard sale. Serve donuts. Get to know the neighbors. That'll be fun, and we can generate a little buzz before we put the house on the market."

Lydia shook her head slowly and grinned.

"Look," Greg assured her. "We might have to make a few repairs, but this is win-win. We didn't invest anything, so it's pure profit even if we sell it for less than it's worth."

"Greg," Lydia said. "Please do one thing for me: Stop looking on the bright side. Even one month in this place is going to be hell."

She took a seat in the overstuffed corduroy recliner. She tugged the side handle and her feet came gliding up on the footrest.

"Tired?" Greg said. "Take it easy. I'll unload the car. You look like you could fall asleep."

Beneath the fringe of shaggy brown hair, Lydia's eyes had closed. Now the right one opened and glared at him.

"Everything here is hideous. Indoors and out."

His voice took on the soothing tone she was learning to anticipate and loathe:

"We can make yard sale money off anything you don't want to use while we're here, and entertain ourselves by meeting the neighbors at the same time. Then we ditch the last of the furniture and move back to Seattle. It's all good."

"Hideous. If I have to live here six weeks, I'll kill the neighbors," Lydia warned with a crooked smile.

"Well, aren't you nasty for a pregnant woman? We're going to be so popular here."

"Buy a gun, an automatic rifle, and I'll shoot them," she said.

"That's a great idea, honey," Greg told her. "So you take a little rest, there, and think about how to dispose of the bodies, and I'll bring in the suitcases. Then I'll get you some more water, and we'll talk funny again, okay?"

"Mm," she said. "Me talk funny and kill people."

As soon as he was out the door she hit the speed dial on her cell phone. She needed to hear a friend's voice, even if it was from far away. No answer, and then the voicemail picked up. She decided not to leave a message. Not today. She felt too pathetic and worn out. She nestled into the comfy, ugly chair and closed her eyes again.

A ratcheting squeak told her Greg was taking their suitcases out of the car trunk. She knew he would check the bumper again for blood and scratches from the rabbit. He probably wanted to show her enough damage to justify his reaction on the road. He held onto things like that.

The air was sweet and cool for the moment. All day the temperature had fluctuated but the humidity had remained insufferable. Lydia was tired. Her breasts were swollen and they ached. She knew her eyes were closed, but she couldn't tell if she was awake or dreaming. It sounded like someone was trimming hedges, or edging their yard, in the distance. The steady, thin buzzing was like a lullaby. This was how summer had sounded to her in the lazy suburbs where she grew up.

She became aware of singing. A thin, high voice in a singsong rhythm, a rope-jumping song.

Lydia opened her eyes in time to spy a child racing across the lawn. A cluster of blond hair above a smile flashed in a ray of sunlight and quickly folded back into the shadows. By the time Lydia sat forward in her chair, the kid was gone. For some reason a long forgotten family expression came to mind:

"Lickety-split."

She wasn't sure of its etymology. She made a mental note to look it up online. Then she sighed and closed her eyes again.

A neighbor's child, she thought, playing alone in the woods. How sad and sweet.

Marietta

Marietta edged into the house and closed the front door as quietly as possible. She didn't want to disturb her daughter-in-law, who had one of her headaches today. Both women suffered from migraines, and took turns nursing one another back to health.

The foyer led to a wide hallway. Double doors opened onto the living room with a floor-to-ceiling window at one end, exposed rafters, built-in cedar benches and shelves. An elk's head decorated the wall above the stone fireplace. Facing it at a right angle were two deer heads mounted on plaques.

Everything about the house was overdone, the living room most of all. It was too big, calculated to make people think an outdoorsman made his rugged home here, when nothing could be further from the truth.

Marietta lived here with her son Henry and his wife Alicia, but she never thought of it as home. She would never have made such a home for herself.

Alicia and Henry had never hunted. Yet in addition to the mounted heads they collected elk and deer hooves under a set of small glass domes. An antique, sawed-off shotgun was on display over the living room door. They had purchased it at an estate sale and had it professionally cleaned and restored.

To Alicia living in the country was an adventure. She collected baskets and filled them with dried flowers and leaves. She made potpourri. She sponsored bake sales to support Henry's church, and joined a quilting circle at the Longview women's club. She gravitated toward all things natural and down-home. Marietta's beekeeping was the only thing Alicia had refused to adopt, and only because she was highly allergic to bee sting.

Alicia's family owned real estate on the west coast. They had a chain of hotels and a couple of theme parks. She might have lived anywhere, but Henry had staked his claim here in Skillute. So here they were, and they insisted that Marietta live with them.

"Family ought to be together," said Alicia whenever the topic came up in conversation.

Years ago they had stopped urging Marietta to sell the little bungalow where she had raised Henry. They accepted her reluctance to sell as a sentimental eccentricity. Anyway the land around the old place was strangled by blackberry bushes and weeds that ruined any appeal it might have to a buyer. It would take an awful lot of work to restore the land.

Marietta was as nice as she could be to Alicia. In truth, she felt sorry for her daughter-in-law. The woman was twelve years older than Henry. She was tall, broad-hipped, and a little awkward, as if she were still getting used to her body, like a girl who sprouted several inches over one summer. She smiled a lot and laughed eagerly. The way she recounted her life to Marietta, she had been a lonely child, shuffled between boarding schools and divorced parents, acquiring and discarding fashions and hairstyles in a constant effort at fitting in. Here in Skillute she had put down roots with a vengeance: building a large brick house on three acres of land, and eventually buying and decorating the double-wide unit that served as Henry's church.

The light waned and Marietta sat in her favorite spot, tucked into the cedar window seat surrounded by embroidered cushions. She sipped tea and watched the complicated shifting of shadows across the meadow that separated the Colquitt house from its nearest neighbor.

The view in this direction took in wildflowers, tall summer grass, and devil's club skirting the forest. It included vine maple, orange honeysuckle, and wild blackberries. From the other side of the house she could see the Sanders and Jasper homes. Both views excluded Henry's chapel, which was just as well.

Marietta didn't like to gaze on the church her son had built next door to his home. The glossy trailer and the Astroturf made it stick out in a neighborhood that was mostly residential and rural. A ground level, brightly lit marquee told the world that Henry and his savior were open for business, like tire salesmen. People were afraid to stop by, Marietta thought, because it looked like the Lord Himself was on duty at a gas station twenty-four hours a day. She wondered when Henry would get the idea to hand out coupons for discount salvation. He had tried just about everything else to bring in recruits. Everything failed.

Marietta didn't share the faith of her two loved ones. She didn't believe in a God who listened, let alone protected or cared, but she went along with as many of Henry and Alicia's activities as she could stomach: Christmas and Easter service, and a few baptisms each year. She attended these as she had attended Connie Sara's memorial: Quietly, politely, without closing her eyes or bowing her head during the prayers.

Once Alicia had enlisted her in a prayer circle. She tried to beg off, but the woman wouldn't take no for an answer. They were meant to pray for Alicia's fertility following a discouraging report from her doctor in Portland. Marietta was relieved when Alicia's next examination proved she wasn't capable of conceiving. For a short time there was talk of finding a surrogate but neither Henry nor Alicia had enough enthusiasm to carry out a search. Marietta kept her mouth shut and soon the subject died altogether.

Henry's holiday sermons brought in the poorest of their neighbors, young couples with no money and no inclination to join a real church. When the collection plate came around they didn't feel saved, only humiliated. Broke and mostly uneducated, they hauled sickly infants to Henry's church, the Chapel of Christ's Mercy, for a perfunctory blessing. As often as not these babies would die from the complications of simple things like colds and flu, or because they suffocated in their blankets in the middle of the night, and Henry would deliver the funeral service.

Ethel had been a recipient of Henry's kindness because her husband Burt was so often out of work and doing odd jobs to make ends meet. Their daughter wasn't sickly, had never been sick a day in her life. It was unnatural, people said, how quickly the girl had grown and how strong she had become, roughhousing in the meadows and the woods, pulling pranks on the few children whose parents allowed them to play with her.

Now the girl was gone, and no one talked about the terrible way she had died. In fact, they never spoke her name. They didn't pull down the road signs with her name on them. No one would touch the signs, or even look at them.

Ethel had left town right after the memorial and the burial. No one had heard from her since. Burt had stayed on in their house for a while, but loneliness and grief caused him to drink more than usual. Pretty soon he was sleeping outdoors. Then he started camping out full-time. Maybe it was easier for him than living alone in the house he had once shared with his family.

The girl was to blame for it. The thing that took her form was to blame. Connie Sara was what Burt and Ethel called her, what they had named her at birth, but Marietta knew she had other names. The girl had lived here, in some form, for longer than Marietta had been alive. The terrible thing, buried for years, woke up the day Marietta and her friends took their oath in the woods. From that day it wanted to be alive again. It had forgotten what it once was. Now it only wanted to live, and it would kill anyone who stood in its way. This thing didn't pass on with Connie Sara. That much was clear from the way Beverly had died.

The coroner decided the cause of Beverly's death was a heart attack. Maybe it was. Nobody questioned it, because

Rex and Beverly had never made a secret of their rich diet. Rex had gone the same way. It made sense, so everyone believed it.

The thing that didn't make sense was why Beverly had spent the last minutes of her life piling chairs and cushions and end tables against the grate of her fireplace. People who didn't know Beverly laughed when they heard that, but Marietta knew it was something her friend would never do in her right mind. She was too house-proud to risk damaging her nice things unless she was fighting for her life. She wasn't easily frightened, either. She had stayed on in the house Rex built for her, alone, for years after he died. She never complained about being afraid there. The only complaint she had was against the girl, Connie Sara.

Marietta felt a rush of guilt each time she remembered the plan she had made with Beverly. She didn't regret what they had done. She was only sorry because it was clear to her now that they had failed. They didn't kill the thing that had come back as Connie Sara. It was still here, waiting, working a new strategy in the dark.

She had heard that a couple was coming to claim Beverly's house. She had had her suspicions. Now she had gotten a brief look at them, and her worries were confirmed.

They were city people, so she hoped they wouldn't stay long. Maybe they only wanted to sell the house.

When she'd seen the woman, and the woman's condition, she understood that Beverly's death wasn't simply revenge. It was part of a plan.

Lydia

That weekend, sweating in a bright blue sundress and fighting an urge to belch after a late breakfast of pancakes with maple syrup, Lydia sat in a canvas chair on the lawn and watched her only customer pick gingerly through a box of picture frames. It was impossible to guess the exact age of the woman with raven hair and violet eyes. She seemed fragile. She also seemed familiar, but everyone looked slightly familiar at the moment.

These had been a busy few days, with a trip to her interim doctor, then to buy hardware, a long trek to a home supply store and then a grocery store in Longview. Then came the Welcome Wagon: tiny spinster sisters who drove a wood-paneled station wagon and wore matching sweater sets despite the humidity. Later there was a brief but memorable appearance by a real Avon lady, a brisk, handsome woman named Odelia Farrow who left fragrance samples and a lilac business card despite Lydia's assertion that she and her husband were only visiting and would be gone in a month.

On separate occasions the pastors of two local churches stopped by to say hello and leave pamphlets that looked like vacation brochures. One of these was named Henry Colquitt, and he made an impression without inspiring Lydia to sample his sermons.

Lean, almost freakishly tall, stooped at the shoulders, with dark, straight hair and eyeglasses, and dressed not in a traditional suit but in jeans and a white shirt with button-down collar, Pastor Colquitt explained that he had no bias against any religion or lifestyle and welcomed everyone to his church. Lydia couldn't get over his resemblance to a young Stephen King. She kept thinking he was about to jump at her and say, "Boo!"

The funniest part was that the church in Pastor Colquitt's brochure looked like nothing but a trailer surrounded by fake grass. It reminded her of the idyllic, mundane pictures that gave Lydia and her childhood friends the creeps when they were sent to vacation bible school. The churches portrayed were impossibly pretty and tidy, and inexplicably frightening. Nothing that placid could be real. The emerald grass and yellow sun must be a distraction from something wicked, just outside of the frame.

It had taken Lydia and Greg a few hours to clean and dust and move all this junk onto the lawn. Then Greg had loaded up the kitchen set Lydia hated more than anything else in the house and headed off to the nearest dump. Since then no one had made an offer on any of the spare furniture or knick-knacks. Several times people in cars and trucks had slowed down then cruised on past the front yard where Lydia sat sweating and smiling.

No doubt about it: Greg had gotten off easy this time, hauling away a fake colonial dining set Lydia said no one except the wife of Satan would buy. She expected a great takeout dinner for doing the yard sale solo.

"Those are a dollar each," Lydia said gently.

The dark-haired woman stopped, fingers poised like spider legs over the box of ornate frames. She gazed at Lydia with a fierceness that made her uncomfortable. Then she nodded. At last Lydia recognized her from Misty Mart on the day she and Greg arrived in Skillute.

The loud twang of a country radio station cut the air. Lydia flinched. The source of the music, a red and white pickup truck with tiny American flags attached to its hood, pulled up at the edge of Lydia's yard and stopped. The passenger door popped open and Kristy Court slid out, landing on both feet at once with a loud crunch of sparkling white and tangerine tennis shoes in gravel. She walked toward Lydia with an exaggerated femininity, not quite swinging her hips, a less than subtle imitation of woman-hood. The effect was further distorted by the braces on her teeth and the broad chewing motion she made, working a piece of gum to the brink of extinction.

Chewing her cud, Lydia thought.

"Hey again!" Kristy called out to Lydia, who managed to force a smile at the girl.

"Hi," she said.

The raven-haired woman didn't look up until Kristy called out in her direction:

"Oh, hey, Miz Colquitt! Hey there!"

The name caught Lydia's attention at once. Briefly she entertained the notion that the woman was married to Pastor Colquitt, but the raven hair was a dead giveaway. She had to be his mother.

Now the woman raised her head and turned, her face softened slightly by a good-natured grin. It took Lydia by surprise, and she wondered if she had misjudged the woman, assuming she was hostile when she was merely half-witted.

"Kristy," said the woman. "How tall you look nowadays, and how pretty!"

"Thank you, ma'am," Kristy replied.

A short honk from the truck indicated that the driver, a burly middle-aged man Lydia assumed to be Mr. Court, was losing interest in the scenery.

"D'oh! I got to go," Kristy said to Lydia. "I'm late for my shift at the store."

"You see anything you like?" Lydia asked and blushed.

She knew they would never unload all of this ugly junk. Greg would have to drag the chairs and the end tables from the lawn back into the house when he came home. And she would have to camp out in a house where she pre-tended not to see the hideous decor right in front of her. The thought made her sleepy.

"Oh," said Kristy. "I don't think we need anything today.

We just wanted to pull over and say welcome to the neighborhood and stop by Misty Mart any time! We've got baby supplies for sale, my mom said to tell you, and we're open most holidays except for Christmas, Thanksgiving, and Easter."

Lydia was acutely aware of the two strange women, the raven-haired nut and the frizzy country teen, staring at her. She wondered if they found her weird, too: dripping sweat, her belly beginning to swell and throwing off her center of gravity, a pair of smart, square sunglasses shielding her eyes. Mothering her yard sale like a crazy lady.

"Okay," she told Kristy. "Thanks for stopping by."

Pastures beyond the woods, bovine hips in all of those pastures. All the girls say: "Moo."

She had to stop. She was driving herself crazy. She had spent the previous afternoon trying to get friends in Seattle to answer email, while trying not to seem pathetic.

They were busy, all of her friends, and she was only waiting, now: Waiting for the baby, waiting for the house to sell, waiting for Greg to find work, and waiting for life to become good again. When was that going to happen? Or was it over? Was her real life done, finished? Would she spend the rest of her days cleaning up after someone else?

As the truck took off, grinding gravel under its tires, Lydia turned her attention back to the dark-haired woman. She had moved along to a small table covered in knick-knacks, little objects Lydia had found in the drawers and cupboards.

"How much do you want for this?" Marietta asked.

She held up a red ceramic bowl.

"Oh," said Lydia. "I don't know. Fifty cents?"

Marietta fetched two quarters from her purse and handed them to her. Then Lydia surprised herself by saying:

"Would you like to come inside for an iced coffee?"

Greg

Greg had driven off around noon, back seat loaded with four chairs and a disassembled table Lydia couldn't stand to look at. It had been a lovely day, warm and bright. He was now returning, victorious, with an empty car.

This drive through a landscape he had never seen felt illicit. Zipping along in the car, venturing down dirt roads and dodging potholes, flying past the woods, the meadows, it was crazy. It made Greg want to sing one of the pop songs his mother used to like. Something about a green tambourine, or a girl with flowers in her hair, in the rain.

What was so bad about this place, anyway? The whole situation was temporary. Why couldn't they relax and enjoy the adventure? They had worked as hard as anyone they knew, saved as much as they could, put off indulgences, and it all came to nothing. It was all shit, finally. Their reward for being good was unemployment.

Out of the blue, with no effort on their part, they had an inheritance. It was insane. Neither of them had family money. No trust funds or estates, no investments. Greg had worked his way through a state college waiting tables. Now they had this lucky break, this windfall that nobody ever gets, and Lydia acted like it was a curse.

Granted, it wasn't a very cool house. But it was theirs, free and clear, to sell. Pure profit. No sentimental attachment. Lydia didn't show the slightest interest in finding out about this Dempsey woman, who might be her mom. She was pissed off when he suggested they ask around and see what people remembered about Mrs. Dempsey.

What could be better than inheriting something

valuable you never expected in the first place, no strings attached? Considering how bad their prospects were at the moment, with so many companies going bust and the ones that managed to stay in business announcing hiring freezes, they were lucky. They had squeaked by on his severance pay until they got the news about the house. Now they had just enough to live on until he found another job. And they had their health.

Greg had never owned property. He expected to work his ass off just to make the down payment on a condo in the city. Now he had a place of his own, they had a place, and wasn't that better than where they were a few weeks ago?

No, he just didn't get Lydia's point of view about the house. He made allowances for her condition, the new responsibility and the hormones, the challenge of this trip, the feelings she must have about her relation to Beverly Dempsey, and he still couldn't see what the big problem was. Something doubting and negative had started to surface during her pregnancy. Maybe it would go away once the baby was born. Until then, he was trying to ignore it, because he wasn't sure he liked it.

On certain bad days when Lydia stormed around saying things he couldn't understand Greg wondered if he, too, would someday become an unbearable sight to her, a thing to be hauled away and dumped. In the car, he laughed at the idea. It was silly. Of course they belonged together. They were made for each other. All of their friends assured them it was true.

Both Greg and Lydia had been gun-shy from failed relationships. Both had waited until they were over thirty to marry. Both were surprised by the pregnancy, several years into their life together, but they adapted quickly enough. If Lydia seemed unhinged at times, that was only natural given her condition. He was trying to understand. He loved his wife more than ever, and he wanted all of this to work out.

Yet more and more, time away from her felt like this, like escaping in the car down an unknown country road. It felt like a guilty pleasure.

He first noticed the sensation entirely by chance. This was before they had received the letter about the house and decided to drive down to Skillute. Greg had been sweating through a second round of interviews for another job he knew he wouldn't get.

They were broke, but Lydia was in one of her moods and suddenly they had to buy a crib, the perfect crib. Nothing else would satisfy her. They had to jump in the car and take the freeway to a shopping center and bring home the world's best crib.

They went to a mall about fifteen miles from their apartment, in an industrial area south of the city. Greg expected the place to be deserted. He had automatically come to assume that most people were in the same boat, struggling. They found the place teeming with families, full of the buzz of people, hungry and over-excited, entertaining themselves by eating junk food and buying stuff they probably didn't need.

After the ordeal of the freeway and the parking lot, it felt good to walk. Greg loved the release of being able to stride along indoors.

"Would you slow down?" Lydia asked, loud enough to attract the attention of several people nearby.

He did slow down, and he let her catch up to him. He took smaller and smaller steps, until it seemed he wasn't walking at all but hovering. No matter how he tried to drag his feet, he would edge ahead of her again after a minute. He thought: she must be dragging her feet too, pacing herself so that she could not keep up, so that she could gripe at him again.

"Would you please just slow down?"

Soon he was exhausted, worn out by the effort it took to move at an abnormally lazy pace. He refused to admit the other cause of his weariness. He was stifling an impulse to shout at her, to stride away and leave her there.

No. He could cope. He told himself he had lived alone with his mother for fourteen years after his father died. If he could cope with his mother's mood swings, he could handle anything Lydia had to throw at him. It was while he was thinking of this, and recalling his mother's habit of scattering her hair products and toiletries all over the bathroom, that an odd thing occurred. Greg lost track of Lydia.

Unable to find a satisfactory crib for their child-to-be, Lydia had wandered into a boutique. Never mind that she couldn't fit into any of the snaky little dresses they sold. The mannequins were hipless, breast-less creatures with down-turned lips. They reminded him of Lydia before the pregnancy.

Daunted by the vacant stares of four of these emaciated plastic models, Greg had stood outside the shop waiting. He knew his wife would soon come stomping back to him complaining about her new hips, her new breasts, all that he considered benefits of her pregnancy, the way her body seemed to be unfolding without permission. It was too bad. She seemed sick of it, ashamed of the newfound curves he found sexy.

He wandered along in the wake of a group of teenage girls, chatty and skinny, their jeans barely clinging to their butts; tiny curlicue of a tattoo peeking over a silver-studded belt; body oil wafting back to him, not patchouli, less spicy, maybe citrus and something else, mixed with the aroma of cigarettes. One of them, the tattooed one, the leader, her skin taut, slightly tan, fragrant, she turned suddenly, let go of her friends, whirled around in the opposite direction, still talking away and wham!

"Jesus! Sorry!" She shouted.

Wicked sweet smile on her as she sidled around Greg, her hands patting against his chest, gliding past him, not so much pushing as pinching gently. The other girls turned and followed her, the alpha, the fragrant beauty, surrounding her with their knowing smiles and a cascade of giggles. They all linked arms again and laughed out loud as they retreated and disappeared into the crowd.

All he could do was smile stupidly. He wasn't even embarrassed, not really.

Greg found himself at the door of a music shop and went in. The guy at the counter mumbled a standard dude greeting and went back to listening to the current store selection: Menomena, the CD cover propped next to the cash register. The track was "Ghost Ships."

There was something Greg had been thinking of buying recently. It was on the tip of his memory, awakened by the waves of eerie music spilling out of the speakers. What was it he had been thinking of buying? Not Deerhoof, something equally hard to find, though, and almost as good. He strolled down the middle aisle of the shop, loosening, smiling, setting his mind free to tinker and find its way to something. What was it?

Lydia.

Greg glanced up from the stacks of CDs just in time to see his wife walk right past the shop window. She was looking for him in the crowd, probably getting angrier by the second. When he caught up to her she would yell at him, as if he had no right to wander off and shop without her, as if he were her son and not her husband. The tongue-lashing he anticipated made the muscles in his neck tighten. At the same time, he had a new, tiny discovery he didn't want to share: He had forgotten about her.

He had traveled alone, if only for a few hundred feet. For the first time since they were married Greg had completely and absolutely forgotten that Lydia existed. He had slipped into his own world by himself, where he used to be all those years when he was single, between living with his mother and living with his first real girlfriend. He had wandered into his old life. And it felt good there. It felt wonderful.

Today was good, as well: Sun breaks between frothy

clouds, with a loamy scent beneath the cedar. Here the clouds gathered and parted and changed color all day, and then they might suddenly burst into rain in the afternoon. Everything could change in only a few minutes. The landscape might break open and let another world right in, at any moment. He liked this, too.

Ridiculous. He felt ridiculous, and also pleased with himself. A simple trip to the transfer station and back, alone, had left him giddy.

Lydia

Lydia sat on the back steps of her new home, puffing on a Lucky Strike. She raked the fingers of her left hand through her shaggy brown hair, and ruffled her bangs. She let the forbidden smoke roll out in a languid breath. It spread over the grass and hung there like fog.

Ahead of her a large catalpa spread its spindly branches. To the right, closer to the woods, there was another Japanese maple. She wondered what it might be like to watch these two companions change colors through the seasons. She caught herself daydreaming about the bright yellow catalpa and the scarlet fall leaves of the maple. It was idiotic wanting, even for a second, to linger in Hooterville just to watch the leaves turn.

Greg hadn't come back from the transfer station, the dump, whatever they called it in Skillute, USA. He would make it back before dark; the days were long now and there was plenty of light left.

That wasn't the point. Lydia was sick of telling him what time to come home. He had promised to come right back, but he hadn't, and there was nothing she could do about it. If she got sick, she would be on her own. Better yet, once the baby came, there would never be anything she could do about it. She would be busy every minute from now on, and Greg would be doing whatever the hell he was doing at that very moment.

She tried to free her thoughts. She wanted to avoid dwelling on a comparison between her state of mind and Greg's. It might enrage her and make her open a bottle of chardonnay to go with the Lucky Strike.

She placed her cell phone on the step beside her. She hadn't been able to get a signal for an hour. Greg had neglected to have their landline hooked up. He said something silly about the initial fees and how they were only signing up for a month or a month and a half. As if that mattered while she was producing their fucking child. As if he had to tell the phone company his life story. As if they cared. As if that were the point. Cut off like this, she might as well be living in the backwoods, in the 1940s. That was the point. Her state of mind was the point.

She could log on to Facebook and let people know she was alone, but that was lame. She wasn't in danger. She was fine. She wasn't battling a real threat. She was battling fear, the kind that had never entered her conscious mind until she got pregnant.

Before that she had savored her privacy, especially those afternoons when she didn't have to go online or talk on the phone at all. She couldn't recall ever being afraid when she was on her own. Now, for the first time, her life consisted of backup plans, breadcrumbs home, and emergency exit signs. It was tiring. It was maddening. She had circles under her eyes from waking up several times each night to make new lists of things that might go wrong.

She added negligence and tardiness to the ever-expanding list of reasons why Greg wasn't cut out to be a father. The words themselves made her feel like a matron or a schoolteacher, and this set off a new wave of irritation.

She decided to contact the telephone company tomorrow and schedule the hookup herself, even if it meant making a trip to the dreaded Misty Mart to place the call. Surely she would get a cell signal again soon. But right now she had less practical matters on her mind. The strange woman at the yard sale had given her plenty to think about, although she wondered how much of it she should take seriously and how much to attribute to premature dementia.

Lydia couldn't identify her discomfort. It gathered and then stretched. She put out the cigarette by crushing its tip against the ground. She left the butt on the step, to be flushed down the toilet later.

Marietta Colquitt had accepted Lydia's coffee invitation, and the two women sat down for what Marietta called "a neighborly chat." Lydia had made the offer in part because she expected to be interrupted soon by Greg, who never showed up.

Two hours later Lydia was trying to make sense of the visit. Now, sitting on the back step, she believed that Marietta had come to talk with her on purpose. If her assumption was correct, she wondered why Marietta pretended to be interested in the yard sale, instead of simply stopping by and introducing herself. What a strange, old bird.

Up close Lydia marveled at the woman's skin, translucent yet weathered, with the fine grain of onionskin paper. Her black hair appeared natural without a hint of silver. Her eyes didn't remain violet but changed color from one light source to another: Now dove-gray, now shot through with a purplish light. Looking into her eyes was like watching a harbor on a rainy day.

"I see you got rid of that dinette set," Marietta said on first glance at the kitchen, which was now furnished with two folding chairs and a couple of crates.

Lydia wasn't comfortable with people watching while she cooked or made coffee. She never asked strangers into her home, certainly never invited people to visit without a purpose. Something about Marietta's manner had put her at ease in person, and then troubled her after the woman was gone.

"Greg took it apart and carried the whole set to the dump, with a couple of rugs that were too worn out to sell," she explained.

"Beverly kept meaning to replace that table," said Marietta. "She would've been embarrassed to know you had to haul it off. Oh well."

Lydia ran tap water into the teapot and put it on one of the stove's front burners.

"So you were friends with Mrs. Dempsey?"

She poured the last coffee beans into the grinder.

"You might have to switch to a coffeemaker," Marietta said.

"Sorry?"

"I've got a French press, too," she said with a nod toward the glass pitcher on the counter. "My daughter-in-law ordered it from a catalog. I like it, but there's no place that sells whole bean coffee in Skillute. You'll have to drive into town, I mean Kelso."

Lydia laughed and let the grinder whir for a couple of seconds.

"I never thought about that," she said.

"I've experimented with Maxwell House in the French press," Marietta told her.

"How was that?"

"Not too good."

Lydia laughed again, and realized it had been days since she had even smiled without effort.

"So, is Misty Mart the only store in Skillute?"

"Oh, no," said Marietta. She grinned. "But it's the best one."

They settled on the sofa in the living room with iced coffee and a plate of macaroons. Then Lydia asked again:

"Did you know Mrs. Dempsey?"

Her guest said: "We knew each other in school. We got to be good friends. Later on, after she married, we were friends and neighbors. Her husband built this place on some land that used to belong to his family."

Marietta stopped and seemed to study her for a moment.

"You plan to sell the house?"

"We have some work to do, but, yeah, as soon as we can. If you know anybody who's looking to buy, send them our way."

Marietta gazed out the window, across the front yard. She had a quizzical expression.

"Am I cutting the yard sale short?" She asked.

"No," Lydia said. "You and Kristy were two of exactly six

people who stopped by all day. A few trucks slowed down, but I think they just wanted to get a look at the freak from the city."

She asked where Marietta lived.

"You can't see it from here, although technically speaking we're on the same road. At least by name."

"I was wondering about all those handmade signs," said Lydia. "Was that the name of somebody who used to live around here?"

Marietta added another macaroon to her plate. Then she went on without acknowledging the question.

"We're about two miles east. Take the left turn at the junction, go about five hundred feet, and we're on the right side of the road," she said. "You might have seen my son's church. It's a double-wide trailer with a marquee out front on the grass."

"Oh!" Lydia recalled the church from one of Pastor Colquitt's brochures. She'd made fun of it to Greg only the day before.

"Well," she told Marietta. "You have a good-sized piece of real estate, there. Sorry if I'm being presumptuous."

"That's all right," her guest said. "I live with my son Henry and his wife. My daughter-in-law's a good gal. I like her. She comes from a family that's pretty well off. The land we live on didn't cost too much, though. It used to be a farm. Alicia got a good price at the auction. She knows about that kind of thing."

Marietta smiled. Her eyes caught the light in the room and faded again. She asked:

"Have you had many other visitors, before today?"

Lydia turned her attention from the window and faced Marietta. Her hands and face grew warm.

"A few," she replied. "Not if you mean neighbors. Is that what you mean?"

Marietta put her plate on the coffee table and folded her hands in her lap. She took a breath before speaking.

"Anybody unusual. Maybe someone's come up to your

front door," she said. "Maybe you've seen somebody you didn't recognize, but felt like you should. That kind of thing."

In Lydia's peripheral view the sunlight shifted outside, rippling swiftly across the lawn. The wooden windmills puttered in the breeze. She had no idea how much time had passed.

"I saw someone right after we got here," she told Marietta. "But I was tired from the drive, and I kept dozing off. I might have been dreaming. Why? Is Skillute dangerous? It seems pretty quiet around here."

"It's always good to be cautious," Marietta said. "This is a nice little house. The property once belonged to Beverly's in-laws, the Dempseys. They moved off the land a long time ago. They didn't have enough money to keep it. They might have thought Beverly would leave it to her husband's family. I wouldn't know."

Marietta paused for a sip of iced coffee and then continued:

"The Dempseys don't own much, so they don't like to let go."

"We have all the legal papers."

"Oh, there's no legal question," Marietta said. "Leaving this house to somebody from out of town, that's just the kind of thing Beverly would do. She'd like to know the Dempseys were in an uproar over something she did."

"Maybe we should sell it to the Dempseys," Lydia suggested.

"The rich ones moved away years ago. I doubt any of the family that's left could afford it. Also, they might not feel like paying for it. They might consider it to be in the family already."

"So, do we need to keep a shotgun by the front door?" Lydia joked. She lost her humor when she saw the serious expression on her guest's face.

"Nothing to worry about," Marietta told her. "I'd be cautious, but not worried, if I were you. As long as you plan to sell soon and move back to Seattle, I wouldn't worry about it."

Two hours later Lydia sat on the back steps smoking and worrying about it. Who were these backward, backwoods cousins, and what the hell did they want? She thought of a children's picture book she once owned: rodents in a hut full of rags and twigs, feasting on cheese stolen from a neighbor's trash, working at it with their mole hands and sharp teeth. It was weird to hear Marietta refer to a bunch of hillbillies skulking in tents and trailers, practically in her back yard. They sounded like a feral clan from a horror movie. They were probably old hippies. It was probably nothing but a ploy to get Lydia and Greg to lower the price of the house. Pastor Colquitt would stop by with an offer any day now.

Marietta talked about Beverly, the woman who was very likely her mother. She had a sense that Marietta knew this but never alluded to it, and she wondered why. She could have asked point blank, but she didn't know how much she wanted to learn. While clearing out the cupboards and shelves of the house she had discovered a few photos and numerous ornate frames, but no pictures of Beverly. Not even a wedding photo. She wondered if Marietta had helped herself to whatever she wanted before the attorneys sent an appraiser.

What was it about Marietta that appealed to her, despite the odd manner? When she finally realized what it was, she had to laugh: Marietta was the first woman she had met who didn't show the slightest interest in her pregnancy. All the time they were together talking, and despite the peculiar turn the conversation had taken, Lydia had felt like herself, her old self, instead of a woman carrying a baby until it was ready to be born.

Clouds gathered swiftly in the afternoon sky, and the temperature began to drop. The shade descended along tree trunks and swallowed the bright green bristles of the yew shrubs that grew between the back steps and the woods. When the last glimmers of warmth and sunlight were extinguished Lydia heard a faint, tuneless whistling out on the road, at the far end of the house. She decided it was time to go inside.

Never mind the rest of the yard sale. Whatever was left tomorrow, Greg could clean it up. Or he could leave all of it on the lawn and let it rot, for all she cared. She picked up the crumpled cigarette butt and went inside to lie down.

Marietta

Marietta had offered as much warning as she dared. If she came right out and told Lydia what she suspected, and what she and Beverly had done, what good would it do?

She sat in the deepening dark of the late afternoon watching the meadow from her spot at the living room window. This was the center of the world she had made for herself in her son's house. Floorboards creaked overhead. Henry would be pacing, practicing his next sermon. He had mentioned it at supper: Something about forgiving hearts and the release of envy, something about not coveting. She had forgotten the gist of it.

Alicia was such a good person. Marietta was glad she'd found Henry. Who else would have taken her son, with his need to save the world? Where did all of that come from? It wasn't from her. Maybe she had been wrong to let Bonnie sit with Henry all those times when he was growing up. Or maybe there was a strain of insanity in John Colquitt's family. She would never know.

Butterflies hovered over the wild flowers. Marietta smiled. The world would just go on when the human part died off, someday. It would be like we never existed, and that would be a blessing. People were greedy and selfish. They lied best about things they loved and wanted to own. Even an innocent desire could lead to something terrible. Good intentions, like Henry's, mostly failed. The weak prayed for mercy, and they were wasting their breath. The strong preyed on the weak as often as they could get away with it. That would never change until all the people on earth were gone.

The meadow and sky and trees wouldn't miss anybody. She wondered, when all the people were gone, would this thing that had killed Beverly die off? Or would it still be here? Did it know what it was? Maybe it was trying so hard to live, it didn't realize it wasn't supposed to.

Beverly was dead. Ethel was gone. Marietta had decided not to tell Lydia what she knew. She had told Beverly too much, and the knowledge didn't protect her. This thing had killed her. Now it would try to kill those young people and their baby.

Anyway, Marietta thought, the more she said, the less they would believe. Beverly had loved the conspiracy, the sneaking around to lay a trap. But maybe she didn't believe what she was told, not entirely. She thought the girl was dangerous and evil, but by that she meant crazy. Once Beverly had an idea she wouldn't let it go. They were setting a trap for a little serial killer in the making. Beverly didn't realize the danger she was in. Even after she had heard the story of Harriet and Flora she wasn't as careful as she should have been.

Aside from all of these speculations Marietta had confirmed during her conversation with Lydia that the young woman was Beverly's daughter. She could tell that Lydia knew too, but didn't want to talk about it. She was curious about the woman who had left her a house to sell, but something held her back.

Being in the same room with her was disconcerting. The way she rolled her eyes when they talked about her hillbilly neighbors, the way she touched her forehead with the back of her hand to dab away the beads of perspiration, something in the timbre of her voice, was pure Beverly.

Lydia

She must have dozed off. Greg had dragged himself to bed in the middle of the night. Now he was snoring away in his loud, happy animal slumber. A single bead of saliva clung to the corner of his lips. She thought of slapping the back of his head. It served him right. Then she sat still for a minute thinking about smothering him with her pillow. No. It was too good for him. What an asshole. Maybe she should poison him. She made a mental note to look up local herbal poisons online. Then she laughed at the high drama of her mood.

She was wound up and brittle with pain and worry. Her joints creaked when she moved. So she moved as little as possible, and yet she still ached all over.

The baby had been growing relentlessly for weeks, gaining momentum. There was no way out. No jumping ship at this point. In the early days she had kept track by the calendar on her computer, silently noting the passage of the safety zone, finally admitting that she wasn't going to lose it, and that she was actually having a real baby.

With the meticulous methodology of an editor Lydia had read half a dozen current books on parenting. The word made it sound like a game or a sport! Who were these half-wit authors who didn't realize it was a relentless responsibility that she had finally accepted? She wanted some goddamn credit for what she was committing her mind and body to. She was eating well and she wanted to sleep well. She didn't know if she wanted a child, but she couldn't condemn a baby to sickness by being negative or stubborn and not taking care of her health.

That had been her mother's gift: an ability to inspire illness in her children and to blame them for keeping her stuck at home during her "good years." She never tired of saying (sometimes to strangers at airports, and often to hair stylists) that she had given up a modeling career for stretch marks and a series of inadequate patios. The truth was, two of her three children were adopted and the modeling career was limited to one underwear catalog. Lydia laughed again.

"What a loon," she said to the empty living room. "Maybe she lied. Maybe she said I was adopted, when she really was my mother. I definitely inherited her attitude. Thanks, Mom."

She laughed at the sound of her voice contained within the rectangular room. She was sitting on the sofa, staring at the fireplace at two a.m., thinking she could feel the mad thing in her womb growing.

The first time this had happened, back home in Seattle, she had called 911. She still flushed with embarrassment at the memory of lying on the bathroom tiles in their apartment, hyperventilating. The building manager, Paul, let the paramedics in and begged Lydia to go to the hospital. Someone checked her pulse and temperature. By that time she was breathing normally. The crowd of paramedics recognized her at once as a non-emergency, a woman who had freaked herself out just by thinking about the child growing inside her. The word "hypochondriac" was written on every face. They had started taking other calls on pagers and cell phones almost as soon as they arrived.

"You'll be fine, miss," the ginger-haired, chubby paramedic had said. His grin faded when he answered his pager and prepared to face a real emergency at the next stop.

She felt like an idiot. At the same time, even now, thinking too much about the whole, live body that nested inside her could make her feel dizzy and sick. She needed constant distraction.

Sitting there on the sofa she wondered: What did the Dempsey family look like? Would she know a Dempsey if she saw one?

"Dempseys. Dempseys."

She said it so many times it sounded like the name for a fantastic creature with dollops of flesh for arms, rolling past the house at the speed of a runny marshmallow. Should she invite the Dempseys down the hill for a barbecue? She could host a barbecue with pulled pork sandwiches and chardonnay. She could get gardening and weeding tips from the Dempsey clan, and offer to baby-sit. Maybe the Dempsey women had a knitting circle.

This was how people lost their minds in the country. Her friends had warned her: Outside the city it's solid dark at night and there's no traffic so you can hear every tiny, insignificant noise. Crickets yawning. Owls farting. Madness dawning.

She heard a scratching noise. She turned from the fireplace to the window and froze. Only fifty feet away a child stood watching her through the window, a slender girl with a tangle of blond hair.

The front door opened smoothly for Lydia, but the glass and aluminum security door shimmied with a metallic sound. Then it stuck on the welcome mat. She had to pull it loose.

She shook the door into place and looked out at the spot where the girl had stood. No one was there. The air was mild against her face, and it carried a hint of cedar. The fragrance reminded Lydia of something, the hope chest her grandmother kept in a closet, filled with little treasures and souvenirs, reminders of the most entrancing days and nights of her life. A fleeting acknowledgment: her mother and grandmother weren't connected to her by blood, and this woman with awful taste in furniture was. Lydia shivered and then laughed.

She went to the kitchen and found a flashlight. Then from the front door she scanned the yard. All she could hear was the chirping of crickets in the grass. Yet she kept sweeping the light back and forth, doing her duty as a responsible adult, rehearsing the good mom she must impersonate in all the years to come. Finally she gave up searching for the child, locked the door, and went back to bed.

Greg

Coffee. The scent of coffee quickly mingled with the aroma of bacon and toast. He kept his eyes shut to savor the dream reeling him back to the kitchen of his childhood. He ate Pop Tarts and cereal before school, but his mother cooked a huge breakfast on weekends, waffles and bacon, while he watched cartoons.

He stuck his nose out of the bedding and gave an exploratory sniff. The scent of bacon was real. The clock next to the bed told him he was still running late. It was almost one o'clock in the afternoon.

He couldn't remember the last leg of his drive home. He only became aware of the house, the driveway, the evening sky, Lydia's face relaxed for the first time in weeks, framed by the sheet she unconsciously gathered up at night, the heavy quiet of the night coming on. He must have taken a wrong turn on the way back. He must have been lost. How else could the time have passed? How else could he arrive home after dark?

He remembered drinking beer when he got home. Two bottles. Then he had tumbled into bed next to his wife, whose peaceful sleep was a blessing.

He followed the bacon scent along the hallway, into the kitchen, where Lydia sat reading. Without the discarded dinette set they had to sit on folding chairs and eat off of plastic crates. Greg opted to stand at the counter and Lydia poured coffee, half a cup for herself, a hearty mug for Greg. He helped himself to breakfast.

"Real bacon. You went shopping again."

"I thought we could use a change," Lydia said. "A

little more protein."

"A little!"

"You don't have to eat it," she told him. "Throw it away."

"No! It's great. Thanks, honey, you didn't have to do this," he said.

"No," she said.

"Sorry I got back so late yesterday."

"What qualifies as late in Skillute, America?"

"Sorry."

"I didn't notice. Time flew where I was. It flew right out the fucking door."

"Really screwed up. I don't even know how I got back so late. I was driving and it was light outside. Then, I guess I got lost, because by the time I pulled into the road the sun had gone down."

"Say it."

"What?" He asked, but he knew.

"Stop calling it 'the road.' It sounds so weird."

"I'll come up with a better name."

"Why don't you call it by its name?"

He didn't want to, and this bugged him. So he forced himself:

"Connie Sara Way."

Lydia said:

"I'm having the landline hooked up on Monday, Tuesday at the latest. Don't worry about it, I'll take care of everything."

"Great. Do I still get my allowance?" He was kidding, but she didn't smile.

She stomped off to the bathroom to shower. He ate his breakfast because he suddenly felt ravenous. It was better than anything they had ever eaten.

Late on Sunday afternoon Greg answered the doorbell and found Henry standing outside wearing a sheepish grin. He was holding another one of his accordion-folded color brochures. Greg blinked.

"Afternoon," Henry said. "I met your wife last week? And I think you know my mother. Marietta Colquitt? My name is Henry."

"Oh! Sure," said Greg. "My wife knows Marietta. I mean, she said they had coffee. Would you like to come in?"

They shook hands. Greg thought he detected hesitation before Henry crossed the threshold and entered the olive and beige living room that Lydia railed about every day. That seemed a bit snooty. Greg couldn't see any problem with the decor. It looked all right, better than their old apartment, better than the office where he used to work, with its computer boxes piled up in corridors and reference books propping up desk corners.

Lydia wouldn't know about that. She had the luxury of working from home, on the rare occasions when she still took a freelance assignment, which she hadn't even considered since she developed migraines. She obviously considered being pregnant a full-time job, and Greg didn't know how to argue with her. It would have to wait.

"Honey!" Greg called over his shoulder. There was no answer. He grinned at his visitor. It seemed silly, in such a small house, to admit that he had lost track of his wife.

"I brought some literature about us," Henry said, and held out the brochure. "I gave your wife, Lydia, one of the old ones, and I said I'd stop by with something more up-to-date. These just came in on Friday."

Greg knew it was another church come-on, but he accepted the brochure and even managed to flip through it casually, smiling. He was wondering how a preacher had time to visit his neighbors on a Sunday afternoon. Then he realized he hadn't been to church in so many years, he had no idea what time services took place. He closed the brochure and smiled at Henry.

"We're not really believers, you know."

"Oh," said Henry. "No pressure. I mean that. Just in case you ever need anything, we're nearby."

"Sure," said Greg. "Thanks. Sorry! That's great. Would

you like to sit down?"

"Thank you," said Henry. He made himself at home on the sofa and looked at the coffee table. He glanced around at the rest of the room with apparent discomfort.

"Lydia!" Greg called.

There was no sound from the bedroom or the kitchen. He excused himself and took a quick survey of the house: bedroom, storage room, bathroom, kitchen, and back to the living room. No sign of Lydia, which was odd. He'd spent the last two hours on the sofa, reading a tattered copy of *House Selling for Dummies*, and he didn't hear her leave the house.

"Ha!" Greg shook his head. "I guess she went for a walk. Would you like a beer? Oh. No. Coffee?"

"A beer would be great, actually," Henry said.

Greg went to fetch two bottles of ale from the fridge. He was still wondering when Lydia had slipped out and where she might have gone in a neighborhood she hated.

Lydia

The weather was mild. There might even be a sprinkling of rain later. It was one of those unexpectedly dark days of Northwestern summer. The season seemed to pause. Then came terrible humidity, the shifting barometric pressure that caused headaches, the sudden storm that ruined outdoor parties.

Lydia had spent far too many hours online the past week, writing email and endless, banal status updates promising to return to Seattle in time for Bumbershoot. She had reached a point where no one replied with comments, and she didn't know if her friends were too busy or simply sick of her.

Every one of them worked full-time. Not just jobs but careers at ad agencies and software and game design companies. All they could manage were a few innocuous or enigmatic one-liners during the week. On the weekend they went backpacking and hiking. They didn't have time to respond to Lydia's barrage of news about every inch of her house in Skillute. She caught herself taking the walk down the driveway and across the road to the row of metal mailboxes, checking for snail mail two or three times a day, like a retiree anxiously awaiting a social security payment.

She had company several times during the week, but not the kind she wanted. Misty Court dropped off a batch of coupons and sold her a box of candy for Kristy's high school. The Avon Lady stopped by with a seasonal sale catalog.

So the week had gone by, wasted. They had spent two weeks in this awful place, with nothing to show for it.

While Greg read his manuals and plotted how to unload a tiny house with no special features in the middle of nowhere, she sat on the back step sneaking another cigarette. When she heard the doorbell ring, she caved. It was just too much. She bolted. She did the only thing she could do in this place: She went walking in the woods.

Five more minutes of making nice with one of the locals and she would have started screaming. She would kill them all. She knew it. She would drive "downtown," to the only intersection, with its fifteen shops and a rusty train station. She would walk into Buck's Rifles Guns 'n' Ammo and say to Buck:

"I need a big gun, Buck. I want to kill my neighbors."

Would the lanky man with weathered skin standing behind the counter in jeans and a camouflage t-shirt, smoking a Marlboro, understand? She thought he would, and she thought he would sell her a gun 'n' ammo, because that's why he existed. This was who Buck was: the man who sold people the means to kill what they wanted dead.

Greg wasn't remotely qualified to sell the house. He didn't know how. He didn't have time to figure it out. He was emailing three different versions of his resume several times a week and calling his colleagues to follow up on job tips. He stayed busy every minute of the day, not only as a display of his loyalty and responsibility, but as though his sanity depended on it. He was still insisting that they could handle the house without a real estate agent, but this was beginning to sound crazy.

Since the day of the yard sale Greg had been more distracted: running errands, leaping to his feet to fetch Lydia anything she wanted at any hour. He said it was the least he could do, after the sacrifices she had made. Although she would never say this to him, she felt that he wanted to get away from her, and any excuse would do.

She found herself letting him take care of things. Pick up the groceries. Drop off cards and letters at the post office, three miles away, instead of leaving them in the mailbox across the road. He seemed happier when he was in motion, so she gave him reasons to move.

Meanwhile Lydia was wandering, drifting, losing ground. She had never decided to have a baby. She had forgotten to avoid it. Then she got drunk and broke the news prematurely to a couple of friends. The cards and emails had started pouring in: comfort, congratulations, surprise, elation, all before she had made up her mind about the baby. She was cornered. She couldn't believe the things people started saying to her. Out of nowhere, all of her friends wanted more than anything for her to have a beautiful baby. They wrote such tender notes. She cried over a few of them because no one she knew had ever said such heartfelt things to her. Were these messages for her or for the baby? She didn't want to know.

When she told her mother the news by telephone the answer was bright, forceful, and immediate:

"Where are you registered?"

Once Lydia had given her the information she needed and a license to shop, the conversation was pretty much over. A few flourishes, orders to keep in touch, eat more often, her mother's signature "mwa" kissing sound, and they were done with each other for at least a month.

When Lydia had received the news about Beverly Dempsey's house, she had said nothing to her mother. She couldn't bear to provide the material for a round of high drama. It wouldn't end well. So Lydia told her mother that Greg inherited some property from an uncle. The rest of the story she told was true, leaving out Beverly altogether. Lying to her mother was a habit she had perfected by first grade.

She wasn't close to her siblings, never had been. She let them think she and Greg were still in Seattle until they finally noticed one of her pitiful status updates and called her.

"Well, that was lucky, Greg getting a house from a relative he didn't even know."

"Yeah," said Lydia. "How about that?"

No one needed to know, certainly not anyone in her family, with their phantom aches and pains, their happy hours, spa memberships, group vacations, and over-the-limit credit cards. They had enough to deal with, just waking up in the morning. By lunchtime they were exhausted from putting up with the foibles and stupidity of all the people around them. One more thing to think about might kill them.

Lydia had come to a clearing in the woods. She stood before a cottage, painted robin's egg blue with white shutters. She didn't know how far she had walked, or in which direction.

"Flora!"

Lydia flinched at the name, shouted by someone inside the house. From the far corner of the yard, where it bordered the line of fir trees, a girl came walking toward the house, her arms full of weeds. The door to the house opened. A tall woman, with hair as red as a fox, stepped outside onto the flagstone walk. She wore crimson lipstick, a gold silk dress with high heels. The girl went slouching toward the door.

"What is the matter with you?" The woman yelled. She caught the girl by her hair and slapped her. The ring on her left hand grazed the girl's neck and she cried out.

"Stop!" Lydia shouted. Neither the girl nor the woman noticed.

The woman shook the girl and marched her toward the cottage, all the while gripping her hair so that the girl was drawn back in a contortion of pain. As the two passed, Lydia saw the girl more clearly. She could not have been more than thirteen or fourteen years old, with long blond hair that was matted and dirty. Even from where she stood, Lydia could see that the girl was pregnant, probably expecting around the same time she was. Other than her protruding belly, the girl might have been starving. Her skinny arms and legs reminded Lydia of a spider.

"Lydia!"

She turned just as Greg caught up to her.

"Where have you been?" He asked.

"She's crazy," she said. "She crazy, Greg."

He put his arm around her. They started walking together. He seemed to be protectively guiding her away from the woods, back toward home.

"Who's that, honey?" He asked. "What are you talking about?"

She only had to glance over her shoulder to know that there was no house where she had been, only the deep, wide shadow of the woods.

Greg

"I'm not going," Lydia announced at the front door.

Greg had his keys in his hand, and they were on their way out. It was the first time he noticed that she was still wearing the stretched-out t-shirt and knit skirt she had worn all day. She hadn't showered or brushed her hair, and he had never thought about it until now.

"You never intended to go, did you?" He asked.

"Yes I did," she said, getting defensive right away, as she usually did when he confronted her.

"No, you never planned to go," he said. "You ran out the back when the guy came to visit yesterday. Then you said sure, let's go have dinner with the old crazy and her family, and today you didn't do one thing to get ready. You never intended to go with me, did you?"

"So what? I'm tired. I'm fucking pregnant, Greg, I get tired at the end of the day. It's bedtime for me. Why didn't you say we could only come for lunch? The guy said dinner."

"Supper. They call it supper."

"Who cares? And you said, 'Sure! You bet, Pastor Cockhead!'"

"Okay."

"You didn't ask me. You told me you accepted the invitation: Two different situations. Did you tell him we want to be baptized, too? Maybe we should stay here until the baby comes, so he can throw some holy water on it. Or did you say he could have the baby, because we want to be neighborly?"

"It was kind of embarrassing, you know? 'Oh, sorry, I have no idea where my pregnant wife is. Maybe she's having our baby alone in the woods. Let me go check.'"

"That's your defense? You were embarrassed? Well, Greg, I'm so sorry you had an awkward moment. It isn't like I've been carrying an extra burden, or anything, for five fucking months!"

Greg watched her stomp through the house straightening things up. She picked up cushions and slapped them into place on the sofa. She moved each framed photo a quarter of an inch to the left or the right. She went to collect sheets from the dryer.

"I'll call it off," he said. "Who cares? It's just dinner, we can do it another time."

"No!" She shouted and stomped back into the living room. "It isn't dinner, it's supper! You're going. I'm staying. You said yes, I didn't. Can't you take a hint? I need an evening alone, okay?"

She said this with such ferocity he decided she was right.

"Cell working?" He asked.

"Yes."

"Charged?"

"Yes!"

"Call me?" He asked, and kissed her cheek.

"If I pee more than once, or if a leaf blows into the yard, I'll call to let you know."

At times like this her sarcasm lost its limited charm and made him wonder how they would ever get through the next few weeks together, let alone the rest of their lives.

Fortunately they were not dining in the room where the animal heads were mounted on the walls. That would have been more than Greg could handle with a straight face. The dining room was closed off from the rest of the house by double doors at both ends. Painted saffron, with white and maroon trim and overhead fans, this room was by far the most comfortable one in Henry and Alicia's house. The four of them were gathered at one end of a table that could seat fourteen.

"He said he'd been praying," Henry said as he scooped a spoonful of broccoli onto his plate. He passed the serving dish to Alicia.

"In the woods?" Alicia said. "By himself?"

"I guess that's where he lives now."

Greg felt Marietta watching him while he served himself. Yet every time he looked across the table he found that her eyes were fixed on her own plate and she was eating instead of staring at him.

"I'm sorry," Greg said. "Who is this, again?"

"Burt Sanders," Henry explained.

"Poor man," Alicia chimed in. "We could let him sleep in the chapel, Henry. He isn't dangerous to anyone except himself."

"He has a house of his own, right across the road. He just doesn't want to stay there. Says he can't stand to be indoors."

"Poor man," Alicia said again. "He's lost his family. First his little girl died."

Marietta poured herself a glass of water from the pitcher.

"That was terrible. Terrible for everyone, for Burt and for Mr. Jasper, and the poor child."

"Was it an accident?" Greg asked.

The silence told him this was a bad question, despite Alicia being the one who brought up the subject. Greg shook his head.

"Sorry," he said. "No. Please go on."

"It was an accident, but nobody knows how it happened. The child was in a coma, and then she passed away. Burt was in a bad state. Then his wife left him," Alicia said. "Right after the memorial. Ethel walked away from the grave, and drove off! There we all were, saying a prayer, and off she went. Since then, nobody we know has heard a word. Well, you knew her, you used to be very close, isn't that right, Marietta? If she contacted anyone in Skillute it would be you, wouldn't it?"

Marietta looked at Greg now, but her eyes told him nothing.

"Burt just wanders around," Alicia continued. "At first, I think he was looking for his wife, but now I just don't know."

"He's a pitiful soul," Henry said. "I've tried ministering to Burt, but he lives in the past, in his head. He's got some delusion that his daughter is still alive, and he spends his nights outdoors, sleeps there, drinks."

"When did you see him last?" Alicia asked.

"A few days ago," said Henry. "I was in the car, actually. Making my rounds, and I saw Burt out by the freeway, you know where they closed the on-ramp?"

"Is this recent?" Greg asked. "I'm still finding my way around."

"Greg," Alicia explained. "There used to be an entrance to the freeway not far from here, a lot more convenient than driving to the one in Kelso. The department of transportation closed it, though."

"Five accidents in two years," Henry chimed in. "Anyway, that's where I saw Burt, stumbling along with his shotgun in his hand, obviously didn't know what he was doing. I pulled over, stopped on the shoulder, and got out. I asked what he was up to. I offered him a ride. I told him he didn't want the sheriff or the highway patrol to see him like that, half drunk with a firearm, wandering around. So he got in the car, and I drove him to the next exit. Before he got out, while I was driving along, you know what he said?"

They all looked at Henry. Alicia said:

"What did he say to you, dear?"

"He said he didn't need God any more, because his little girl was on her way home."

Alicia shook her head.

"Poor man. Do you think he meant she was on her way to heaven?"

Greg thought again of Lydia, at home, probably cursing him, most likely still sulking because he hadn't shown the backbone to say no when Henry invited them over. She was right, although the Colquitts were pleasant enough. Greg didn't belong here, and neither did Lydia. They should try to borrow money against the house, turn it over to a re-altor, and head back to Seattle. Trying to find a job long distance wasn't working, anyway. His plan wasn't working out for either of them, and now his wife was home by her-self, fretting about things that were his fault.

"When is she due?"

Greg was startled by Marietta's question. These were the first words she'd spoken since they sat down to dinner.

"November, " he told her.

"It's a shame she couldn't come for supper," she said.

He decided her lavender eyes and her frown told him what she thought of him for leaving his wife alone at night in her condition. Under her gaze he flinched and turned his attention back to Henry.

"How long have you had your church here?" He asked, feeling stupid because he was sure Henry had answered the same question when he stopped by Greg's house and invited them to visit. Now Greg wondered if the idea had been Marietta's rather than Henry's. If so, why was she so quiet? If she wanted to get acquainted, she wasn't trying very hard.

After Henry provided another verbal essay on his made-up religion, his feelings about God and free will, and his ongoing efforts to save Skillute, the conversation turned back to "poor Burt Sanders." Alicia seemed to think she was the only person in town who understood what the man had been through.

"Absolutely horrible," she said. "I can't imagine losing a child, and in that way. But it wasn't anyone's fault."

"What happened to her?" Greg interrupted.

Marietta answered now, in a measured tone that un-nerved him.

"She was teasing the neighbor's pit-bull. The dog got loose."

Greg, Henry, and Alicia stopped mid-bite. Marietta went on eating.

"She was an adventurous girl," Alicia said. "A tomboy."

Marietta spoke without taking her gaze from her food.

"She wasn't right. They sent her home from school. And two children disappeared."

Alicia adopted a soothing tone:

"Those rumors didn't help anyone. Nobody knows what happened to those poor little ones. Connie Sara Sanders wasn't going to that school any more."

"Because she broke a little girl's collar bone and pulled another one's arm out of its socket," Marietta said. "Ethel had to take her out then. She didn't have a choice."

"For home school?" Greg asked.

"Ethel never home schooled her daughter. She didn't like to be alone with her, as far as I could tell."

"Well, then," said Henry. "I'll bet you're about fed up with our tales of Skillute, Greg. We must seem like gossiping hens."

Marietta glanced at Henry but said nothing. She filled her glass again.

"Oh, no," Greg said. "Small towns are interesting. Local history. In fact, I wonder about the house my wife and I have been staying in."

No one took the cue. Greg helped himself to another biscuit and said:

"Lydia tells me you knew Beverly Dempsey, the woman who owned our house."

"She was another friend of my mother-in-law, and Ethel. They grew up together, right?"

Alicia smiled at Marietta, who said:

"The doctor told us Beverly had a heart attack. She was confused when she died, that's why she left things the way she did."

"How's that?" Greg asked. He helped himself to wine and discovered it was a Chateau Margaux.

"Mother found Mrs. Dempsey and called the sheriff's office," said Henry. "Then my wife and I went around to clean up, once the sheriff said it was okay."

"Clean up?"

"Oh," Alicia said, fluttering her fingers and then letting them rest on her husband's hand. "It wasn't like that. There was no mess. She must have been disoriented."

"Confused," said Henry.

"She had stacked some of her furniture against the fireplace, that's all. We put it all back where it belonged. She would have wanted that, I'm sure. I didn't know her well, but she kept a very tidy house. A woman doesn't want to be judged by her last moment."

Her look around the table faded on Henry, who blushed and said nothing. Greg wondered what kind of life Henry had had at age six, or again at age sixteen, with a mother like Marietta. He thought: So that's where preachers come from. Then he felt ashamed at judging Henry while enjoying his hospitality. He also marveled at these people who swooped in after a neighbor died and straightened up her home to make it more presentable. It seemed both decent and interfering. No wonder Henry had been so uncomfortable in Mrs. Dempsey's living room.

"I should call my wife," Greg said.

Lydia

She wasn't sure this was the right direction. She was feeling her way along instead of following signposts. She didn't know what kind of trees or plants grew here, and wouldn't recognize them. She only noticed one of the rotting pieces of shingle, with the name of the road painted on it. The letters had faded and worn away. She reached up and ran her fingers across the letters.

The night was still, the air pungent and warm. The scent of roasting meat drifted on faint smoke. Ordinarily this would have brought memories of family nights by the pool. At the moment the smell of meat made Lydia feel nauseated.

Underfoot the dry leaves and twigs crunched. Ferns swept across her ankles. It seemed that she had walked a much greater distance this time, when she stepped into a clearing and saw the house: robin's egg blue, with white shutters and cedar shingles. The blue-black night reflected in tall windows.

She flinched at fluttering wings and a woofing noise overhead. She looked back and saw the outspread wings of an owl in flight, down the unmarked route she had taken.

All of this, the blue-green shimmer of fir, the cottage, the clearing, carried a hint of memory, a fairy tale, or a recurring dream. She was smiling at this when she heard the first scream.

At once she knew it was the girl she had seen before. Instinct told her, with a thrill in her gut, that the girl was in pain. Before she could think of danger, Lydia headed for the cottage. With each step she could hear more distinctly the cries of the girl.

Lydia followed the walkway. She opened the door to the house, and went inside. Immediately she realized that this was not the front of the house as she thought, but the kitchen. The girl lay on a cot. The woman with fox-red hair stood on one side and on the other an older woman assisted. They were holding the girl down. They had pulled the covers away to reveal her legs, which were splayed and struggling against the sheets. Her abdomen was swollen to full term. She was in labor.

Another ear-splitting scream shot through the room the two women had prepared for delivery. Both wore aprons over their clothing.

Now Lydia could hear them, although they took no notice of her.

"This will only hurt as much as you make it hurt," said the woman Lydia had seen before. Under her apron, her dress was black with gold trim, and she wore gold earrings. Her hair was swept up in a French twist.

The other, older one, whose hair was tucked into a white cotton bandana, was trying to reach between the girl's legs. She might be a nurse or a midwife. Every time she reached, the girl screamed and wrenched away.

"Poor little thing," the midwife said. "I'll have to use the forceps. You know that. You have to settle down."

"Do you have to do that?" The other woman asked. "You might hurt it."

"Stop!" The girl shouted and struggled against them. Then she doubled up, in too much pain to make a sound. Her mouth hung open, drooling.

"There it comes," said the midwife. "Hold her."

The redhead in the black and gold dress followed her instructions and pinned the girl to the cot by her shoulders, draping her own torso across the girl's.

"No! No! I can't breathe!" The girl screamed.

The midwife grabbed her legs and quickly tied her

ankles to the corners of the cot. She looked to the red-head, who made a frantic gesture to hurry up. The midwife reached with both hands toward the girl.

Lydia couldn't move. All she could do was hold her belly. She was trying not to vomit.

Writhing under the weight of the woman, the girl was crying and screaming at the same time. She gasped for air. The redhead screamed at her to be quiet. Then she grabbed a washcloth and stuffed it in the girl's mouth. The midwife gave a tug, just as if she were opening a package and taking out what was inside it.

Blood and amniotic fluid ran like snot, soaking the sheets and the midwife's apron. Her arms were bloody and dripping when she stood up grasping the infant in cupped hands. It was so small and wrinkled it hardly looked human. It wasn't moving at all.

Now that the baby was outside the girl, the red-haired woman who had held her down let go and left her. She reached out for the baby, but the midwife wouldn't relinquish it.

"What's wrong? Why isn't it crying? Let me have it!"

The midwife held the baby in one crooked arm and massaged its chest with her fingertips. She turned away so the redhead couldn't take hold of it.

"Give it to me!" The woman said. "It's mine! Give it to me!"

The girl moaned and whimpered, on the bed. She was still bleeding. The washcloth fell from her mouth along with vomit and saliva. The bedclothes were sodden, scarlet with white streaks, and the room smelled of blood, wet and metallic.

"She's not breathing yet," the midwife said. "Stand back. See to the girl."

"Give her to me, I'll make her breathe."

"Don't touch her!"

The girl was shivering. She held her abdomen with one bloodstained hand and with the other she grasped feebly at the sheets, her splayed fingers trying to pull them toward her, to cover herself. The sheets were slick and they kept slipping out of reach. Blood ran down the sides of the cot and dripped onto the tile floor. The girl looked up and let out a sigh, and then she stopped moving. She lay there dead in the mess, with her eyes open, looking at the women.

They didn't notice the girl at once. They went on shuffling and arguing, with the baby still clenched in the midwife's arms, until a phlegm-coated cry rang out from the infant's throat. The baby coughed and then broke the air with a shrill, wide-mouthed scream.

Greg

Greg was halfway home when the wheeze in the engine started a second time. He drew a sharp breath. With one hand on the steering wheel, he tried the cell phone. No luck. Now he kicked himself for leaving Lydia by herself. What was he thinking? What was he trying to prove by going out alone to dine with people they would forget about in a couple of months? They would never see these country bumpkins again, and yet he had said yes without hesitation. He had been pleased when Lydia refused to join him. That was the part that made him cringe. His first thought was freedom. Now Lydia was alone and he couldn't reach her to say he was on his way.

Adding a gargantuan red cherry to his day, the car was threatening to stall. Probably just overheating, but who the hell knew? He could walk from the Colquitt house to his own. It wasn't that far. He just hated having car trouble when they were already strapped for cash. Now that he thought about it, why had he taken the car? It wasn't raining. It wasn't cold. He needed the exercise. Yet he had driven to the Colquitt place. Served him right if the car broke down, but Lydia would never understand.

He passed one of the road signs, a "Connie Sara Way" marker made of cedar, nailed to a tree trunk. He wondered: if the transportation department knew this place had been dubbed by Burt Sanders, resident drunk, would they pull the signs down and give the road a real name? Could he make an anonymous call to the county, or would his neighbors know? How terrible to be known in a town this small as that guy from Seattle who called the authorities and had a grieving father's tribute to his dead daughter torn down.

It was dark out, with no traffic lights, no street lamps, just the road flanked by tall trees. He was tired. All he wanted was a shower and bed, clean sheets, a happy wife. He hoped Lydia had done laundry while he was gone, and then he kicked himself for being a jerk again. She must have been bored to death the past two weeks.

There was the wheeze again, a woof-and-whine. This time it held on and grew louder. A shadow across his peripheral vision made Greg shiver and slow down. That's when the engine died, and the car glided to a stop.

The trees on either side of the road looked flat and opaque. The last faint threads of daylight had given way while he was indoors, in perhaps the only room in the Colquitt house without windows. Greg tried the cell one more time, and gave up. With clenched jaw and a determination not to dwell on the tongue-lashing he would get when he arrived at home, he got out of the car.

He propped the hood open. When he stared down at the engine he wondered how many men had done this, since the car was invented? How many men had stood gazing down at this incomprehensible shit, trying to figure it out by magic? He shook his head and laughed. The whole night was ridiculous. Lydia would think so, too. The way he would tell the story, she would laugh. Thinking of this, knowing he was grasping at straws, he became aware of the road shifting.

On second thought, it wasn't the road that was changing but the air around him. It seemed thicker, viscous and heavy. Silver shadows moved on all sides and folded in on themselves. Greg squinted, refusing to believe what he was seeing. From the trees and empty fields, from the forest down to the blue-black asphalt, narrowing to the car and a bit of ground around it, came fog.

"No way," Greg said out loud.

Then he laughed. It was preposterous. What else, in this stupid town? What next?

For a moment he wished and hoped like hell that Lydia would see this rolling in. He imagined her standing at the window in the living room. He remembered the way she had danced with delight on their first foggy day together in Seattle. He was momentarily lost in the beauty of it.

He wondered how this could happen in the summer. He couldn't see the mountains from this spot even during the day, and he didn't know how close the nearest body of water was. He tried to work out an inversion theory, and then realized that he was distracting himself. In fact it was hard to keep his mind on what he needed to do. He had to finish the trip on foot. He had to walk home, and he needed to get started, but the fog was so dense and beautiful.

"No friggin' way," he said, shaking his head.

Pearl-gray tendrils of the fog went scuttling across the road. Reluctantly Greg started walking. He trained his eyes on the path that kept disappearing ahead.

The fog swelled and enveloped him. No cars passed. No lights.

All right, he said to himself: No problem. He tried the cell again. His call didn't go through. One great, weird thing happened and he couldn't even share it! His view of fog rolling up onto his feet made him shiver. He put his cell away, and kept walking. By now he could only see a couple of feet in any direction.

Beyond his view, nocturnal animals were stirring. Now and then a shadow would dart from one tree to another, into the underbrush or the leaves of a maple with a quick, sharp rustle.

Greg trudged along, thinking that he must be close. It seemed that he had been walking long enough to reach the driveway. Then he wondered if he had passed it. He was going on instinct and the knowledge that his house was just up the road and on the left. He had never taken the route on foot.

After a few minutes the noises on either side of him died away. Then there was no stirring at all, not a sound. From the thickening fog, he heard nothing.

When he stopped and looked back, he couldn't see the car parked on the narrow shoulder. He couldn't see the shoulder. He couldn't see anything. If he reached out a hand, it would fade away before he stretched his arm to full length.

He was sorry he had decided to leave Lydia at home. She had refused to go, but he could have canceled. Why did he feel compelled to be nice to the Colquitts? They didn't mean a thing to him, the preacher who made up his own religion and his horsy wife, with their trophy house.

He could still picture the hallway lit by the living room, crowded with animal heads, the room's amber light shining around the crazy one, Marietta, when she stood in the front door watching him leave.

"I'm sorry Lydia decided not to come, too," she had said. "It would have been good if she had come with you."

That seemed like an accusation. Yet it was true. What could he say?

She had offered more wine, then dessert, and finally insisted on wrapping up a piece of cake for him to take home to Lydia. Marietta had still been there, watching from the door of her house as he backed the car out and turned and headed down the road. Later when he got out of the car and started walking, he had forgotten the slice of cake, left it on the seat.

While he was remembering the details of the evening, someone joined him. Simply and distinctly he became aware that someone was walking, to his left, keeping pace with him. He hadn't heard or seen anyone approach, but there was someone, no more than an arm's length away, in step with him. Yet when he glanced down and to the left, he saw that this was impossible because there was a trench alongside the road, where the person would be.

With all of his might he resisted the urge to run. This was pure instinct, overwhelming and negating his reasonable need to find out who or what was there in the fog beside him.

The fog. In a movie theater or watching a DVD in his living room, it would be ludicrous. He would have laughed. But he was alone and the only sound was the tread of his shoes, and the scrape and tap of the other one's step.

He kept walking and he tried to breathe normally. He tried not to speed up. If he panicked and broke into a sprint; no, he must not do that, no matter how much he wanted to escape, no matter how crazy it felt to him. He imagined a dangerous animal, so close it nearly touched him. He had to keep walking and stare straight ahead.

His skin tingled. He had broken out in a sweat. His breathing grew shallow, but he couldn't help it. The air was thick and vaporous. He tried to think how far he must have traveled, but he had no idea. He didn't know the landscape, not that it made any difference. He was walking blind.

All at once he had to pee so badly that everything else seemed unimportant. He had to pee. How could he do it? He would have to unzip his pants in the dark, in the fog, and stand there, not knowing what was about to happen.

What the hell was it? Was he freaking himself out with his own shadow? The sound? It couldn't be an echo. It wasn't possible.

His nerve broke. He bolted. He ran hard, with arms pumping. His feet began to sting, soles of his shoes hitting the asphalt in a wild rhythm. He wasn't breathing so much as gulping air, breaking out in a full sweat and trying not to scream.

Lydia

Waking from feverish sleep, Lydia moved slowly through the house. The rooms felt natural to her now. For the first time she didn't feel homesick or bored. She decided to take a bath. Greg had not called, or if he had she was asleep. It didn't matter. He would be home soon.

She ran the bath water. She undressed slowly, being gentle with herself. From now on, she would do this: She would treat herself the way a woman in her condition ought to be treated. It was that simple. It was all very simple.

She eased herself into the bath, using the handles built into the wall, and thought: At least the old lady who lived here before was good for something.

This was a fine house, actually, though not robin's egg blue. Where had she seen a blue house, with a shingled roof?

The water was a joy to touch. She splashed the surface like a baby taking her first bath. Then she leaned back, rested her neck against a rubber cushion, and let her belly rise until it broke the surface. She relaxed and tried to let all the muscles in her body recover from the day. Everything took so much effort. By night she was worn out even if she hadn't accomplished a thing.

She tried to find the center. It felt like a knot. She wanted, more than anything, to let go, to unclench the fist at the center of her body.

When she got her energy back she would redecorate. She would paint the living room goldenrod and cream, or hire the Dumpy Dempseys to paint. Then it would be so beautiful.

Bitches. That's what the women of this neighborhood were, all of them. Especially that one with the crazy eyes, who had a lot of nerve to come around telling weird stories and upsetting her. Bitches like that ugly fat girl who worked in her Misty Mommy's store up the road. She smoked outside next to the trash dumpster where her mother didn't see her, and she thought she was so smart. Bitch-cow. Her hair was dry as a haystack and she smelled of cow milk.

The longer Lydia reclined in the bath, stretched full length, heels pressed against the end of the tub, the warmer the water became. It was a luxury, really, being like this. Why get so wound up? Before she knew it things would be back to normal. Everything felt good, when she thought this way. It was all so good.

Lydia woke and she couldn't tell how long she had drifted. She couldn't say if it was nighttime, although the house beyond the bathroom door was dark. Then she heard it, the sound that must have awakened her. She sat perfectly still and listened with her whole body.

Front door. That was it. The doorknob rattling, then silence. Someone was knocking, lightly. Greg wouldn't knock. Someone, not out front, no, but at the back door, tap, tap, tap.

Lydia held her breath. There was nowhere to hide, nothing she could do now. Something seemed to be circling the house, wanting in. Worst of all was the feeling, no, the certainty, that this, every sound, every moment, had already happened. But how could it? How could it?

Now the tapping came from the front door again, and this time, this time, she heard the lock tumble, the lock was giving way. It wouldn't hold against whatever wanted in. It was coming in, and she sat frozen, stuck in the animal heat of her own body, trapped in the center, in the light, with whatever it was coming closer.

It was walking along the hallway, to the door at the center of the house. Lydia looked down into the water. She found she was sitting in a bath of her own blood, not pink but crimson, dark, thick, and warm.

Greg

Greg was out of breath when he stumbled up the driveway, fumbled with his keys and opened the front door. He had never been so grateful to finally reach home.

Only the outside light was on. Indoors it was pitch black. He made his way carefully to the nearest lamp and turned it on. Then he tiptoed to the bedroom and confirmed that Lydia was sleeping. It was after eleven.

He wasn't sure what had happened out there, on the road. By the time he recognized his own yard, and sprinted up the drive, the fog was gone completely.

Right now, safe at home with Lydia, he didn't care that there was no reasonable explanation. His fear and the energy it took to make the dash home had left him sweat-drenched and exhausted. Nothing was more important than sleep. He would pick up the car tomorrow.

Greg undressed, climbed into bed and nestled close behind his wife, listening to her steady breathing. In a way, he was glad she wasn't awake. He didn't want to have another one of those conversations: why couldn't he reach her by cell phone, and why had he gone to dinner with the Colquitts in the first place? They were having too many talks like that lately.

He had just closed his eyes and started to feel the tug of sleep, when he heard his stomach growl. He had eaten everything offered at dinner, and finished with a slice of that cake Marietta foisted on him, just to prove his appreciation.

He tried shifting his weight. He craved silence and sleep, but he was plagued by wild images darting through his mind every time he shut his eyes. He returned each time to the rabbit lying still on the asphalt. The heat from its insides made its eyes open. He rolled over and felt a wave of nausea. He managed to get out of bed and into the bathroom just in time.

Five minutes later he was still crouching in front of the toilet, heaving. The worst part, the most sickening part, was knowing that everything was just as bad as Lydia said it was. He was letting her down, in every possible way.

Once he was certain he had thrown up all the food in his stomach, and the dry heaves had subsided, he stumbled back to bed and curled up under the top sheet. Despite the comfortable temperature in the house, his teeth chattered. He cursed himself for being so childish. Why was he trying to make friends with people he would never have given the time of day under normal circumstances? Now he had gotten what he deserved: food poisoning. He lay under the sheet, miserably recounting the mistakes of the last few weeks, vowing to do a better job, to be a better husband to Lydia, and wondering how to get both of them out of this place. At last exhaustion overcame him and he slept.

In the morning he lay in bed letting his mind drift. Maybe he had hallucinated the fog, or the entire drive home. He had been dreaming after sleeping deeply, he was lightheaded and he couldn't say what was real.

He was troubled again by last night's dinner with the Colquitts. Clearly, Marietta was crazy. Greg couldn't get over the way she stared at him, standing there at the front door while he got in his car and headed home. She had followed him outside after he said he was worried about Lydia and needed to go. She had stopped him in the hallway and insisted that he take dessert with him. She was stalling, but why? After all that concern about Lydia, she wouldn't let him go.

"Your wife might be less upset with you, if you take her a slice of Alicia's cake," she said. "It's all homemade, even the coconut frosting. Wait here while I wrap up a piece."

Then, because he was too polite to say no, he had waited while she went to the kitchen and wrapped up the dessert in aluminum foil. He stood there, jingling his keys, dialing on his cell and getting no signal, until Marietta returned. She handed him the cake and said goodnight. Even then she seemed to be thinking of something to say, some way to keep his attention.

Marietta Colquitt was a loon. Greg wasn't letting her or her son, the big geek with his made-up religion and his stuffed animal heads and his gawky wife, get anywhere near Lydia or his baby again.

He thought about last night, and decided he had panicked. His car had broken down on the spooky old road with no lights and no people in sight. He ran into some temporary, freakish weather pattern and his imagination took over. It was stress combined with the strangeness of this place. The sooner they got out of here, the better.

He sniffed the air. Sweet, and pleasant despite his upset stomach the night before. In fact, he didn't feel nauseated. He felt odd, tingling all over.

Unmistakable, now that he recognized the aroma, and a world of childhood came flooding back with it: Gingerbread. Classrooms and chalk, the scrape of desks on hardwood floors in the two-story building where he had gone to school. Finger-paint, bubble gum, pencil shavings, the black tendrils of hair cascading from Didi Schuster's hair band onto the edge of his desk. The clatter of plastic cafeteria trays. The icy bite of January. Skating at Green Lake. Coming home sweaty and exhausted, falling into clean pajamas. The scent of fresh baked gingerbread, the only thing his mother knew how to cook from scratch. This was when he would talk to his mother, while she cooked. They were alone together and he could talk with her about anything.

"Honey? Are you ready for breakfast?"

Lydia was standing in the doorway, smiling, holding a plate with a slice of gingerbread on it and a cup of coffee.

He stared with his mouth open.

"Aren't you hungry?" She asked.

"Yeah," he said. "Uh. Just a minute."

He shuffled to the living room window and looked out at sunlight sparkling in the trees and across the lawn. The Toyota was parked in the driveway next to the house. Before he could think of anything to say, Lydia told him:

"I saw the car a few yards down the road. You were sleeping, so I brought it home."

"You didn't have any trouble starting it?"

"No. I thought you had a flat, but everything looked okay. Whatever you brought home in that foil was a mess. I threw it out."

"Good move," said Greg. "Alicia Colquitt baked it."

"How nice," she said in a flat tone.

"Did you say you could see the car from the end of our driveway?"

"Yes. Why?"

He decided not to tell her about the fog. What good would it do? She seemed relaxed and happy. Why start more trouble?

"No reason," he said. "I just didn't realize I was so close to the house."

"Were you drunk?"

"No. No, I was fine."

"Good," she said. "Have some gingerbread while it's warm."

Burt

Burt stared straight up into the white blue sky. He was trying to imagine the forest as it once was, with its darkened canopy: nettles, branches and twigs entwined and dotted with bits of bark, stray leaves, moss. There were rodents, red voles, living up there. No need to visit the ground at all. Or maybe that was one of the stories the preacher had told him about how things used to be.

Now the sky burned right through. Only a few of the old trees survived. Briefly Burt railed against the men who harvested the wood. Then he lost his train of thought. He was a man in search of a place to hide, to forget, and he could find no sanctuary. Not even in church.

Whiskey burned his throat. He gagged and set the thermos aside. He put his back against the grooved trunk of a fir and walked his way down until he was seated on the ground. He held his rifle across his lap and glanced at the circle of trees. He had been here before, yesterday, or maybe last week. He was traveling in circles, and the trees were mocking him.

Nothing would bring his girl back, the preacher said. But that was a lie, as it turned out. Burt had seen her twice, dashing ahead of him through the woods.

A couple of miles away he had discovered the ruins of an outhouse with a deep trench. Nothing but a hole in the ground, full of shit and mud and dead leaves and a girl with a ribbon in her hair. She wasn't his Connie Sara.

He reached out for the thermos of whiskey. He stared up at the sky.

His daughter stood before him in a black pinafore and white blouse, her hair tied neatly with a red bow. She smiled and her scarlet mouth started to bleed. Blood ran down the sides of her mouth and between her broken teeth.

"Are you my little girl, my baby?" He asked.

And the girl said that she was.

Henry

Henry had to ring the bell a third time. It didn't seem likely that both Lydia and Greg were gone, not with their car sitting in the driveway.

Finally the door opened, and Greg squinted out of the shadows.

"Hi there," said Henry. "I'm on my way back from visiting a parishioner."

Greg said nothing. He seemed to have trouble holding the door open.

"I was passing by on my way home," Henry told him. "I just wanted to make sure everything was all right."

He paused and Greg still said nothing.

"We haven't seen you since you came for supper, three weeks ago," Henry reminded him. "And I noticed there's no 'for sale' sign in the yard yet. I wondered how you and your wife were doing."

"Yeah," Greg said. He coughed. "I've had the flu. It's okay, I don't think I'm contagious any more."

Greg's eyes were bloodshot. He stood back to let Henry in.

As he stepped forward, Henry had the immediate sensation of passing from light and warmth into the darkness of a cave, where it was not cold but dank and with a thickness to the air that made him hold his breath. When he could breathe, he realized that his instinctive reaction had been right: The air stank.

Greg took a few steps toward the hallway and called out:

"Lydia! We've got company. It's, uh, Henry."

Henry turned toward the kitchen and the odor hit him full force. Through the doorway he could see the checkerboard linoleum. Breadcrumbs and dust were visible from where Henry stood. One corner of the countertop was covered in plates and glasses, all of them coated in layers of food scum. The hum of scattered flies told him the portion of the kitchen he couldn't see was in the same condition.

The longer he stood there, and he wondered how long he would be able to, the more Henry's olfactory glands were able to distinguish between foul odors. He could detect, apart from the decay of unwashed dishes, the aroma of human sweat mixed with blood, and the funk of urine and feces lingering somewhere unseen.

The living room was in disarray with soiled linen lying everywhere. The fabric on most of the furniture was stained. Ashes spilled forth from the fireplace into the middle of the floor.

Greg excused himself and walked away down the hall, calling his wife's name. Henry stepped forward enough to get a better view of the kitchen, confirming that every surface was coated with food and grime. In the center a soft circle of fruit flies formed a living cloud shaped like a twister, and a couple of fat blue flies wandered from one spot to another.

Henry had seen homes like this many times before. He had gone on charitable visits: to the ill, the mentally unstable, or those who simply couldn't wrestle with despair any more. He had seen poor families crammed into tiny quarters, apartments with no doors and no air conditioning, where people cooked their meals on a hot plate and the corridors reeked of fried fish and teemed with half-clothed children.

Yet in most of those places, on the faces of most of the people he found there, no matter how little he judged or how fairly and compassionately he doled out food, blankets, clothing, or the word of the Lord, he saw something that he didn't see in Greg's face. He saw shame, whether fleeting or constant, and often mingled with dignity and the knowledge that they were blameless. It was always there to some degree. Not here.

Greg returned a minute later, and shrugged.

"That's funny," he said. "I don't know where she went. She must have gone out for a walk. I guess. She's been cooped up here, taking care of me."

"How long have you been sick?" Henry asked.

"Oh, uh, I guess I started coming down with it right after I got home from your house," Greg said. "First I thought maybe the rich food disagreed with me, but it keeps hanging on. I've got a bug."

"That was a few weeks ago," Henry said.

Greg frowned.

"Was it? Oh, right. You told me that."

Henry studied Greg's expression and said:

"Greg, if you need anything, if your wife would like some help, you should know that my family is at your disposal, all three of us. You know, sometimes, getting ready for a baby, it can just over-whelm people. There's so much to do and to think about, one person, even two people, can't handle it all. I'd be happy to lend a hand. My wife would love to help."

Greg stared at Henry. He blinked. Then he said:

"All right. Well, we'll keep that in mind if we ever need it. Thanks a lot."

As Henry followed the driveway out to the road he took an-other look and realized that most of the grass had gone dry and yellow. The tulip bed had been plowed up, and the windmills and wooden geese lay in a heap at the far corner of the yard.

"Good riddance," Lydia said from the bedroom door.

"Shit! You startled me," Greg said. "I thought you went out for a walk."

"In this weather?"

"It's warm out."

"Too warm," she said with a wicked smile. "I can't stand the heat, right now. Let's stay inside and play."

Marietta

Marietta had a feeling Henry was doing what she had asked him not to do. Just that morning he had expressed concern about their neighbors. Alicia was, if possible, more innocent than Henry. She wanted him to pay the couple a visit, to check and see if they needed anything. Marietta warned them:

"We don't know these people, so if they want to keep to themselves, we ought to mind our own business."

Naturally Alicia objected. She had the thwarted instinct of a childless woman.

"They're out of their element here in the country," she said. "All the more reason why we should help in any way we can."

"Some people can't be helped," Marietta told her. "They won't take good advice when it's offered."

"Marietta," said Alicia. "This is Henry's calling, to reach out to people in need. You know that. No one is beyond hope. I think that's why you spoke with Lydia in the first place, isn't it?"

Her daughter-in-law's kind smile told Marietta that she had no idea why the older woman had changed her attitude toward their new neighbors. That was just as well. Marietta's words to Lydia had had nothing to do with reaching out or helping people in need.

She had given Lydia a warning, and that warning had been ignored. She knew that Lydia was lost the night she failed to show up for supper. Marietta was prepared, that night, to tell her everything. If Greg and Lydia insisted on lingering here, if they weren't going to sell their house and escape, she had decided to tell them the whole story. She owed that much to Beverly.

Then Lydia had snubbed the Colquitts. She had stubbornly stayed at home while her husband paid a social call. That was the night, then. That was what the girl had planned all along, and nothing Marietta had done could stop her.

Now Marietta drew a new line, a new circle around Henry and Alicia. She would protect them as well as she could. If Greg would listen to reason, she might be able to save him too. Lydia was already beyond reach. She had stupidly invited it right into her home.

Ever since Beverly died Marietta had been rising before dawn to perform the rituals Delphine had taught her. She mixed herbs and she burned sage and repeated the words Delphine had used, to keep the thing at bay. She did this for the safety of her two loved ones. This, she knew and Delphine had known, was the extent of her power against the thing that was invading Lydia and Greg. The best she could do was to keep it from her family and let it take the form it wanted, which might be Lydia's baby or Lydia herself if it had the strength. It wanted to be born. It wanted to be strong. It also wanted what Lydia owned. It had slowly made its way to her, and now it was at home.

"Did you talk to the wife?" Marietta asked Henry when he finally returned from making his rounds.

"Lydia wasn't there," Henry said.

Marietta considered this.

"Mother, I don't want to scare these people away," he said. "I think they need help."

Marietta nodded. She sometimes wished she had a son who could see what she saw, or at least listen and understand and not respond by locking himself in his room at night and whispering prayers to fall asleep. She accepted Henry as a decent and righteous man who both believed in a merciful savior and was afraid of the dark.

"It's all right, son," she told him. "You did a good thing, checking on those young people."

Henry paused and then said:

"They need help, but Greg didn't seem to care. It was strange. Maybe he just didn't notice because he's been sick with a flu bug or something. He's been sick since the night he visited with us, but he hasn't seen a doctor. Everything seemed so uncared for. Not only the kitchen and living room, but the yard, the grass."

Marietta waited. She held back any comment until he finished.

"I drove past their place about half a dozen times in the past three weeks, and I never noticed the grass going yellow. Maybe I saw what I expected to see. Maybe I wasn't paying attention. I don't know. What do you think?"

Marietta nodded. If this was the explanation that gave Henry peace of mind, so be it. He couldn't handle any more than that.

"You did all you could," she told him. "And we'll be here if they need us."

Greg

By the end of his third week of illness, Greg was too weak to drive. He asked Lydia if she felt like giving him a ride to the doctor, but she said the car was acting up again. She asked if he wanted her to call an ambulance, because she would be happy to. He couldn't bring himself to do that, so he said what he had been saying for weeks:

"Maybe I'll feel better tomorrow."

Lydia fluffed his pillows and cooked homemade lentil soup. She read him the news online and kept an eye on his email in case of job offers or interviews. There were none. She cleaned and baked, and she kissed him on the forehead and checked his temperature. She called the doctor while Greg snoozed, and she reported his latest advice.

Every morning he felt more tired. His joints ached and he ran a constant, low-grade fever.

"I'll have to get up and go to the store soon," he said one afternoon.

The light outside wavered, the color of lemon water, and began to fade with the coming dusk. The midday temperature was still uncomfortably warm, but by nightfall it was mild.

"No need," said Lydia.

She shook out the thermometer and placed it under his tongue.

"I had one of those Dempsey kids pick up what we needed from Misty Mart. We're stocked up."

She smiled down at him. She was wearing a yellow smock embroidered with red and yellow flowers. In the last rays of sunlight from the high window in the bedroom, she was the picture of summer: glorious, golden, her skin slightly tanned and her dark hair sparkling.

"Poor little things, those kids love to run errands. They'll do anything for five dollars. We never have to go shopping again."

She laughed and brushed the hair back from his forehead. Her fingers were cool and slender with slightly bulging knuckles that only made them seem more fragile.

"You know," she whispered. "There's no hurry. We can sell this house any time we want. We could even stay here. We could live here all winter, if we want. It's cozy and beautiful."

He was so lucky. Everything he could want was here, after all. And one day soon their baby would join them. It was all just perfect, he felt, as he drifted off again.

When Greg woke up he didn't know what day it was. He felt that he had been sleeping for years. His head throbbed. He was shaking as he stood up and pushed himself away from the bed. The sheets were sodden with sweat.

"Lydia!" He called, but there was no answer.

He noted that it was odd to wake up and not find her waiting by the bed. She always seemed to be there, patiently nursing him through this.

It was awful, the worst flu he'd ever had. He wasn't vomiting since that first night, or sniffling or sneezing. The symptoms were fatigue and confusion, and an all-over ache. He had sore throat and swollen glands, sore muscles. Nothing made it better, or worse. His illness just went on and on.

Now, suddenly, he was tired of being tired. He felt bored, and restless. For the first time since he had come down with the bug (right after visiting the Colquitts, as Lydia had reminded him more than once) he allowed his desire for a change of scenery to override his lethargy. He walked unsteadily from the bedroom to the front door and opened it.

The shock of sunlight swept over and blinded him. The heat felt so good on his skin, he opened the security door and stepped out onto the tiny porch.

The tulips were still blooming. How odd, he thought. A slippery breeze ran through the wooden windmills in the yard. The maple, the emerald grass, and the lush fir trees, the dark shaded ground under a line of hemlock trees, light glancing off the ferns, the beauty of it all made him swoon. He felt, for once, that he could spend his whole life on this very spot.

When he felt the need to sit down and turned to go back inside, he saw the envelope. It was manuscript-size, sealed, lying on the mat next to the door. There was no marking on the outside, no name. He looked around the yard and the driveway, the road. No one was there.

He tore open the envelope and found several pages of handwriting. He sat down on the porch and started reading what seemed to be a fairy tale. He read the story of someone named William Knox and his wife Harriet and the baby girl they adopted, a girl who burned down their home and died in the fire along with Mrs. Knox. At the end of the story Greg found this message:

"You may not know what to make of all this. I'm not sure you'll take the advice of an older person who seems so different from your friends and other people you trust and rely on. I hope you will think, though, of all that has happened since you've been here.

"Growing up, most kids thought of Miss Knocks as a fairy tale, meant to keep us scared out of the woods where we might get into mischief. I was just a girl when my aunt told me that the story of Harriet and Flora was true and had happened right here where we all lived. The girl had rested until my friends and I came along. We didn't wake her up on purpose, but that doesn't matter.

"I wasn't sure what to make of my aunt's rituals and precautions, until I saw the thing come back. I saw it with my own eyes.

"When Ethel Sanders' daughter was born, I knew the girl was something bad that came back, not to make peace but to cause damage and to take what she felt had been stolen. I thought Connie Sara's dying settled things, but I was wrong.

"Beverly, your wife's birth mother, kept something she ought to have thrown away. That may be the reason she died. Then you and your wife came, and now I see there was a plan all along. I also know it's a bad thing to keep this from you. It's too late for your wife and maybe too late for your child. You have to face this although it's hard, but I can't let this thing kill you for no good reason. I've searched my conscience and now I've told you what you need to know.

"Don't ask yourself to believe me. All I ask is that you step outside of your house, beyond the threshold, where you can see things the way you have to, and look at your wife as she is. Find some way to do that. It's the only thing you have to do. Then you'll decide for yourself."

Greg finished reading the manuscript and tore it in half. He was certain now: Marietta Colquitt was completely insane. She had no right to interfere with his family, and when he was well enough to drive again he would go to see the sheriff. Skillute wasn't far enough off the beaten track that he couldn't get a restraining order.

Imagine that bitch coming up to his home and leaving this thing on his doorstep! What if Lydia had read it?

Greg would fight to keep this hag away from his wife and his baby. First he would call Henry and give him a warning to get control of his mother or he was going to the sheriff. No. First he would tell Lydia that she was never to see or speak with Marietta again. Then he would call Henry. Then he would speak with the sheriff.

He would talk with Lydia. He wouldn't tell her about the manuscript. He would just say that he had given it a lot of thought. He was sure there was something seriously wrong with the Colquitts. It was best if he and Lydia avoided their neighbors.

They would be heading back to Seattle as soon as he could turn the sale of the house over to a real estate agent. He didn't care any more about getting the best price. All he wanted was to get his family out of this place.

No matter what Greg had to do, take out a loan, sell the house for far less than it was worth, it didn't matter. They had to get back to the city, where the crazy people were easy to recognize from a distance. He longed for the eccentricities of the man who lived down the hall in their old apartment building and announced the start of every spring by donning a taffeta dress and walking his Chihuahuas in the park.

Greg dragged himself indoors. In the living room, he shredded the manuscript and tossed the pieces behind the grate in the fireplace. Then he went back to the door and peered out. The sun drifted behind luminous clouds.

He felt a desperate need for another dose of fresh air. He went outside and stepped gingerly onto the grass, which felt stiff and dry between his toes. The windmills and all the other yard ornaments lay in a heap in the far corner of the yard. He was sure he had seen them in their usual places, earlier. Lydia must have taken them down, thinking that a more neutral look would help sell the place.

He looked down. Now that he stood on the grass he noticed it was dying. He had taken it for granted, expected it to be the way it was when they moved in. Why would it look like this? Lydia said she was taking care of the yard while he was sick. He must be imagining things. He was delirious. The story he'd read came back to him full force and made him nauseated again.

He heard the back door slam shut. He walked unsteadily beside the outer wall of the house, to the crook where the living room joined the kitchen, and stopped. From inside came the sound of humming. He could hear Lydia humming a tune in the kitchen. He knew she wasn't in the house when he stepped outside, so she must have just gone back in. He had assumed she was out back, taking a walk in the woods while he read that horrible story from Marietta. The car was parked in the driveway, and Lydia wouldn't have taken it anyway. She said she was paying a neighbor's kids to do her shopping. She said the car wasn't working, probably needed a tune-up when Greg was feeling better.

He took a few steps closer to the window, and then found himself crouching. Not hiding, he thought. Not because he was hiding. Only because he knew what he was doing was foolish. It was the fever, his illness. He was confused, he told himself.

Lydia's humming grew a little louder when Greg reached the open window, directly above him. A tune from high school, a ballad that sounded silly and disconnected pouring from an open window in the middle of the day, surrounded by the dying lawn and the trees and sultry clouds.

Marietta Colquitt was a nuisance and a witch. He was only proving it, because when he did what she said and nothing happened, he would have the edge. He could tell her to leave his family alone, and she wouldn't find any sympathy with Lydia. So without thinking, like diving into a pool, he stood up and peered into the kitchen window.

He meant to catch a glimpse and go right back into the house, where he would kiss Lydia and fall into her arms and tell her the hilarious story of the crazy, irritating woman who played him for a fool. Instead he froze, unable to move in any direction while he felt the metallic surge of bile rise in his throat.

The red cotton dress with black stitching belonged to Lydia, and the slender arms and shaggy brown hair. Everything else about her bore only a passing resemblance to his wife. The skin was gray, almost purple, shot through with darkened veins and bulging at joints that seemed ready to burst through the skin's surface. This was some animal, a living thing trying to pass itself off as Lydia.

It dropped a knife onto the floor. The knife skidded across the checkerboard linoleum and hit the far wall. The thing reached, and reached, and reached its arm, stretching all the way across the kitchen floor to grasp the knife and yank it back to the counter.

It made a sputtering noise, like a drowning laugh. It dipped its claws into a casserole with green fungus growing on top. Flies crawled over the rotting food, and hovered in the air. Greg could hear the buzz and drone of the flies from where he stood.

The thing turned away, and started searching for something in the drawers, without bothering to close them. It dragged out more and more silverware and kitchen utensils, and threw them on the floor in frustration. It let out a long sigh and angrily shook its head.

From this angle Greg saw that the thing was bleeding. A cloud-shaped scarlet stain was imprinted on the back of the dress that belonged to Lydia, and a long, glistening cord hung down like a tail, its end coated in dust and grime from sweeping along the floor whenever it moved. With the bile churning in his throat, Greg realized that it wasn't a tail but an umbilical cord.

He collapsed onto the ground on his ass, and sat there, breathing, his pulse pounding in his neck. He tried to take a deep breath, but this made him sob. He threw himself forward onto his hands and knees and scuttled around the side of the house, dirt and weeds catching between his fingers and cutting his skin.

When he reached the back corner he began to heave, but nothing came up. He felt his stomach muscles contract, and he retched up a viscous brown clot onto the grass. He tore at the grass nearby and held it up, to make sure it was dead. The lawn was nothing but yellow and brown scruff with intermittent tangles of twisted weeds. Around the back steps there lay piles of rotting food, broken dishes and glasses.

Inside the kitchen the humming had stopped. Something was moving, with a growling noise, working its way through the house toward the back door.

Soaked to the bone with cold sweat, Greg was running. He fell twice and kept moving on all fours until he could grab hold of leaves and pull himself upright. He caught a licorice fern and stripped it, getting a deep gash across the palm of his hand. His bare feet were cut and bleeding. Every step stung like a lash, but he kept running. Behind him he could hear the snap of twigs and the rustle of leaves, and he didn't dare look back.

"Gre-g-g-g!"

The sound of his name echoed around him. He pressed on. His heart ached and his lungs felt constricted.

"Gre-g-g-g! Where are you?"

The voice thrummed like a machine or a mass of insects, not like a human being, not like his Lydia. It wanted him, wanted to get inside him.

"Gre-g-g-g! Come ba-ck!"

He was vaguely aware of thirst, and acutely aware of cuts on his face and hands and forearms as he tore his way through shrubs and trees, up through a bank of flat rocks, and on. He never looked back. He never considered stopping.

He didn't feel the ground give, or think of falling. He fell so suddenly and swiftly, all he knew was the rush of blistering branches all around him. He heard his clothing rip while he slid down a trough of mud, his feet scrambling wildly for purchase, sliding down, covered in mud and sliding down, helplessly. He hit a hard surface with a sick-making crunch.

He was dazed, then grateful not to be falling, and just as this idea formed in his mind, he heard and felt the crack of wood giving away under him. Both his arms hit something solid, breaking at the elbows with a shattering sound as he plunged into absolute darkness.

Greg had no way to measure how much time went by while he lay in the filth and mud, cold creeping damply through his clothes. The air was so fetid, so nauseating he had for a moment the sense of being turned inside out, of wearing all the blood and organs of his body exposed. He gagged but there was nothing in his stomach now, not even bile. He listened for any sign to tell him where he was. There was only a drip, and the awful twitching of worms in the slime all around him.

His arms were broken and he couldn't reach, but he tried to move an inch or two from side to side. A sharp pain struck his right side. He struggled to free his feet from the muck while sidling over. He thought he must have landed on tree roots or fallen branches. He tried to rock sideways but the pain shooting from his arms into his chest made it impossible. He rested in agony with his head back in the cold filth. His eyes took in the skull and scant remnants of skin and hair next to his face. He screamed, and the more he tried to stifle screaming, the more the trapped sound choked him. Tears ran down his face and he began to sob.

Greg called out in the depths of this place, begging for mercy, for light, for God. Like an answered prayer, suddenly a light opened above him. It was faint, weak as a distant whimper, but as he watched it grew brighter until he could see what he knew to be actual sunlight shining down, full and flashing with a golden haze.

In this burst of late afternoon light, he had time to see two things clearly: the rotting corpse of a child lying rent and crushed beside him, so decayed she must have been long dead, and the man wearing overalls and a dirty baseball cap, standing above him in the glow of this glorious day with a rifle pointed down directly at his head.

Burt

The rifle blast knocked Burt down. When his head cleared he crawled over to the hole and peered deep inside.

The devil was down there. He knew this the way he knew his own name. He knew it the way he knew how to breathe. Only he couldn't say how he knew, or when he had begun to know. He had done the right thing. He had put the devil down. This was what he was supposed to do. He told himself these things. He told himself to stop crying.

He sat on his ass in the clearing, before the pile of cedar shingles he had built as an altar. When he had gathered up enough, she had come back to him: His beauty, his baby, his child Connie Sara. In the soft pile of wood he could still make out two of the signs with "Connie Sara Way" painted on them.

If he sat like this, quiet, next to the hole in the ground, while the blood flowed from the devil down there, down into the roots and the mud and filth, his child would come to him again, and she would stay. He was sure of this. Only one more thing needed to be done.

He wiped the tears off his face. He picked up the rifle and set it at an angle, braced against the ground with the barrel pointed up at his chin. He worked the angle until he could reach the trigger. When he was ready he looked up at the sky. A branch high above shivered and the sharp-edged leaves looked like dancing angels. Burt smiled. A strand of saliva ran down the side of his jaw just before the trigger clicked and the rifle blew his face away.

Marietta

The husband was dead. She had seen his face in the mud and slime. She had known this would be the end of everything, and she couldn't make it stop without a sacrifice. There was no spell she knew that would accomplish this.

She asked to borrow the car and when Henry wanted to know where she was going, she said Misty Mart. This ritual was nothing to do with Henry and Alicia. They would never understand. With all of their prayers and kindness to others, they would never believe her if she told them the truth. Only Marietta knew what to do.

She parked the car on the road and opened the trunk. She walked the rest of the way carrying the heavy canister steady so it didn't splash.

The familiar path, the walk up the driveway to Beverly's house, brought too many memories of her friends. Their rides to Long Beach and the secrets they shared, even the ones they knew but didn't speak out loud. All of their life together seemed to gather about Marietta like a cloak. It gave her strength. She let that strength carry her as she spread the trail of gasoline all the way around the outside of the house.

When she was done she stood on the parched grass and gazed up the front steps and across the tiny porch. She regarded the security door, propped open with the welcome mat. The front door stood wide open. This was an invitation she would no longer resist. There was no reason to hold back, now.

She couldn't see into the living room, but she could hear a restless breathing, an agitation, inside. It must be hidden in the shadows just beyond the threshold, waiting.

Marietta held the canister in both hands. The trail of gas had been enough to encircle the bungalow. Now she splashed a thin stream across the porch. With a sharp breath she upended the nearly empty canister and let the last of the noxious liquid pour over her shoulders and her clothes. She took the wooden matches from her pocket and struck three of them together.

The fire shot up all around her. She bit her tongue, tasted blood and gasoline. She swallowed the tip of her tongue, bitten off in her mouth.

The dead grass acted as kindling. Fire raced up the outside walls and climbed onto the roof. In seconds the whole place was engulfed and the smoke rolled up more than fifty feet into the sky.

Flickering out of consciousness, consumed by pain, Marietta fell forward. Her eyes roasted and popped. Her skin sizzled. When the fire hit fat and bone, it crackled. She let herself scream, and couldn't stop. Like a siren the scream rose with the flames.

In her mind she saw Greg's face and the blood-spattered tree trunk where Burt lay. She saw the tiny body of her daughter stuffed inside a metal box. She saw the girl she herself once was, running, all elbows and knees, running from the burning forest. She saw the dress Ethel had sewn for Connie Sara's funeral shroud. She saw the black and yellow and green, the falling gravel, the hot summer day when John Colquitt died. She saw Beverly's furniture piled against the fireplace in a panic while the thing that was once a child slithered down the chimney after its helpless prize.

She had only a moment to think of these things. Then the charred claws lunged out through the open door and she was seized, torn from where she stood and thrust into the open maw glistening with spit and blood.

Epilogue

Epilogue

The Box

Far behind her the girl heard voices. They were calling her name. There were two of them, a boy and a girl, and they were slapping at the grass with sticks.

"Ruthie! Where you hiding, girl? Say?"

She had run as far as she could, stopped only by a chest-high barbed wire fence. She followed the fence for a minute, but it seemed to go on for some distance. It probably encircled this piece of land. She would never get around it by the time they caught up to her.

She was heavyset and she felt overheated in her knit slacks and sweater top. These were worn at her mother's insistence. Ruth knew they made her look chubby. Her mother found this funny, and told her friends Ruth didn't get her looks from her side of the family. Then they laughed.

They laughed at every new family portrait. Ruth's mother sat in the center, sucking in her cheeks and looking hungry, flanked by two handsome sons who were away at college and her doting husband who had gone flabby and bald. Ruth was positioned next to her father, almost out of the frame, turned at an angle that the photographer assured her mother was the most flattering he could manage.

"Ruuuuuuthie!"

They were getting close. With trembling hands Ruth held the lines of barbed wire apart and carefully climbed between them. She was all right until she stood on the other side, on one leg, and started to pull the other one through. Then she panicked and let go of the barbed wire, which nicked her ankle with a white-hot gouge only an inch from her Achilles tendon.

"Ow!"

She got to her feet and began brushing the tall grass and weeds aside. Most of the vegetation was just over her head. Her heart beat crazily and she prayed that her tormenters would be too cowardly to follow. The grass was brittle. It snapped her in the face as she rushed through it.

"Where did you go, Ruthie?"

The voices sounded farther away. They were losing ground. She was getting away. She pressed on until she stumbled against a fortress of wild blackberries tangled up with the grass. She squinted and saw that there was something else, something underneath the blackberry bushes. It might be a rusted-out tractor or a truck.

Pinching and pushing aside the grass she ducked down and sat on the ground in a clearing just big enough for her. Thinking this spot was sort of a miracle, she tried to slow her breathing and rest.

She looked around at the ground. It felt hard and flat and cold. She moved aside and saw that the dirt was worn away in the place where she had been sitting. She scratched the dirt with a twig and found what looked like a metal door. Not a door but a lid, with a slim handle in the middle. She brushed away the rest of the dirt and freed the handle. It was metallic, too, and stained.

She listened for a moment. She couldn't hear the boy and girl. She thought with a rush of hope that maybe they had given up.

She dusted off the handle and pulled. It wouldn't open. There must be a latch still buried in the dirt. She kept pulling. She pulled so hard that she thought she might break a sweat. She began working the lid from side to side, until it snapped loose in her hand.

She stared at the lid and saw that the rusty latch below the dirt level had broken off. The whole thing looked like a cymbal in her hand, the kind she had seen in the school marching band, except it was rectangular and had black streaks all over.

She turned back to the hole she had just uncovered in the earth. Not a hole, but a sort of chamber, a box, a metal box full of something charred that smelled the way she imagined a dungeon might smell.

Ruth poked at the charred mess with the twig and lifted it. What she found on the end of the twig was a tiny blackened skull, no bigger than a fist.

She only had time to draw breath. She would have screamed if she had not heard the rushing sound behind her and looked up to see the blond girl's scowling face bearing down on her.

"Ruthie," the girl said. "Why did you hide from me?"

Acknowledgements

Thanks to my husband Cory James Herndon, for making everything possible. And thanks to my friend Suzanne Morrison for all the encouragement, support, and brilliant editorial advice, and to my agent Danielle for loving the book.

About the Author

S.P. Miskowski's stories have been published in *The Absent Willow Review, Identity Theory, Horror Bound Online Magazine, Other Voices, The Stranger, New Times,* and the anthology *Words to Music,* and will appear in *Supernatural Tales 21* and the Omnium Gatherum anthology *Detritus.* A member of the speculative fiction group Wily Writers, she writes Shock Room, a blog dedicated to horror fiction and films. Her darkly comic collection of short stories *Red Poppies: 7 Tales of Envy & Revenge* is available for Kindle. You can contact the author and comment on *Knock Knock* on our Facebook page or at the author's blog:
http://d-o-cat.blogspot.com

The cover design and illustration for *Knock Knock* are by Russell Dickerson. You can find more of his work at Darkstorm Creative:
http://www.darkstormcreative.com

For more books by S.P. Miskowski and other Omnium Gatherum authors visit:
http://omniumgatherumedia.com

Lightning Source UK Ltd.
Milton Keynes UK
UKHW022010271118
333080UK00023B/665/P